REACH
FOR
YOU

Also by Pat Esden

A Hold on Me

Beyond Your Touch

Published by Kensington Publishing Corp.

REACH *FOR* YOU

A Dark Heart Novel

PAT ESDEN

KENSINGTON BOOKS
www.kensingtonbooks.com

KENSINGTON BOOKS are published by

Kensington Publishing Corp.
119 West 40th Street
New York, NY 10018

All Kensington titles, imprints, and distributed lines are available at special quantity discounts for bulk purchases for sales promotion, premiums, fundraising, educational, or institutional use.

Special book excerpts or customized printings can also be created to fit specific needs. For details, write or phone the office of the Kensington Sales Manager: Kensington Publishing Corp., 119 West 40th Street, New York, NY 10018. Attn. Sales Department. Phone: 1-800-221-2647.

Kensington and the K logo Reg. U.S. Pat. & TM Off.

eISBN-13: 978-1-4967-0010-0
eISBN-10: 1-4967-0010-4
First Kensington Electronic Edition: July 2017

ISBN-13: 978-1-4967-0009-4
ISBN-10: 1-4967-0009-0
First Kensington Trade Paperback Printing: July 2017

10 9 8 7 6 5 4 3 2 1

Printed in the United States of America

For Joann

So much of this story is for you:
the beauty, the love, the kindness, and the sorrow.
(And, because I know you would have loved them, the sexy parts)

Acknowledgments

First, I'd like to thank my friends, readers, and family who listened patiently to my insane myriad questions over the years. Thank you for putting up with my writer babble and helping me bring this series to life.

Thank you to my brilliant editor, Selena James. I've never met anyone who can impart so much wisdom in so few words. You are amazing.

Thank you to Jane Nutter for your guidance and support. And a huge round of cheers for the rest of the Kensington gang as well. I'm privileged to have such a wonderful team behind my books.

Thank you most of all to Ginger Churchill, Jaye Robin Brown, and my agent, Pooja Menon. Your unrelenting support, sharp eyes, and honesty mean the world to me.

I'd also like to give a quick nod to authors with a lot more experience than I who took the time to extend their hands. Whether you realize it or not, your gestures of kindness supported me. You are shining stars.

A Note to the Reader

In *Beyond Your Touch* (Dark Heart #2), my Note to the Reader mentioned that the quotes I created for the beginning of each chapter offered a glimpse into the mysteries in this series, hints about characters' motives, and things to come. This is true, but perhaps even more so in this book. Read the quotes carefully. Even the Note to the Reader in *A Hold on Me* (Dark Heart #1) whispers about things that even Annie isn't aware of, at least not yet.

CHAPTER 1

ठ· β·⸱₉₇⸱⸱ ₚ·⸱₍·₉⸱₇₇ ⸱⸵ⁿ˃ ⸣⸱₇₇⸱₉₇

We journey. Ceaseless and hungry.

—Carved into stone tablet. Tenerife, Spain

The campsite was ominously silent. Then a breeze lifted and my ear caught the faint clank and rattle of the bones and knives hanging in the pine trees behind us.

"You don't think they're both dead, do you?" Selena whispered.

I scanned the dilapidated camper ahead of us, a do-it-yourself RV created out of an old bread truck. Despite the midafternoon warmth, the doors were shut tight. The tent behind it, barely visible from our angle, bowed under the weight of rain that had pooled in its canopy. There was no campfire smoke. No trampled grass. In comparison to when we'd come here last week, the place looked deserted.

Goose bumps pebbled my skin. I gave the camper another once-over. "Zea was really old and sickly. He could have died—or if the kidnappers came here first looking for Lotli, they could have found him. They might have—"

Selena cut me off with a glower. "You mean, *supposed* kidnappers."

My jaw clenched. *Yeah, that is exactly what I meant.* I understood why my cousin didn't like that everything we'd discovered pointed to her boyfriend, Newt, being involved in Lotli's disappearance, and perhaps Zea's as well. But I thought we'd gotten past that, like a bunch of times already.

I swiveled toward where we'd parked our Land Rover. The Professor stood rooted next to it, a mixture of disgust and apprehension crinkling his face. From his scholarly glasses and sandy brown hair all the way down to his polished loafers, he looked anything but ready for our reconnaissance trip out here on the back roads of Down East Maine. An afternoon of research at Oxford University would have been more appropriate. "You want to check inside the tent while we look in the camper?"

His gaze flicked to the soggy tarps. He cleared his throat, then—as posh as ever—said, "Don't get me wrong, I'm not totally against the idea. But the thought of discovering a rotting corpse is a teensy bit abhorrent."

"Would you rather discover one in a closed-up camper?" I snapped. It was lucky we'd driven into the campsite from the main road instead of walking like we'd done the last time. I'd assumed the Professor had an adventuresome spirit to go with his young Indiana Jones good looks. Especially since he was an archaeologist, though this summer he was tutoring Selena's eleven-year-old brother as a favor. Still, and despite how eager he'd seemed to come with us, the Professor had freaked the second we started past the creepy stuff Zea and Lotli hung in the trees to scare people off: the knives and bones, pieces of copper pipe, broken mirrors, and doll parts. Frankly, I was surprised he'd even gotten out of the Land Rover at all.

I pasted on a smile. "Sorry. I don't much care for the idea myself. Let's just hope he's napping or something."

The Professor wiped his hands down the sides of his chinos. "I truly hope you're right."

As he headed for the tent, I tramped toward the camper with Selena close behind. If only Chase were here now. The creepy stuff hadn't bothered him at all, and the fear of Zea being dead would have only driven him forward faster.

My chest tightened, my longing for Chase aching inside me, raw and unrelenting. If it weren't for me, he would be here now. Instead, both he and my mother were trapped in the djinn realm, prisoners of his father, Malphic. If it weren't for me, Lotli wouldn't be missing either.

"Well?" Selena jerked her head at the camper door. "Are you going to just stand there?"

I raised my hand and knocked. One second passed. Two seconds. I rapped harder. Nothing. I tried the doorknob. It turned beneath my grip. I opened the door a crack, hesitated, and took a deep breath before pushing it open all the way.

A wave of hot, musty air rushed past me as if the camper had been closed up for days.

"Hello?" I said, sticking my head inside. I gave the air a cautious sniff. No dangerous odors, like a leaky gas stove, permeated the air. No rotting-trash smell—or decomp.

Selena nudged my shoulder. "What are you waiting for?"

I swallowed hard and stepped forward.

The place was cramped, a gypsy wagon on steroids. Tassels and prisms curtained the windows, letting only faint streaks of light inside. Miles of fuchsia and turquoise fabric draped the ceiling and walls. Animal skulls, feathers, and nubby candles clustered inside miniature altars. The fridge, table, and chairs, every surface that wasn't fabric covered, was painted purple or black. Stars decorated the ceiling. An antique bed piled with crimson quilts and an avalanche of pillows took up the camper's entire backend. It was cozy enough, I supposed. But I couldn't begin to imagine what life had been like for Lotli, apprenticed to Zea as a child because of her magic abilities, essentially indentured. Not that I thought a devout shaman like Zea would have been cruel to her. It was just so different from anything I'd experienced.

"Zea, are you here?" I called out. "We need to talk to you about Lotli."

I minced my way deeper into the cramped space, working my way toward the back of the camper. Cold sweat carved a trail down my spine. I crept past a tiny kitchen and dining nook, then the bathroom—one toothbrush in the holder, a washcloth draped over the edge of a yellowed sink.

I returned to the front of the camper and pulled aside the curtain that divided the living area from the bread truck's cab. Seats for the driver and a passenger, seashells glued to the dash, insulated coffee cups in the holders—

Something brushed the back of my neck.

I yelped and jumped sideways, whipping around to see what it was and smacking my elbow against the wall. Pain zinged up my arm. I glared at Selena, standing barely an inch behind me.

"Shit," I said, rubbing the sting from my arm. "You scared the hell out of me."

She gave me a sheepish pout. "Sorry. I thought you knew I was there."

"I didn't think you were *that* close." It wouldn't have hurt half as bad, except I was already sore and bruised from being thrown out of the djinn realm earlier in the day.

Her pout transformed into a smug smile and she flipped her blond hair over one shoulder. "Looks to me like Zea and Lotli might have pulled a vanishing act after all. Huh?"

I stopped rubbing. "Or the Professor's about to find something disgusting in the tent."

"Want to bet?"

I closed my eyes, struggling to regain my composure. We couldn't afford to waste time discussing the same thing over and over again, any more than I could have afforded the luxury of staying home to nurse my aches and pains. Chase and Mother were in danger. And I couldn't go back to the realm and rescue them until we found Lotli. Without her and her flute-magic, it would be too risky, perhaps even impossible to enter or escape from the realm.

I shoved past Selena and strode to the tiny bathroom. "While we're here, we should find something personal of Lotli's that you can use to scry and see where they're holding her."

Glancing around, I spotted a scruffy hairbrush. You couldn't get much more personal than that. I grabbed it and brandished it toward Selena.

She stood just inside the bathroom doorway, hands on her hips, eyes narrowed. "Cut it out, Annie, I've had enough of you talking like Newt kidnapped Lotli, the innuendos and little jabs. Maybe his family's hiding something, but Newt doesn't have anything to do with it. So quit acting like he's evil, okay?"

I mirrored her stance. "He told you his dad was a stock-broker, that they owned their summer home. Those were lies. His brother is a registered creep. No matter what you want to think: Newt's not innocent."

She turned her back on me, her voice bordering on hysteria. "I don't know why I bothered coming. You're so, so . . . You always have to be right—" Her voice died and she slowly faced me. Angry red blotches mottled her face. But tears rimmed her eyes.

My anger drained. She didn't look pissed. She was trembling like she was about to fall apart. Earlier today, when we'd first heard about the lies Newt and his family had been telling, I'd seen something in Selena's eyes, something beneath her disbelief.

"What is it? Tell me," I asked gently.

She raked her hands over her face. "Nothing. You just need to trust me. I know Newt couldn't be involved. And he wouldn't have let his brother do it either."

I leveled my gaze with hers and toughened my voice. "What makes you so certain? Tell me the truth, Selena."

Her chin quivered. "I just know."

Tucking the hairbrush handle first into my hip pocket, I stepped closer. I pushed her hair back from her face. "You're my cousin. Please. Tell me."

"Nothing. He just wouldn't do it. He loves me."

"I get that. But—"

She shoved my hand away. "No, you don't get it. I *know* he loves me. Like forever." Her eyes pleaded for me to understand what she couldn't bring herself to say.

A possibility seeped into my head. My hands went to my mouth, covering a horrified gasp. She couldn't mean. She couldn't have. "What did you do?"

"I kind of—I put a . . ." Her voice faded and she looked down at the floor.

"A spell?" A month ago, the idea of witchcraft being involved would never have occurred to me. Now it seemed more than likely.

"You can't tell anyone. Mom, Dad, Grandfather—they'd kill me." She curled her arms over her head, her shoulders shaking as she crumpled down against the wall.

I crouched and put my arms around her. "Whatever it is, it'll be fine. It can't be that bad."

"It is," she sobbed.

CHAPTER 2

Spiderweb surrounds candles white. Blood stains
petals red. Chamomile. Caraway. I bind thee with
willow. Love me now. Love me forever after.

—Persistence Freemont (1989)
The Compendium of Witchcraft (Vol. 2)

"I cursed him to love me forever," Selena said, tears streaming down her cheeks.

Stunned, I released her and sat back. "Cursed? Aren't curses evil?"

"I was going to use a love spell to attract him to me," she sobbed. "But that might have attracted other guys. He was the only one I wanted."

"You can remove it, right?" I bobbed my head, as if by doing so her head would nod yes as well.

She cringed. "Maybe."

"You need to try, right away. It's not fair to him."

"I know." Her tear-damp eyes met mine. "You remember that night when you were worried about Lotli coming on to Chase and I told you if you kept him satisfied he wouldn't look at other girls?"

As I recalled she actually suggested I do kinky stuff to keep Chase happy. "What does that have to do with this?"

"I almost told you about the curse then. But, I don't know, maybe I was jealous of what you and Chase have. You didn't have to do anything to make him like you." Sniffing back tears, she hung her head. "I wish I'd said something."

My chest squeezed. Chase—

I clenched my teeth, cutting short the surge of sadness and worry that threatened to overwhelm me, and steered the conversation in a more rational direction. "The thing is, Selena—whether Newt loves you or not doesn't matter. Loving you wouldn't keep him from doing something to Lotli, especially if he thought she was a danger to you."

She blinked. "I never thought of that."

I got to my feet and pulled her up with me. "There's only one way to know for sure if Newt is innocent. We have to find Lotli."

Footfalls sounded from the other end of the camper, followed by the Professor's voice. "Absolutely no sign of anyone in the tent, alive or otherwise."

"No one here either," I called to him. I wiped a few stray tears off Selena's face and gave her shoulder a reassuring squeeze.

"My goodness, this place is quite fascinating," the Professor continued. "My heavens, I believe this Maya bowl has some serious age."

"Really?" I slipped past Selena, emerging from the bathroom and giving her time to regroup before the Professor saw her.

He held out the bowl. It was red and orange with glyphs around the rim and filled with—"Are those bird skulls?"

"I believe so, along with those of a few unlucky mammals." Grimacing, the Professor set the bowl back into its altar. "However, I also believe my first evaluation was wrong. More likely it's a quality reproduction, judging by its weight."

"It's still nice," I said.

Selena came out of the bathroom, her face wiped clean of tears and her complexion back to normal. She scanned the camper as if looking for something. "I could scry for Zea. This place is full of his stuff."

"I was about to suggest the same thing." I pulled the grungy hairbrush from my pocket and held it out to her. "I'm guessing this is Zea's, since Lotli didn't take it with her to Moonhill."

She snatched the brush. "Perfect. If they both used it, then I should be able to pick up on Lotli, too. It won't be as exact as using a dark mirror to locate them, but it'll be quicker." She pressed the hairbrush between her palms and closed her eyes. Her eyes flashed open. "Just so you know—if he or both of them are . . . If they aren't alive, then scrying like this might attract their spirits."

Fear weakened my legs and I sunk down on a dining nook bench. The idea of attracting ghosts or spirits didn't bother me. If Zea were dead, it wouldn't be a shock, considering he wasn't that healthy to start with. Not that it would be a good thing either. But Lotli—we needed her and her flute-magic.

I took a deep breath, calming myself, as the Professor settled onto the bench across the table from me. Selena sat down on the floor cross-legged, clutching the brush between her hands. She closed her eyes and began to slowly sway.

For a long moment, silence weighed heavy in the camper. I became keenly aware of the lumpy cushion beneath my legs and of a faint aroma of curry and fennel, spices Lotli and Zea must have used a lot. And a hint of mildew as well. Selena's head bobbed forward. Abruptly, it snapped back up. Her eyes flickered open, showing nothing but the whites.

The Professor flinched and jerked back. I bit my tongue to keep from gasping. I'd seen her do this once before, but that didn't make it any less frightening.

The nerves in her face spasmed, then stilled. "Not dead," she mumbled. "He's nearby, but not that close. Drifting, sleeping, meditating, maybe."

"And Lotli?" I asked, barely daring to speak.

Selena's head rolled on her shoulders. She shuddered, her breathing becoming loud and labored. "Not with him. She's— I sense rope, wooden beams . . ."

I leaned forward, ears pricked so I wouldn't miss a word.

"Ouch!" Selena yelped as if burned. She leapt to her feet and slammed the hairbrush to the floor. "Son of a bitch that hurt."

The Professor and I both scrambled out from the nook.

"What happened? Are you all right?" I took her by the shoulders, peering into her eyes to make sure they were back to normal. They were, though her pupils were dilated like she was terrified.

The Professor patted her arm. "You're fine. There's absolutely nothing to worry about."

"No, I'm not," Selena said, her breath still ragged. "The hairbrush—it bit me. I was almost to her. Then I felt this presence."

My gaze darted to the hairbrush. "Bit you? What are you talking about?"

"I thought I was approaching a riding stable. There was this electric fence around it. Only it wasn't that kind of fence. It was the presence of a fence. A magic fence. Powerful, enclosing Lotli. I touched it—and *zap*." She eyed the hairbrush. "I'm not going near that thing again. But we should take it with us, so we can see what Mom and Kate sense."

I nudged the brush with my shoe to make sure it wasn't going to do anything to me. I had no ability to scry or sense things, and it hadn't done anything before, but there was no reason to take a chance. Certain I wouldn't get zapped, I scooped the brush up and shoved it handle-first back into my pocket. "We should probably take a few other things, too, don't you think? So your mom and Kate have a variety of stuff to scry with."

Selena nodded, then glanced at the Professor. "Would you

mind getting my water bottle from the car? I'm so dry, I can barely swallow."

"Oh, yes. Absolutely." He flew out the door and Selena and I started opening drawers, looking for things to take with us— Lotli's bras, panties, socks, scarves, a large box devoted to jewelry. I stopped. "Selena, are you finding anything that looks like it might belong to Zea, like pants?"

"He's probably sworn to a life of poverty. Shamans do things like that."

I surveyed the chock-full trailer. "You really think so? I mean, all this and not even one pair of pants for him, really? Why would he allow Lotli to have tons of stuff?"

She shrugged. "It doesn't really matter anyway. We know he's alive and we've got the hairbrush. It doesn't sound nice, but, honestly, it's Lotli, not him, we need to find."

"You're sure he's all right, though?"

"Definitely. He probably got lonely with Lotli gone and went to stay with some local friend."

"That makes sense." It was also entirely possible that the kidnappers had come here first looking for Lotli and that's why he took off.

The *thump* of the Land Rover door shutting sounded in the distance, undoubtedly the Professor was on his way back with the water.

Selena bit her bottom lip, her eyes filling with worry.

I lowered my voice. "If you're thinking I'm going to say something in front of him about what you did to Newt, forget it. My lips are sealed. But I'm not ready to declare Newt and his family innocent. Do you think there's any chance they're involved with magic?"

She snorted loudly. "Are you crazy? Of course not."

"Then how about we prove it?"

Her eyes narrowed. "What are you thinking?"

"We're near Bar Harbor. Newt lives there, right? If we

were to make a little side trip—like say to his neighborhood—
would you be able to tell if we were closer to this magic fence?"

"It depends. Probably not. But"—she took out her phone—
"I'm all for doing some snooping if only to prove that Newt and
his family are innocent." Her lips curved into a devious smile and
she began typing.

I lunged forward, sandwiching her hands and phone between mine. "Not so fast. Who are you texting?"

She shimmied her phone out of my grip. "That was a good
move, but it's the Professor's phone you need to grab, not mine.
We don't want him calling Kate or Mom and telling them what
we're up to."

"I'm not doing anything until you explain." I folded my
arms across my chest. "All I'm suggesting is that we drive by
the house, so you can check for any trace of magic."

She turned her attention back to the phone. "Trust me. I
know what I'm doing."

"Selena," I said warningly. But I was curious what she had
in mind. To be honest, at this point I was up for anything. I
craned my neck, glancing at her phone. Newt, of course—who
else would she be texting?

U still home? I've got the car, if you've got the time <3

She sent the message, then looked at me. "He was all over
himself apologizing this morning because he can't see me for a
few days, something about his cousin getting married. They've
got rehearsal this afternoon, then a dinner. The wedding's on
Friday. His whole family's involved—that means no one will
be at their house right now. We could peek in a few windows."

Her phone buzzed and she held it up so I could read Newt's
response.

Sorry, babe. Already left. Sunday, U and me?

She raised her eyebrows. "What do you think?"

I toyed with my necklace for a second, mulling over the idea.
We'd been led to believe Newt's sleazebag younger brother,

Myles, had kidnapped Lotli based on a previous attempt that I'd interrupted. Information we'd gotten from a local plumber had convinced us that Newt and his family were lying about his dad's profession and who owned the summer house they were living in. The truth was, even if we didn't discover anything related to magic, a peek through the windows might go a long ways toward confirming or eliminating this secondhand information.

"Okay, let's do this," I said. But in the back of my mind I could already hear the scream of police sirens and the click of handcuffs closing around my wrists. *Unlawful trespass.* Not exactly the kind of thing that enhanced college résumés.

CHAPTER 3

*He followed the sleepwalker through the dark tunnels
and into the necropolis. But what he sought and where
the sleepwalker led were two very different things indeed.*

—James William Freemont
The Tale of the Sleepwalker's Hoard

It was around five when I drove past Newt's house, an older
two-story cape near the end of a sparsely populated cul-
de-sac. Even without any other evidence, the fact that Newt
had never invited Selena to their so-called summer home or
introduced her to any of his family—other than sleazebag
Myles—made it likely that this place contained at least a few
secrets.

I reached where a tall cedar hedge marked the end of their
property. Just beyond it, an access road went down toward the
ocean. I backed into the access and parked where we could see
the front of the house through the hedge. One bay of the
house's attached garage was open, but there were no people or
cars around.

Selena leaned over the front seat and cuffed the Professor's
arm. "See, I told you, no one's home."

"They're here, somewhere. No one in their right mind
would leave without closing the garage doors," he said.

I unhooked my seatbelt. "They probably were distracted and left in a hurry."

"You really believe that?" He raised an eyebrow.

Doubt hovered in my mind, but I wasn't about to let him know it. However, I also wasn't totally foolish. I pulled his phone from my pocket and held it out to him. Following Selena's suggestion, I'd confiscated it from him back at the campsite, so he couldn't call Kate. Now that he'd calmed down a little, it seemed wiser to give it back.

Selena lunged for the phone. "Are you crazy?"

I outmaneuvered her and slipped the phone to the Professor. "He can call us if he sees a car pulling in or anything."

"At least one of you has some sense," the Professor said. "And just to be perfectly clear, I'm not convinced this idea doesn't have merit. I am, however, against either of you taking any unnecessary chances."

"Don't worry, we won't." My voice might have been filled with confidence, but I was fully aware that just parking here had put us at risk.

I grabbed a flashlight from under my seat. It might help us see into the basement windows, a good place to start since that's where the plumber found his evidence.

Selena and I hiked up the street and down the driveway toward Newt's house, as casual as if we belonged there. I didn't dare say anything to Selena, but I was starting to feel woozy along with stiff and sore. The truth was, if Chase had been with us, he'd have told me to take it easier. No. He would have made me stay home and rest.

A small black metal sign on the garage caught my eye: PROTECTED 24/7 BY SAFEHOLM.

I moved in close to Selena and whispered, "I can't see anything. But they've definitely got some kind of security system."

She lowered her voice. "Newt told me he used to cover a

camera and sneak in through a bathroom window when he got home late from partying."

"He could have just said that to encourage you to sneak out and meet him," I said.

She flashed me a dirty look, then lengthened her strides and marched swiftly toward the darkness of the open garage bay.

A warning prickled the back of my neck. *Too convenient.*

I hurried my steps and followed her. "Do you sense anything—like the fence?" I asked louder than I'd have liked, but it did make her stop and glance toward me.

While her brow wrinkled with concentration, I quickly scanned the shadows. A short flight of stairs led up to a back door with a security keypad next to it.

There was a rolled-up garden hose. A pair of old swim fins. Pieces of copper pipe and a toolbox with DOWN EAST HEATING AND PLUMBING stamped on the side. For the most part, the place was neat and disturbingly empty.

Ahead, a dust-smeared window framed a view of the backyard and an immense array of huge antennas and satellite dishes, enough for a small military installation or a TV studio, way more than the basic Wi-Fi.

I tilted my head, weighing if I should point them out to Selena or wait for her to spot them on her own. The information that we'd gotten from the plumber claimed a guy named Jeffrey White owned this house, instead of Newt's dad. Jeffrey White hosted a TV show about history and ancient aliens—in other words, he was the kind of guy who might have a huge antennae array.

"I don't sense the fence or anything," Selena said. "Not a trace. Which isn't a surprise since they aren't—" Her voice tensed and she stopped talking. "Fucking Newt," she snarled. "The bastard lied to me. He stinking lied!"

She kicked a doormat, sending it flying across the floor.

I grabbed her by the arm, squeezing. "Shush. Calm down," I said, but even at a distance, I could see what had pissed her off. WELCOME TO THE WHITES' HOUSE was printed in bold letters across the doormat.

She shoved my hand away and pointed at a sign hanging beside the back door. "It says *White,* too. I can't freaking believe it!"

I softened my voice. "I know. It's awful. But we don't need the neighbors calling the cops."

"How could Newt do that to me?" Her voice hitched. "He loves me."

I rested my hand on her arm. "I don't think Newt intended to hurt you. After all, he didn't totally lie. His family does live here. It just belongs to someone else." I nudged her toward the garage door. "Come on. Let's look around out back."

The name pretty much proved Newt and his family were liars. However, I wasn't totally convinced all the plumber's claims were true. He swore Newt's dad wasn't a stockbroker, but instead made his living running a blog about snake wrestlers. That sounded a bit far-fetched. But, whether the snake wresting was true or not, there had to be more here, something to link Newt and his family to magic. If we could uncover that connection, it might bring us closer to figuring out *why* they'd taken Lotli, and that combined with the scrying could lead us to *where* she was being held.

We dashed out of the garage and around to the backyard. Unfortunately, other than the electronic equipment, there wasn't anything out of the ordinary to be seen. No stone circles or ritual fire pits. No mound that could hide a bunker. Not even a witchy herb garden. Only a very average deck attached to the house and a standard metal bulkhead that undoubtedly protected an equally normal basement entry.

Pushing aside my disappointment, I led Selena up a flight

of stairs and onto the deck. We peered through a set of sliding glass doors and into a family room: hardwood floor, exposed beams, walls decorated with photos of Acadia National Park. To the left, there was a kitchen, modern and clean.

"We're not going to find anything else here," Selena said. "We should get going."

I relented and headed back down to the lawn, but uneasiness twitched in my stomach. One of the things I'd learned from my years of dealing antiques with Dad was that the best cons appeared innocent on the outside—not that Dad and I did illegal stuff, but there were a lot of crooks in the business, and Dad had taught me to watch out and trust my gut. Right now, it was screaming that something was out of kilter. I just needed to dig deeper.

Frustrated, I stared at the house, windows glittering in the sunshine. "Selena, you really don't sense any magic?"

"Not a trace. And that fence wasn't cloaked, if anything related to it was here, I should sense it."

I nibbled my bottom lip, my gaze lowering to the bulkhead as an idea formed. "What about other things, like books about the occult, witchcraft tools . . . stuff like that—would you be able to sense them?"

"Depends. Maybe. What are you thinking?"

"When the plumber poked around, he was focused on the ancient alien TV things, stuff that had made him geek out and start snooping. He might have overlooked the witchcraft." A renewed sense of energy pumped into my veins as I eyed the bulkhead's metal doors secured with a chain and padlock. "If I had a good stiff wire, I could open that in less than a minute."

In two strides Selena walked over, crouched down, and took ahold of the chain. "I bet I could do it in half that time."

"No way," I said. She had no idea how to pick locks.

She grinned and slid the padlock free from the chain.

"No shit," I said. The lock had been holding the chain's

ends together, but it hadn't been locked shut. "First the garage door, now this?"

"Seems a bit too convenient, wouldn't you say?"

"Exactly." I glanced toward the cedar hedge that hid the Land Rover, then back at the bulkhead. "The Professor will phone if anyone shows up. My gut's telling me to go for it."

Selena paled. "This is a lot riskier than what we planned on doing."

"It could be our only chance." I removed the chain and pulled the bulkhead door open. It was heavy as hell and creaked as if it hadn't been oiled in years. Chase was depending on me. So was my mother. We needed all the information we could get to figure out what Newt's family was up to, and find Lotli. Without her, there was no way to free Chase and Mother from the djinn realm and Malphic's grip.

I stepped into the bulkhead and went down the three steps to the basement's door. Then I took out my flashlight and turned back toward Selena. "I'll meet you back at the car in five minutes."

"Hell with that." She scowled. "I'm coming with you." She hurried down the steps, lowering the metal door shut behind her.

Darkness closed in. I clicked on my flashlight, its beam bright in the cramped space.

"Here goes nothing," I said.

I opened the basement door, and we stepped inside.

Gray light dribbled in through scattered half windows, revealing stacks of boxes with narrow paths between them. It was far too shadowy and dark for my taste, but I couldn't let fear take over. Too much was at stake. Besides, last month I'd discovered my excessive fear of the dark stemmed from witnessing my mother's kidnapping. I could deal with it much better now. I had to.

I fanned the flashlight's beam slowly, starting at the doorway and moving clockwise around the room. It was a technique Dad and I used when we purchased crowded rooms of junk. Don't jump from one spot to another. Be organized. Take your time.

The beam brightened a washer and dryer. A hot water heater. Plumbing supplies . . .

I studied the pipes and wrenches for a second. The way the stuff was haphazardly strewn around made me think the plumber had stopped in the middle of a project and would be back at any moment, except it was after five o'clock and the basement was totally dark. If he was anywhere, he was off having an after-work beer with his friends.

I went back to scanning. A blue tricycle. An old trunk. The light glistened off something moderately tall and narrow. About my size and shape. Wrapped in plastic—

Horror swept through me. I gasped. "It can't be."

Selena moved in close. "What?"

Unable to breathe, I fanned the light again until its beam fell across a plastic-wrapped figure of . . . a person. My body went cold and a sick feeling lodged in my throat. Behind the first figure were dozens more, standing up like they were frozen stiff. *They're mannequins,* I reasoned. But they didn't look plastic.

Selena grabbed my arm. "Ohmigod. They're people. Freaking real people."

Willing myself not to throw up, I took a shaky step forward and swept the beam over the closest one's face. Black hair, dark kohled eyes, high cheekbones . . .

Selena let out a smothered screech. "It's—"

"It's Lotli, isn't it?" I said, my voice barely audible. My whole body trembled, but I forced myself to point the flashlight at her face again. *Please, Hecate, let it be anyone but Lotli.*

The light glinted off a shiny gold-and-black-striped head-cloth crowned with the likeness of a cobra. The eyes were open and as dark as Lotli's, the nose as prominent as hers. But this face had a bold, narrow beard. Definitely not a woman.

"It looks like a wax statue. A pharaoh," Selena whispered. "King Tut or someone."

The tension uncoiled from my spine. Of course, these were what had made the plumber geek out and start thinking about Jeffrey White and his TV show. I fanned the light again, spotlighting the figure next to Tut. The vacant gaze of a Roswell-type alien stared back at me.

I rolled my eyes. "They're TV props."

Selena blew out a breath. "Creepy TV props, if you ask me."

I moved the flashlight beam farther into the room, past a stack of boxes. It brightened a waist-high Ark of the Covenant. Behind it, faces stared out from the darkness, their eyes black and hollow, all glaring at us. Some had bird beaks, others elongated chins, red and black, jagged teeth, fiery hair, flashes of silver metal. *Masks,* I told myself. But another voice deep inside me whispered for me to run. *They have bodies. They are alive,* the voice warned.

"I really don't like this place," Selena mumbled.

"Me neither." I wiped my damp palms on my jeans, gritted my teeth, and inched forward.

Finally, we reached the center of the room. Ahead, the faint shape of stairs led upward toward the first floor. When I scanned under them, the flashlight beam illuminated a door-knob.

"I think there's another room," I said to Selena.

She snuggled in closer, her whole body trembling. "Probably a dungeon."

I laughed, like it was a joke. But part of me worried that was exactly what it might be. I shoved that aside and lifted my chin. Enough of this bullshit. This was all fake. A Halloween funhouse that I didn't have time to get caught up in.

I strode the rest of the way across the room to the door. It was normal, no fancy keypad or signs of alarms. I opened it. Nothing but darkness, pitch-black and solid.

I swallowed hard. Was an unlocked door a good sign or a bad? Probably the latter, I decided. Worse still, I was certain the smell permeating the air was not musty or stale, but fresh, a man's cologne mixed with peanuts. That meant the room had been recently used.

"I can't see anything," Selena whispered.

"There has to be a light switch." I stepped inside with her close behind me, located a switch, and flicked it on.

The ceiling lights sputtered to life, slowly brightening the room. Medium size. A drop ceiling. Wall-to-wall carpet. An office.

I shut the door and began scanning the place as quickly as I could.

One wall was covered with blown-up satellite images of the Nazca Lines and various Stonehenge-like structures. There were also sketches of petroglyphs, a timeline with elongated skulls stationed along it, images of Maya gods, Easter Island heads, a Hindu temple, and star charts. On another wall, bookshelves rose floor to ceiling. A glass-topped desk was piled with files and framed photos that I assumed were of Jeffrey White on the set of his TV show. There was an open can of peanuts on the desk next to a half-empty bottle of water. Computers, printers, other electronic devices . . . Loads of stuff, but not one pentagram or anything that screamed witchcraft.

"What the hell?" Selena pressed her fingers against a blown-up photo that hung next to one of the satellite images. "Newt took this. I thought . . . He sent me a copy, but it didn't look like this."

I hurried over. Selena was in the photo, or rather the side of her head was. Clearly, the original had been enlarged and cropped to focus on the crowd standing behind her. I leaned in to take a closer look, but jerked back in surprise when I realized who the image now centered on.

"That's Lotli," I said.

She was playing her flute in front of a small fire, its smoke rising like a spellbound cobra. Chase and I had been in the crowd that day, watching Lotli's performance. It was the day before we went to the campsite and Zea agreed to let her come back to Moonhill with us.

Selena's eyes went flinty, teeth grinding in anger. "I was so into Newt, I didn't even notice the show. Damn bastard—apparently, the curse didn't stop him from having other things on his mind."

I took out my phone and snapped a couple of shots of the image.

"We have to go upstairs," I said, heading for the door. Now that we'd discovered this photograph, I was feeling hopeful. We were right on track. We just had to follow the evidence to where it led. I was sure we'd discover something else. "We'll start with Newt's room."

Selena cuffed the peanut can off the desk, nuts flying everywhere. "I fucking hate Newt."

I glanced back. "You okay?"

She gave me a pained look. "I don't know. Let's just get out of here."

My chest tightened as we crept up the stairs toward the first floor. I knew how she felt—betrayed, embarrassed, responsible, angry. . . . Last winter, I'd had sex with my best friend, Taj. We'd been close through years of homeschooling and even when he'd started interning at the Metropolitan Museum. It had felt wonderful. I'd thought it was the beginning of something amazing. Then I found out he had a girlfriend and the hurt had been almost unbearable. Selena's situation wasn't exactly the same; still, I felt horrible for her.

At the top of the stairs, a door opened into the kitchen, as clean and modern as it had appeared through the sliding glass doors. We tiptoed down a hall, through a dining room and up a carpeted staircase to the second floor. Straight ahead was a bathroom. To the left was a short hallway with three closed doors. A hallway with just two doors jutted off to the right.

I turned to the left. "I'll check these rooms, if you do the other ones."

"Newt's will be the one labeled *jerkwad*," she said, flinging open the door closest to her.

I tried the first door on my side. A stench of body odor and Axe cologne smacked me in the face, and the memory of dancing with Newt's brother, of him rubbing his crotch against me, sent nausea crawling up my throat.

I yanked the door shut. "This one belongs to Myles."

"This room's their parents', I think," Selena called. "The next one looks like a guest room."

I opened another door. No reek of body odor or cologne, just a light, spicy scent. "Found it," I announced, stepping inside.

The room was tiny with a single twin-size bed. Its navy blue spread was tucked in with military precision, the thin pillow perfectly centered. A poster of a black Mustang hung squarely in the middle of one wall.

I shuddered. It looked exactly like Newt's Mustang—and exactly like the car I'd found Lotli tied up inside, during the previous kidnapping attempt. If only I'd been as certain that night of Myles and Newt's guilt as I was now.

Pushing my regret aside, I went to his desk. Above it photographs of Selena and a couple of guys in lacrosse uniforms hung next to an award plaque.

Selena came up beside me. "Look at this," she said, waving a stiff piece of paper in front of me. It was an invitation done in a fancy cursive font. Doves and raspberry-pink ribbons were embossed across the invitation's top edge. "At least Newt didn't lie about everything. Apparently there is a wedding this Friday."

"It also means he probably is at the rehearsal right now." I snapped a photo of the invitation, then turned back and took a shot of the plaque. It was an award for excellence, given to Newt last winter. The emblem in the center was a snake, twisted up like a pretzel.

My mouth dried. It was an exact replica of the tattoo on Newt's wrist, except this was surrounded by a motto written in what looked like Latin. "Selena," I said sharply to get her attention. "You better come take a look at this."

She bent in, studying the image. "It's his team logo—or at least that's what he told me. But he never mentioned a motto."

"Can you translate it?"

She nibbled her bottom lip, then began enunciating each word slowly. "*Open minds with eyes on the heaven.*" She straightened back up, a puzzled look coming over her face. "It's the same motto that's on the home page of his dad's blog. Only it's in English." She hesitated. "Not that I knew about the blog before. I only looked at it earlier today, after we found out about the lies."

"Isn't that kind of a weird motto for a blog? I mean, especially for a blog about snake wrestling? The whole idea is pretty strange if you ask me."

She laughed. "You haven't looked at the blog, have you? It's not about *snake wrestling*. It's *The Snake Wrestler*."

A faint rumble sounded in the distance and I held up my hand to silence Selena. "Did you hear that," I whispered.

Her eyes went wide. "Shit. It's a car. In the driveway."

"But they're at the rehearsal dinner," I said. Then it hit me. The police. We'd tripped a silent alarm.

The jangle of her phone echoed in the room. Selena snatched it super fast and listened for a second. Then she crammed it in her pocket. "That was the Professor. We've got to get out of here."

We sprinted for the stairs as fast as we could. But by the time we reached the first floor, the slam of car doors sounded in the driveway. We were too late. The outlines of two SUVs were visible through the windows on either side of the front door. Crap.

I grabbed Selena and made a dash through the dining room, shoving her along in front of me. My pulse hammered in my ears and panic gripped my throat until I could barely breathe. But I forced myself to focus. I needed to get us out of here. The front door was out of bounds, so was the backdoor, since they'd parked in front of the garage. There was the basement. But the sliding glass doors were closer. I took off, hauling Selena along. We were almost to them when a burly guy in green workclothes walked up onto the deck, followed by another man.

Heart in my throat, I yanked Selena through the closest open door and out of sight. I shut the door behind us.

We stood in a small half bath. Was it the one Newt used to sneak in at night? We couldn't be that lucky, could we?

I flew to the room's only window, almost tripping over a sweatshirt and tool pouch that lay next to the sink. I shoved the window up, then the screen. Below was the lawn, beyond that the cedar hedge and the Land Rover.

"Go," I said to Selena.

She shimmied out feetfirst, holding on to the window ledge for a heartbeat before dropping down to the ground.

The scrape of footsteps and voices reverberated from somewhere inside the house.

"I'll be right there!" a man shouted. "I left my tool pouch in the bathroom."

Shit. I dove for the window.

CHAPTER 4

Even when the sun rises, the stars rule the sky.

—Imprinted on clay tablet

I dropped to the ground and shrank back against the house next to Selena. Even if the guy noticed the open window and screen, staying in the shadows would keep us out of his line of sight. That was as long as he didn't stick his head out the window and really look around.

Selena nodded toward the hedge on the far side of the lawn. I raised a finger to tell her to wait a minute. I could still hear the man shuffling around inside the bathroom, putting on the sweatshirt or doing whatever.

After a long couple of minutes, the shuffling stopped and Selena and I catapulted across the lawn and through the gap in the hedge. The second we got into the car, I put it in gear and pulled out from the access road. As we passed the house, a sense of relief washed over me and I blew out a breath. But my throat clamped shut again when a man appeared in the open garage bay, his attention fixed on us as we drove by.

"Do you think he saw us?" Selena said, hunkering down in the backseat.

The Professor swiveled away from the side window, hiding his face. "This isn't good, not good at all."

I stepped on the gas. "If he wasn't suspicious before, he is now with you two hiding like that. At least they weren't cops."

"Are you absolutely sure about that?" The Professor glanced toward the house.

"Definitely. It was the plumber and some other guy. One of them was looking for a tool pouch, and there were pipes and stuff in the garage and basement."

Selena hung over the back of my seat. "Why would he be working this late in the day?"

"Who knows? Maybe they're working while the family's gone, so they won't disturb anyone. It doesn't matter anyway. We weren't supposed to be in the house. If they saw us, they'd call the cops as quick as anyone."

I winged out of the neighborhood and took a zigzag route back to the main road. Selena phoned Kate, told her what had happened at the campsite, and gave her an overview of what we'd done and seen at Newt's, a move that ensured we'd get bailed out quicker if the plumber called the police. It also would give her and Olya time to cool down before we got home. Besides, it wasn't like we could put off telling them everything. We didn't have time to waste.

But not a single cop car came up behind us and by the time we got back to the Moonhill, my pulse was subsiding back to normal. However, without the rush of adrenaline, every inch of my sore body began to stiffen and throb, and bone-deep exhaustion settled in.

Tibbs loped out of the house to greet us and I gave him the Land Rover's keys so he could take it to the garage. Tibbs was in his early twenties. He lived on the estate and did tons of things for the family, all the mechanical work, security, and weapon maintenance. . . . He even helped his mother, Laura, in the kitchen and with household chores. He also was the person who uncovered the information about Newt's family by grilling his local friends, including the plumber. This initiative upgraded him in my aunt Kate's eyes. Unfortunately, the only person Tibbs wanted to impress was Selena. Sadly, all she cared about was that he was old enough to buy liquor for her.

He took his cap off and smoothed back his ginger hair. "Kate said you guys went to Newt's house?"

I nodded and lowered my voice to a whisper. "Your plumber friend was right about everything. He also might have seen us."

His gaze shifted toward where Selena and the Professor waited on the front steps, then retreated as if he were afraid she'd shoot daggers at him for screwing up her personal life. "How's she taking it?"

"Let's just say, I wouldn't ask her about Newt right now. But if you could find out if the plumber spotted us she'd—we all would appreciate that."

"No problem," he said. He took a scuffling step toward the driver's door and then glanced over his shoulder. "I almost forgot. Kate wanted me to tell you, she's waiting on the terrace."

Leaving him behind, Selena, the Professor, and I went into the foyer and made our way past the kitchen to the terrace door. We found Kate watering the planters. She was dressed more casual than usual, in her gardening slacks and a pale green blouse. She had a silk scarf wrapped around her neck, covering up a wound she'd gotten about a month ago during a battle with Malphic's full-blooded genie son, Culus, who had taken possession of my dad's body in order to gain entry to Moonhill. She shut off the hose and peered down her nose at us. "It appears that you managed to get home without incident."

The Professor shook his head. "That's a wonderful thought, but we may not be in the clear yet."

Selena waved him off. "You worry too much. Everything's going to be fine."

"I think we're all set, too," I said.

"Let's hope so." Kate's lips pinched into a thin line. "The last thing we need is cops snooping around here."

I got out my phone and brought up the photo of Lotli. I was about to show it to Kate, when an eerie, surreal feeling came over me. Kate and everyone else faded into the background and I became hyperaware of the warmth of the sunlight against my skin, the buzz of a passing bee, the scent of the water evaporating off the terrace's warm stones. It was similar to déjà vu, yet completely different. It was as if I were frozen, while the world whirled on around me. And no matter how illogical, I knew with certainty Chase was there in that moment, right then and there, with me. I couldn't see him. But I could sense the heat of his presence. Smell and taste him, like the lingering fragrance of a candle, a touch of cinnamon and pine—

Something needle-sharp dug into my ankle.

Still dazed, I glanced down in time to see a gray flash of tiger-striped cat racing away. Houdini. He skittered behind the Professor's legs, then stared back at me, tail thrashing.

"I told you that cat was a nasty beast," Kate said.

I blinked at her, not wanting to say or do anything that would take me farther away from Chase, anything that would widen the gulf between us. But time had already moved on. I was back in the world, and what had seemed so real for a heartbeat, now felt impossible.

Kate pried the phone from my grip and studied the photo of Lotli. She moved on to the shot of the invitation. "Interesting. The wedding is *this* Friday."

Selena tsked. "Well, obviously. But that's not important."

I sucked in a breath, to finish righting my brain, then interrupted. "Actually, it is—if we want to get back into the house and take another look around."

Kate handed the phone back to me. "It also confirms our other suspicions."

"About what?" Hope fluttered in my chest. Kate had said she and Zach were going to do some investigating on the Internet while we were gone. It sounded like they'd discovered something.

"There's been chatter on the Dark Net. It seems the Sons of Ophiuchus are gathering this Friday for some sort of special meeting."

"Sons of Ophiuchus? A meeting?" I said, totally mystified. "What are you talking about?"

"The plaque you photographed. The twisted snake with the motto around it. That's their emblem."

"Ah—I'm assuming there's a connection to a serpent wrestler here somewhere?" I said, though I still didn't get it.

Kate scoffed. "Of course. *The* Serpent Wrestler is another name for the constellation Ophiuchus. You are familiar with that, aren't you?"

I cringed. "Stars aren't exactly my thing."

"Don't feel bad." Selena tried to sound consoling. "I knew the constellation had two names and that Ophiuchus is the God of Healing, plus I looked at The Serpent Wrestler blog. But even I don't know what she's getting at." Her eyes sliced toward Kate. "What I also want to know is why no one ever mentioned this Sons of Ophiuchus group to me. If you had, then I might have been at least a little suspicious when Newt told me his tattoo was a lacrosse thing."

Kate lifted her chin. "We didn't mention them because we've never considered the Sons a threat. However, a boy using you to get close to our family has been a concern for some time."

"Don't worry," Selena snapped. "Newt's going to regret this big time."

"I imagine he will." Kate squeezed the bridge of her nose. After a moment, she cleared her throat and continued. "At any rate, the Sons are a rather ineffectual, aging organization—or so we believed. They've been around since ancient times. Doctors, alchemists, men devoted to science to a large extent. It's their conviction—and probably rightly so—that the study of ancient medicine, religious practices, and cultures holds clues to extending life, a sort of immortality that once existed and was lost as we evolved, or perhaps a secret gifted to men such as Sumerian Kings and Nicolas Flamel by visitors from other solar systems."

The Professor touched Kate's arm lightly. "Now that I think about it, I do believe I've run across references to this group. If I'm not mistaken, Ponce de León was involved with them—and Herodotus."

Kate nodded. "Them and many others. According to our family's records, they even provided refuge for witches during the Inquisition. However, we've long suspected those witches suffered far worse fates than the ones who were left in the Inquisitors' hands."

I swallowed hard. Worse than being burned alive? Images flashed into my head: needles being driven under fingernails and into eyes, evisceration, filleting . . . I gritted my teeth, bringing the gruesome parade of ways to get information out of someone to a halt. I met Kate's gaze. "Who belongs to this group now?"

"My best guess is that the Sons have developed a new core membership, perhaps rooted somewhere in the pharmacology industry, that would fit with their goals and might explain their sudden resurgence and financial stability."

The throb and ache of my bruised muscles retreated, overshadowed by the power of a sudden chill. She was talking megacorporations and international ties. Serious power and wealth. I took a deep breath. "Are you thinking they kidnapped Lotli because they believe she knows the secret to extended life? Why didn't they just barter with Zea for the information? She seems willing to do pretty much whatever he asks. For that matter, Zea probably knows the secret, too."

Selena waved her hand like a schoolgirl. "I know. It's simple. We found Lotli and Zea before the Sons had a chance to make their move. Then we brought her to Moonhill. They think we're after the same thing."

Chair legs scraped as the Professor slumped down at the glass-topped porch table. His gaze darted back up to us. "There is another disagreeable possibility. Perhaps they aren't after that secret. They could want her flute-magic—so they can control the veil between life and death. It's another route to immortality."

"That could be," Kate said. "But whatever their reason, it all comes back to Friday and the wedding."

I rubbed my neck, letting everything sink in. "So you think the wedding is really a cover for this meeting the Sons are having?" I asked. I hesitated, then took that train of thought to the next level. "You think they kidnapped Lotli and this meeting somehow involves her?"

Selena heaved a frustrated breath. "We wouldn't have to be guessing about any of this if I could break through the magic fence and see where Lotli is."

"Don't rule that out yet," Kate said. "I've run into fences like that before. They are intended to hide magic from the outside world without disturbing the flow of normal human activities. A person can walk through one without detecting anything, but try to use psychic energy to pass and . . . Well, you felt the results."

Selena straightened. "You're saying we can bypass it?"

"The area encompassed by the fence won't be large, tennis court-size at the most. Once someone walks through the fence and is in the center, they'd be able to scry unhampered—though by that point Lotli should be in sight."

The door to the house flung open and Selena's little brother, Zachary, careened out onto the terrace, his spiked hair jutting out at all angles, his eyes glistening with excitement. The Professor had been asked to tutor him partly because the kid was Mensa smart, but also to keep him out of trouble. A step behind him was his and Selena's mom, Olya, her ratty black cardigan flying out behind her.

Olya's arms fluttered in the air. "Selena, sweetheart, what were you thinking? Breaking into a house! If you had gotten caught—" As if too overwhelmed to speak, her throaty Eastern European accent deepened and she sank into a chair across the table from the Professor.

Zachary snickered. "I think it's cool."

"It was not cool. It was dangerous," Olya said. The worry dropped from her face, replaced by excitement as her gaze swooped toward me. "Oh, yes. We have good news. Your dad—all the men will be home from Slovenia first thing in the morning."

It took a second for what she'd said to register. I'd kind of lost track of time. But this was great. Dad being here would make everything so much easier. "That's fantastic. What time?"

"It depends on traffic or if they can get a private plane up from Boston." She turned to Kate. "They want to go after Lotli right away."

Kate turned away, pacing two steps before turning back. "Then we don't have a choice. Magic fence or not, we need to at least try scrying again."

Selena nodded. "I agree. When I scried before it felt like Lotli was in a riding stable. Part of that was because the magic gave me a shock like an electric fence. But I also sensed lots of wood, rope, and exposed beams like a barn. The invitation said the wedding is at a yacht club. What if I mistook a boathouse for a stable?" She grinned. "Instead of using a personal item to locate Lotli, why don't we just remotely check out the energy around the yacht club? See if we can sense the fence's magic."

Everyone agreed this was a fabulous idea, even Kate. But I wasn't so sure. The idea of focusing on sensing magic rather than scrying for Lotli bothered me. Chase getting trapped in the djinn realm had partly happened because of a humming-bird egg pendant that Lotli had given me as a friendship gift.

Olya had tested it and said she couldn't sense any magic. But later, when I'd broken it in the realm during a fit of jealousy, it had exploded and temporarily nullified the magic oil we were wearing, allowing the genies to see that we were human.

I clamped my eyes shut for a second, wishing I could go back and change that moment. If only I hadn't gotten so angry, then Chase wouldn't have gotten trapped. Mother would be safe, too. Unfortunately, changing the past was impossible. All I could do was move forward and right those wrongs.

"If sensing magic is so reliable," I said, careful to not sound snotty, "then why didn't Olya—or any of you for that matter—notice that the pendant Lotli gave me was magic?"

The Professor leaned forward, his eyes going to Kate. "That's not a half-bad question."

"Fortunately, there's a simple answer," she said. "The egg could have been a conduit designed to absorb magic from outside itself and store it. In other words, the magic went into the egg after Olya tested it."

Selena snorted. "That doesn't make sense. Annie doesn't have any special magic abilities it could have absorbed." Her gaze met mine. "You don't, right?"

I laughed. "Definitely not—though, I did feel better once the pendant was gone."

"That is understandable." Olya swept her hand across the top of the table, as if laying out her logic on its surface. "All living things have energy that can be weakened or strengthened. Magic is nothing more than that energy enhanced innately or through practice." She hung her head. "I am ashamed I did not realize what the pendant could do."

I smiled at her. "Don't worry about it." And I meant it. The anger bristling inside me was aimed at Lotli. Once we found her, I'd confront her about the pendant. I deserved the blame for the failed rescue, but that didn't mean I had to put up with her playing me for a fool. She'd meant for the pendant to suck my energy from me, or to collect power from the djinn realm itself. Put simply, Lotli had used me. But what had she hoped to gain?

I stared past Olya, out toward the gardens and the ocean beyond. There was another thing I couldn't get out of my mind. I'd seen Lotli wrap blue and green strands of Chase's yarn around her flute and then coat them with beeswax as if she were doing a spell. True, unlike the egg, nothing had happened because of the yarn. Still, I couldn't shake the feeling that it served a purpose beyond simple ornamentation, though again Olya and Kate had thought it innocent.

Less than five minutes later, the Professor, Zachary, and I headed inside so Selena and the older women could get into the zone and do their remote scan of the yacht club. When we reached the front foyer, Zach and the Professor turned toward the library and I started up the main staircase.

Dad would be home in the morning. In the meantime, I could rest up and go on my own reconnaissance trip to the yacht club via the Internet. See if I could find out more about its location and who owned it. I could also dig into the Sons of Ophiuchus. Why did secret societies always have such long and complicated histories? Sumerian Kings, Nicolas Flamel, Ponce de León, Herodotus . . . I was good at history, but checking out all those guys was going to be a cross-time-and-culture marathon of history lessons.

I reached the top of the stairs and was about to turn toward my room, when it happened again: The same eerie sensation that had overtaken me on the terrace, dreamlike, languid, time whirling around me. My head felt heavy, yet everything became sharper and more heightened. Dust motes glistened in a gold shaft of light. The far-off gong of a grandfather clock resounded as loud as though I stood right next to it. The scent of beeswax and lemon furniture polish filled my nostrils, surreally intense. I was in this world. I was certain of that. But what was happening? Was it Chase? Was he here, somehow?

Warmth brushed my skin. I didn't dare move as it swept my jawline, down my throat and arms. I could almost smell him, almost taste him, mingling with the beeswax and lemon—

Then, as swiftly as it had come, the moment vanished. The clock gonged one more time, distant, barely audible. The shaft of light muted, dissolving into a hint of brightness as time moved on. There were no smells. Not a trace of anything.

An almost unbearable sense of loss weighed inside me. My chest ached with the need to be with him. Tears burned in my eyes. I covered my face with my hands. There had to be a way to make the moment last longer, so I could really feel his touch, hear his voice. There had to be a special ritual or a time or place—

A special place?

A tingle of hope fluttered in my chest. I turned on my heel and fled back down the stairs, out the front door and to the garage. I snagged the keys to the newest ATV from the pegboard and Tibbs's old work jacket off a hook. The jacket was stained with oil and the sleeves hung down way beyond my hands. But he wouldn't care if I borrowed it, and even if he did, I didn't care right now. I squashed on a helmet and straddled the ATV.

CHAPTER 5

If I give you my heart, if I pledge my soul,
Will you come back, will you be mine forever?
If I reach in the darkness, if I dare the night,
Will you be there, will you be there forever?

From "Forever Mine"
www.NorthTunes.com

A minute later, I was speeding up the driveway. Dusk was deepening, shadows falling quickly. At the main gate, I didn't turn into Chase's cottage. Instead, I steered the ATV in the opposite direction, down a trail-like maintenance road that ran along the southern border of Moonhill's property. The road wound through an overgrown pasture and into the woods, where it dead-ended in a wide spot surrounded by giant pine trees.

I parked the ATV and flew into the darkening woods, the pine's fragrant carpet soft beneath my footsteps. I swept past the place where less than a month ago Chase and I had made love for the first time and out onto a rocky point.

A warm breeze pushed my hair from my face. The scent of the ocean filled my nose. This was Chase's favorite place, his secret clifftop sanctuary, overlooking the broad ocean on one side and Port St. Claire's harbor on the other. The surreal sensation of Chase being with me was gone. But if any place could bring him back, it was here.

Relief settled over me and I sunk down onto the clifftop, sitting with my knees pulled up to my chest. *Chase.* I stared out at the evening sky, letting my head fill with the rhythmic beat of waves against the rocks, the cry of a lone gull, the whisper of the breeze. I breathed in deep through my nose, letting it out slowly through my mouth, the way Selena did when she focused and scried. I brought Chase's face to mind: his ocean-gray eyes, the slope of his jaw, the twitch in his cheek when he tried not to smile. The bristle of his morning beard. The smoothness after he shaved. The taste of water on his lips when we made love in the shower. The way he flinched when my tongue touched the brand Malphic had burned into the skin, just below his collarbone.

My heartbeat slowed, seeming to take on the rhythm of the waves. I balled up Tibbs's jacket. Using it as a pillow, I laid back. Above me, dark clouds rushed across the twilight sky. The warmth of the rock beneath me seeped into my muscles. Despite the breeze and clouds, I was warm. Comfortable. I let my mind drift, trying to go back to that moment in time on the terrace.

I could feel myself relaxing, slipping, closer and closer to-ward sleep. When I was little, sometimes, if I stayed in the place between wake and sleep long enough, I could bring on the dream that I wanted: flying, riding horses into the sea . . . Maybe this time, if I wished hard enough—

The comforting warmth surrounding me grows hotter, hot as if I lay under a midday sun instead of twilight and clouds. Silhouetted against the sky, Chase's outline appears on the edge of the cliff, his blue aura shimmering, marking him as part genie. He wears the leather armor, flowing white pants, and bracers I last saw him in. His tempo-rary tattoos, cryptic swirls and lettering applied for the djinn's full moon festival, glow like blue volcano fissures.

He prowls toward me, more aura than man, a shining comet made of sparks and heat. He kneels beside me, fingers brushing my hair back from my face, his lips nearing mine. I long to reach for him, but I'm drifting close to dreamland and can only lie there, lost in the memory of past kisses, intoxicated by the thought of the dream kiss I'm certain is about to come.

His hands rest on either side of my arms. The weight of him presses against me. Lips graze my throat. He caresses my face, fingertips sending shudders of desire through my body. Chase. My Chase.

I roll onto my side and he's there, lying alongside me, beautiful eyes gazing into mine. He kisses my palm, then folds my fingers around it as if telling me to keep the kiss safe for later, for after dreamland. I rest my cheek against his chest. Leather. Pine trees. Ocean air. The slow, relentless beat of his heart. I slip my fingertips under his leather armor. Warm skin. Firm muscles. Soft belly hair. My fingers sense something else. Slick and sticky. Another smell. Blood.

"I love you," he whispers, his voice full of sadness.

Cold. Something cold pinged my arm. A second later, another ping.

My eyes flashed open. Rain!

Thunder rumbled, wind bent the pines, and the patter of drops transformed into a deluge.

I leapt to my feet, grabbed Tibbs's jacket—and noticed something dark red on my fingertips, vanishing quickly as the rain diluted it, washing away: Blood.

My body went numb. My thoughts frozen.

The thunder growled. The waves boomed against the rocks, their spray hissing skyward and falling all around me. I dropped the jacket and stared at my hands. Blood, now gone.

Logic told me one of the cuts on my arms had broken open. Diluted by water, even a pinprick could look like a gusher.

I ran my hands over my arms, searching for tender spots, torn scabs, or any trace of lingering blood. Nothing.

My breath stalled in my throat. Chase's mother. My mother.

The genie Malphic had visited both of them in their dreams. Malphic had eventually kidnapped my mom and taken her to his harem. He hadn't taken Chase's mom, but she'd ended up in Beach Rose House, diagnosed as insane. Could Chase do the same thing as his father now? Had he reached across the veil to me? That was why I'd come here, hoping to draw him to me.

Horror knifed me in the chest and I clenched my teeth until it hurt. I was such an idiot. If Chase's desire to be with me had allowed him to reach across the veil, it wasn't something that I should have encouraged. It meant, possibly, that he was succumbing to the change. Of all the fears I had about him being trapped in the djinn realm, dying wasn't the worst. It was that his hormones would become too powerful and he'd lose control over himself, and go berserk. Chase was at the age where genies and half genies matured, gaining powers and strength. Sex, fighting, anything that affected his testosterone level or brought on a surge of adrenaline could stimulate that change. When the change occurred, all genies went through a phase of fearless rage and indifference that was a lot like battle-frenzy. It lasted a few moments or one night at the most, except for half-ifrit genies like Chase. Most of them never came down from that stage. They went berserk and were kept in the lowest level of Malphic's fortress, where they were allowed out for fights or to wander the desert at night, full of nothing except rage and bloodlust. Killers, who sometimes became so uncontrollable that Malphic had their life energy drained until they faded and died. I couldn't begin to guess why Malphic would want to push his own son over that edge. But there was no doubt Chase was on the cusp, and I needed to do whatever I could to protect him.

I looked up, blinking against the rain, feeling its chill rushing down my face and neck. I needed to do everything I could to help Chase stay calm and resist the change until we could find Lotli, go back to the realm, and free him. If we could get him home in time, maybe Grandfather and Kate would be able to help him through the change intact. I didn't want to lose him. But more than that, I couldn't bear the thought of him losing himself and becoming nothing but a deranged killer. The Chase I knew was kind and generous. The Chase I loved was gentle and sweet. I had to reach him before he went berserk.

Another thought touched my mind, lightening the weight of my terror for a moment. If what I'd experienced was real and not a dream, then Chase was alive and sane enough to re-member me. For now, at least.

But what about the blood?

There had been so much of it.

What if he'd chanced coming to me to say good-bye?

What if he was on the cusp of death as well as the change?

CHAPTER 6

None is harder to forgive than thyself.

—Epitaph: Henry Freemont's gravestone

The fear I felt for Chase consumed me all the way back to the ATV, and on the dark and rain-driven ride home. But once I'd parked in the garage and put the keys away, my exhaustion took over and my doubts surfaced.

The truth was, the blood I thought I'd seen on my fingertips could have been red sand or dirt from the rocks, or simply part of the dream that my overtired brain had made seem real. It was easy to understand how I might dream about Chase, see his glittering aura. I'd had dreams like that before. In reality, I wasn't just exhausted. I was woozy with the need for sleep, my poor body begging for me to lay still.

I slogged up to my room, stripped off my rain-soaked clothes, and slumped into a warm bath.

I woke up the next morning to a sun-brightened room. It had to be after eight o'clock and I'd intended to get up early, since there was the remote possibility that Dad, Grandfather, and Uncle David had gotten home at some point in the night.

My leg muscles resisted as I climbed out of bed. The bruises on my arms from being thrown out of the realm had turned a darker shade of purple. I had an awful crick in my neck. As much as I wanted to check my phone, I needed to get rid of my aches and pains first.

I staggered to the bathroom, took out my stash of extra-potent willow bark from the medicine cabinet, and popped a strip into my mouth. It was bitter, slippery, and anesthetized my tongue. But I wasn't worried about it causing side effects, like I had been when I first tried it. That time, Selena had dragged me into the solarium and randomly peeled a sliver of bark off one of Kate's experimental willows. She'd all but begged for me to try, swearing it would cure my headache in no time flat. I'd been hesitant, to say the least. Later, I even convinced myself that chewing it had caused me to hallucinate a shadow-genie in the gallery. But in the end, the shadow-genie turned out to be real and the willow proved to be a wonder drug—if taken in moderation.

As the willow worked its magic on my aches, I settled down in a chair beside the window with my phone. My heart sank when I didn't see a text from Dad. There was, however, an e-mail and information packet from Sotheby's about the course in London I'd signed up to take this fall. *Damn it.* I had enough to think about right now without worrying about that. Sure, I should have been thrilled. I'd dreamed about taking one of their courses for years. It was an important step toward me becoming a certified fine arts appraiser. London. By myself. Why wouldn't I be excited?

Maybe because I'd rather spend that time with Chase—if we could get him back.

And my mother. I'd been five years old when Malphic kidnapped her. I wanted time to be with her. And Selena. And Kate, her respect didn't come easy, but it felt good.

Tension pinched behind my eyes. And I moved on to the next e-mail—

"What the hell?" I doubled-checked the sender. I couldn't believe it. It was from Taj.

Since our falling out, I'd only been in touch with him once, last month—and that had been an even worse disaster. It was when Dad and I had first returned to Moonhill and Dad was possessed by the genie Culus. I'd put my pride aside and asked Taj to translate a mysterious inscription on a ring that was involved. Taj pretty much accused Dad and me of stealing the ring from the Metropolitan. I had never expected to hear from him again.

I opened the e-mail.

> Hey Annie,
> I'll be at Old Orchard Beach for the weekend.
> You want to get together? Dinner and a movie?
> Miss you.
> Xoxo, Taj

I slapped my hand over my mouth, smothering a laugh. Oh my God. How stupid did he think I was? *Get together?* Get in my pants was more like it. And that was never happening again.

With a dramatic jab of my finger, I deleted his e-mail. Thanks, but no thanks. Asshole.

My phone buzzed.

A text. From Dad! He was home. In his bedroom! He wanted to know where I was.

Heck with that.

It only took me a second to fling on clothes and sprint to the other side of the house where his room was. Maybe it was more like five minutes. His room was about as far from mine as it could be.

Dad must have heard me coming because he met me in the doorway to his room, pulling me into a bear hug.

"Missed you times a million, Dad," I said, burying my face in his shoulder.

He kissed my forehead and hugged me harder. "Missed you more."

He released me and we went into his room.

I tilted my head, studying him for a moment. I'd expected him to return with bags under his eyes and a few pounds lighter. But—if I didn't count his wrinkled shirt and chinos, and the gray stubble on his neck and chin—he looked surprisingly well for a guy who'd spent a week trapped in the Slovenian mountains. In fact, he looked rested and happy—strange, considering he'd been stuck in a tiny cabin with his father and brother, who he hadn't wanted anything to do with for the last fifteen years.

"You look—good?" I said.

He gave me a questioning glance. "Sometimes, Annie, we get what we need even if it's something we've avoided like the plague." He gave me another hug. "I wish I could have been here for you. I feel horrible about everything that happened. But we've been given a second chance, and that's something most people never get."

I nodded, feeling lighter than I had in ages. I knew instinctively that he wasn't only talking about Chase and Mother, but something more. The time in the mountains had changed him. Dad had never been one to forgive—that was, anyone other than me. But the sincerity in his eyes, his relaxed smile and movements, everything about him told me that he'd let go of the anger he'd held toward his family and moved into a future that included them.

He gently clasped one of my arms and looked down at the bruises. "I'm worried about you, though."

I pulled free and waved him off. "A few scrapes and jellyfish stings. Not bad for being thrown through the sky from another realm."

Without a word, he strode across the room to the desk. Crap. The letter. That's what he was talking about. I'd left it there for him before Chase, Lotli, and I snuck off to the djinn realm. I should have ripped it up the moment I got back, but I'd forgotten all about it.

"Don't worry about that," I said. "I should have gotten rid of it."

Dad's voice was firm. "I'm glad you didn't."

"It was in case I didn't come back. I just wanted to explain why I had to go. It doesn't matter now."

A voice began chanting inside me, low and insistent: *Liar, liar, liar.* And what I'd written to him, the truth put down in black and white, flashed through my head:

> *Dear Dad,*
>
> *I want you to know that my going to the realm is not your fault or anything you could have stopped. I know you love Mother and think getting her back is your battle to fight, but the truth is none of this would have happened if it weren't for me. No one would have needed to lie to you, if I hadn't lied first. Grandmother asked me if someone had been visiting Mama at night and I said no. But I had seen someone. I'm sorry. I wish I didn't have to tell you this. But I saw her with Malphic.*
>
> *I know it will be impossible for you to not worry about where I've gone and what I've gone to do, but give me a chance. I promise, I will return, with Mother. And forgive her, too. She was a victim, just like the rest of us.*
>
> *Love you always. You are the best father any girl could wish for.*
> *Annie*

I pressed my fingertips against my eyes, holding back the sting of tears. If only I hadn't lied to Grandmother, then none of this would have happened. To Mother. To Grandmother. To Chase.

"Annie," Dad said sharply. He yanked my hands from my face and waved the note in front of me. "This is bullshit. You're not responsible for what happened."

My voice hitched. "Yes, I am. I know you don't like it, but it's true."

He ripped the note in half, hands fisting as he crumpled the pieces. "It's garbage. Christ, Annie. You were five years old. A child."

"But I knew it was wrong. I lied to Grandmother."

"You were protecting your mother. Your grandmother was an adult. She could have spoken up at any time. Your mother could have reached out for help. I could have—"

I glared. "You lost the woman you loved. It ruined your relationship with your family. I'll agree that I'm not the only one who is guilty, but you had nothing to do with it."

His jaw tightened. "Why do you think your mother got involved with Malphic? His trickery, most likely. But I was at fault, too. We were married only a few weeks after we met. I brought her to Maine, where she didn't know anyone, to live with people she'd never met, and with all this—" He gestured with both hands, indicating not just his bedroom, but all that living at Moonhill entailed: the witchcraft, the lineage, the mysterious objects, the family business, hidden tunnels and treasuries, so many strange things, so much past. "She got pregnant not long after that. Your mother is beautiful, brilliant, and amazing. She's also creative and high-spirited. I knew that, but I forced her into a strange cage and asked her to be what I wanted."

I lowered my eyes, watching silently as he tore the crumpled note into smaller pieces, watching them drift to the floor.

"If I'd been smart," he said, "I would have moved the three of us into the stone cottage, given her a modicum of privacy at least. I would have insisted on not going away on family business as much—or I could have taken her with me sometimes. I knew this place stifled her. I knew she was lonely. I all but opened the veil and welcomed Malphic in."

In my heart I had guessed all these things. But it was different hearing it from his mouth. It made the truth more potent, impossible to bury beneath my own claim to guilt. *Liar.* The voice whispered inside me. *Liar.* I'd never be able to go back and change what was done, unsay the one word that led to my mother's kidnapping and my grandmother's death. But now something new was building inside me, a battle cry overshadowing a voice that had done more harm than good.

"Dad, it's not your fault either." I raised an eyebrow and slanted a look at the remains of the letter, haphazard white scraps staining the red carpet. "What do you say we forget about that, start over—and blame everything on Malphic?"

He laughed and pulled me into a hug. "Now that's an idea I can get behind."

I wriggled free. "There is just one more thing." I took a deep breath, building up my bravery before I went on. "Why us? I can see how Malphic managed to get involved with Mom. But why her—why our family?"

"That, my dear, is a good question. There have been genies tangled up in our family's history every now and again, ad infinitum. But I have no idea why Malphic targeted your mother. Once she and Chase return, that's something we'll definitely need to look into."

I stepped back and raised my chin. "Dad?"

His eyes narrowed. "I don't trust that look. What's on your mind now?"

"You do realize I intend to go on the rescue mission to the realm, right?"

He grimaced. "I don't like the idea. But, yes, I understand. However"—he raised a finger—"I'm going to insist that you back off and let me plan things out with your grandfather and Kate." His finger lowered and he smiled. "As a matter of fact, your grandfather insisted that you go. He thinks you and I are the strongest team."

I couldn't believe my ears. "He does?"

Dad slung his arm over my shoulders, snugging me tight. "I always thought he was a crazy old man."

I rested my head on his shoulder. "Thank you, Dad." Then I whispered, "I do have an idea about how to rescue Lotli, if she's at this boathouse, like we think."

CHAPTER 7

*I should have left her a note. I should have told her
my real name. I should have said good-bye that
morning in Paris. Instead I took the heartache
with me, and left her alone with the gift of anger.*

—Journal: Kate Freemont

"You think they really are going to let us go to the
boathouse?" Selena asked a few hours later as we parked
in front of a formalwear shop in Bar Harbor village.

I shrugged. "I don't know about your dad, but mine will.
Yours went along with us getting tuxes to wear. That's a good
sign, right?"

Olya's scrying had indicated Lotli was indeed being held at
the King's Pine Yacht Club, a private club on the outskirts of
Kennebunkport, where the wedding reception and the Sons of
Ophiuchus meeting were happening late tomorrow afternoon. Grandfather eliminated the last measure of doubt by
using what he called *electronic sorcery*. It involved tracking
Newt's movements by using texts he'd sent to Selena, phone
sensors, and accelerometers, as well as the satellite system in
Newt's Mustang—in other words, hacking.

I'd suggested we should go to the King's Pine and rescue
Lotli right away; with Chase on the cusp of changing, we
couldn't afford to wait. But after a heated debate, I relented

that planning things out in more detail and waiting until tomorrow when we could blend in with the wedding crowd was
probably wiser. In exchange, everyone admitted that Selena
and I were the only ones young enough to fade into the background at a wedding, especially if we went disguised as waitstaff. They also agreed that Dad was the only older family
member Newt and his family might not recognize. Still, I half
suspected that we'd been sent to check out tuxes in order to
get us out of the way—that eventually it would be Kate or
Olya who went to the boathouse instead of Selena, since either of them could scry and locate Lotli as well.

Selena and I bailed out of the Land Rover and went into
the shop. It was a nice place, brightly lit with pop Muzak playing in the background.

I leaned close to Selena. "Remember basic tuxes. Nothing
fancy."

"Yeah, yeah, I get it. Except—"

Before she could say anything more, a balding man slunk
out from between two racks of mother-of-the-bride dresses
and toward us. He was middle-aged and dressed in a three-piece
suit, complete with a turquoise pocket square. "Good morning,
ladies. Just browsing, or do you need help with something?"

I smiled at him. "We want to rent three tuxes for tomorrow afternoon, for us and a gentleman. Something simple. In
black."

Selena jumped in. "With pink bow ties. Raspberry-pink.
And matching cufflinks."

I shot a hard look at her. "I think we should stick with
black."

The man folded his hands, his face grim. "Color isn't an
issue. However, this is very short notice."

"We realize that," I said. "And we fully expect to pay for
the rush." I pulled my shoulders back and hardened my gaze,
as if I were dickering over a fine antique and not about to

budge. Then I took out my wallet and opened it, allowing him to catch a glimpse of the contents. "Do you prefer a credit card—or cash?"

For a half second my sleeves pulled up and his eyes went to my bruised arms, but they quickly returned to the thick stack of bills. It was impossible to tell what was going through his mind. However, the way he unconsciously rubbed his fingers together made me suspect that he preferred cash and thoroughly intended on pocketing it instead of putting it in the register.

I turned to Selena. "I know pink's your favorite color, but we really need to blend in."

Selena flipped her hair off her shoulder. "We will. Raspberry and black are the color scheme for the wedding."

"Oh," I said, dumbfounded. "Why didn't you say something sooner?"

"I just figured it out on the way here. You know, a little online search—and voilà, there it was."

The man looked from one of us to the other, but he didn't say a word. He'd probably heard tons of people argue over prom dresses and wedding colors. The important thing was, he relented that if we were willing to purchase used tuxes and weren't fussy, he could come up with something for first thing tomorrow morning, raspberry-pink ties and all.

Another thought started to bubble in my head and, as we left the store, I turned to Selena. "Maybe posing as waitstaff isn't such a good idea. I mean, it seems like they'd all know each other. We'd stand out as strangers. If we're going to match the wedding colors, then why not go as photographers, violinists . . . any kind of profession who might get dressed up like that?"

Selena beamed. "You're right. We could be makeup artists or DJs."

"Maybe." I stooped to pick a penny up from the sidewalk

and shoved it in my pocket. We needed all the luck we could get. "There's something else, too. If we want to make sure they let us go tomorrow, we need to come up with an even more foolproof way to keep Newt from recognizing us."

"I'm glad you asked. I kind of already made plans for that." She gave me a sly grin, then strode ahead.

I gulped. I knew that tone of voice and it spelled *trouble* with a capital *T*. "Whatever you're thinking, Selena, just forget it. It's a bad idea."

She winged back and snagged my hand, hauling me down the sidewalk. "C'mon. You're going to love it."

"Love what?" I pulled against her grip, though there was a part of me that was totally curious.

She dragged me around a corner, past a couple of shops and an ice-cream parlor. . . . Just when I thought she'd never stop, she came to a screeching halt and stared longingly through a store window at a display of shoes. I didn't know Bar Harbor well, but I recognized where we were—only a few streets down from Beach Rose House, the permanent care facility where Chase's mother was confined. Before we'd gone into the realm, Chase and I had managed to finagle our way into Beach Rose House to see her. He'd been too on edge to talk with her, but I had. And I'd promised to visit her again.

I hugged myself. I should do it today, while I was in town. But not just because of that promise. Chase's mother was also the only person who might be able to tell me if what I'd experienced on the clifftop was a product of my exhaustion or if Chase had really come to me. After all, Malphic had supposedly visited her in her sleep.

"So what do you think?" Selena's voice jolted me from my thoughts.

I frowned at her. "What did you say?"

"Do you think they're perfect?"

"Yeah, totally," I said, realizing too late that she was talking about a pair of ridiculously expensive pink spikes on the other side of the window glass. The same pink as the bow ties.

"Fantastic. Once we're done, we'll come back and buy us each a pair. After all, King's Pine is very exclusive. Even as professionals, we need to look top-shelf."

Smiling, she hooked my arm and we were off again, this time down an alley between two buildings and into an entryway. Straight ahead, a street-art-style profile of a woman with swirling hair was painted across a metal door.

I ventured a guess. "A salon?"

"Only the best one ever—hair, nails, piercings, even tattoos. We have eleven o'clock appointments." She grinned and bounced on her tiptoes, excitement leaking out every pore. "Newt's never going to recognize us."

Fear twisted in my stomach. "How much of a makeover are you talking?"

"Don't worry, it won't take that long."

I glanced at the door again, weighing the idea. Time was only part of my concern. Her parents would blame me if she did anything too crazy. But changing up our hair was a great idea. Plus, if I went along with this, then most likely she wouldn't object to stopping at Beach Rose House later.

Her expression turned serious. "Speaking of Newt, thanks for not mentioning the love curse to anyone."

I shrugged. "I promised I wouldn't, right?"

"Yeah, but I really appreciate it." Her voice lowered. "I couldn't sleep last night. I was so pissed at Newt. You know, one time he said this actress was ugly because she had too many freckles. I spent the next week bleaching every spot off my skin. When he told me red was his favorite color, I threw out my favorite pink hoodies and all my pink nail polish, and even a dress that I absolutely loved. Last night, I started thinking about everything I'd given up or changed for him. Can you imagine being taken in like that?"

"Actually, I can. It's not your fault either. The Sons of Ophiuchus probably watched you for years and groomed him to know exactly what to do." I cringed. "Sorry. That sounds pretty creepy."

"It is. But what scares me the most is that I didn't even begin to catch on."

A horrifying thought burrowed into my brain. It was unlikely that Newt and Myles were the only guys involved with the Sons. Guys from supposedly good families. I swallowed hard. Smart, good-looking guys like Newt—and like Taj. Was it possible that he was involved with them, too?

"Screw that," Selena said. "I'm not going to let Newt get under my skin anymore." She flung the door open and I followed her inside.

My eyes widened. Industrial lighting hung down from iron beams way above our heads, brightening and showcasing a line of ultra-modern steel chairs. But there was nothing else in the room. Not even a reception desk. No signs of life either, except for the faint smell of hair products and an eerie throb of tribal drums creeping out from two narrow doorways.

"I'll be right back," Selena said, vanishing through one of the doorways.

I tucked my hands in my pockets, shivering as the pulse of the drums sent my mind reeling back to the djinn realm and the moments just before I lost my temper in a fit of jealousy and broke the hummingbird egg, causing the rescue mission to go horribly wrong.

Lotli, Chase, and I had been in the djinn arena for hours, watching performers do their acts while we waited for Lotli's turn. The air was thick with smoke, the audience behind us drunk and rowdy. Lotli and Chase kept whispering about something. I felt left out, angry, and jealous. I told myself he was comforting her. That it was understandable. She was about to play her flute in front of a crowd of half-crazed genies, not to mention Malphic and his cronies.

Lotli had shifted toward me. "It's almost *our* turn," she said, her voice trembling.

I gave her a hug. "Don't worry. They'll love you," I said, but something about what she'd said niggled at my mind, or maybe it was how she'd said those words. I shook my head and shrugged off the uncomfortable feeling. *No more pettiness. It will all be over soon.*

That's when the eerie heartbeat of tribal drums had begun. Chase closed his eyes and rocked in time with the music, every muscle in his body joining in. Lotli blew out loud breaths and stared straight ahead, her chin rising as she focused into the distance.

My pulse quickened with the music's beat gathering energy, and that niggling feeling returned, a fierce uncomfortable twinge in my chest, building ever stronger. What was it that Lotli had said? It seemed important that I remember.

Goose bumps chilled me as Lotli rose to her feet. This was it. She was next. The platform in front of us flared to life, stark and white, surrounded by low blue flames. Wrapped tight in a cocoon of veils, Lotli flowed forward until she stood at its center. Only then did I realize that Chase was already there, crouched, his head bowed, so he was nearly invisible under the fire's dancing light.

Horror-struck, I gripped the edge of the bench. *Our turn,* that's what she'd said, her tongue wrapping around the word *our,* enunciating it with a certain pleasure, different from her normal *we* and *us* bullshit.

He lifted his scarf-covered face, a battle-ready warrior frozen motionless. Thankfully, black smudge still shadowed his eyes, hiding his identity. Still, he looked so fierce, especially with the tattoo-like marks that had been applied to his arms and body—

The memory of those horrible moments in the realm abruptly fled as Selena returned with a Hispanic guy in tow. His raven-dark hair was pulled back in a glossy ponytail, and his black jeans were as tight as his bicep-hugging T-shirt.

"This is Santiago," she introduced him to me. "He's going to do your hair."

"Welcome." He gestured for me to follow him back inside.

I glanced toward Selena. She was already disappearing through the other doorway. I took a deep breath. This was going to be interesting.

As it turned out, Santiago was a traditional stylist and impressively fast. I surrendered to his expertise, sipping a pistachio latte while he deftly put my hair in foil wraps. It was surprisingly pleasant. Except having a man so close made me think of Chase, the warmth of his body, his breath against my hair, strong hands on my shoulders. *Chase.* Yesterday it really had felt like he was with me.

Finally, my hair was washed, styled, and glistening with chestnut streaks. Nothing outrageous, just a subtle change like I'd asked for. I was about to go hunt for Selena, when she bounced into the room, her hairstylist sailing along behind her.

My mouth hung open. Selena's long and preppy-perfect blond hair was gone, replaced by a short pixie cut with razored sides. If I hadn't known she was here, I might not have recognized her at first glance.

She wiggled her fingers through her hair. "I've wanted to try this forever."

I couldn't form words. I was a hundred percent certain Newt would have hated her new look. Still, the joy in Selena's voice and on her face told me this wasn't about him or even just about looking different for the mission. Every gesture of her hands, the tilt of her head, everything screamed that I was seeing the real Selena emerge for the first time. Someone stronger, more confident, and independent.

I clapped my hands, applauding her and the stylist. "It's amazing. Seriously, I love it."

"It feels so good." Selena grinned.

Selena's upbeat mood was so infectious that we were both still super energized when we left the salon. I resisted the urge to mention that her father was going to kill her—and me. I was certain I'd somehow get blamed for the new look, despite the excuse of the boathouse mission.

As we went out into the alleyway, she rested her hand on my shoulder and softly said, "By the way, I've decided I'm not just going to help rescue Lotli. I'm going on the mission to the realm as well."

I felt my face pale and I stopped in my tracks. Going to the boathouse was one thing. But the djinn realm? "No, that's a horrible idea. I mean, your parents will never allow it."

She turned toward me, her face somber. "That's why I'm telling you. I want you to help me stand up to them."

"Selena, seriously. You can't imagine how awful it is there. And dangerous."

"We're cousins. I want to help you." Her gaze trapped mine. "Chase is like a brother to me."

I hooked my hands behind my head, drawing in a long breath. Dad and I were a team. The best team, everyone had agreed about that. We'd worked together for years. It was as if I could read his thoughts, anticipate his moves. He could do the same with me. Cool and synchronized, that was us. Not spontaneous, headstrong, like Selena. Sure we had to take Lotli. We didn't have a choice about that. But we wouldn't have time to look after Selena.

I let out my breath. "I don't think"—*you should go* was what I planned on saying. But the truth was, Selena might have come across as immature sometimes, but when we'd fought the genie Culus she'd proved she could hold her own and be invaluable to the team. She knew a lot about magic. She could think on her feet. She knew the risks. If the tables were turned, she'd be the first one to stand up for me. At a minimum, she deserved a chance to be considered. "Of course, I'll stand up for you. But first we've got to pull off this boathouse rescue without a hitch—that means no crazy stuff."

Her bottom lip turned out in a patented Selena pout. "Can I still buy the pink spikes for us?"

I laughed, but inside my worry blossomed into full-fledged fear. I wasn't totally convinced Selena really was ready to face what waited in the djinn realm. Actually, with each passing second, I was becoming less and less convinced that any of us had the brains and luck it would take to outsmart the Sons of Ophiuchus and rescue Lotli.

CHAPTER 8

The influence these devious beings have had on human history is immeasurable. They stood behind Solomon, whispering in his ear and granting gifts upon the Blacksmith. They secreted the Mamluk warrior into the bed of the Mongol princess . . .

—www.MagicOfDjinn.com

Selena bought the pairs of raspberry-pink spikes. Between that and having everyone we met go crazy over her hair, I figured she'd sail along without objection when I suggested we stop at Beach Rose House for a few minutes. Instead, she whipped sideways in the passenger seat and gawked at me.

"Are you insane?" she said.

My face heated. I narrowed my eyes and clenched the steering wheel, ready to blurt out what had happened on the clifftop, about Chase and the blood, and my fears. But I forced my fingers to relax and took a deep breath. It didn't make sense to get upset or to tell her what I might have experienced, at least not until I was sure it was real.

I glanced her way, my voice steady. "I promised her that I'd visit again—soon."

"Yeah, and I'm sure she'd like that, but it was sheer luck that you got past the receptionist the last time."

The side street that went to Beach Rose House came into

view. My fingers tingled with a desire to steer down it. But a hollow feeling took root in my chest. As much as I wanted to see Chase's mom, Selena was right. It wasn't like they were going to keep letting someone who wasn't on the approved visitor list in to see her. Eventually, they would stop me and, worse yet, notify Chase's stepfather that I'd been there repeatedly.

Selena's voice lifted. "Of course, if we could figure out how to get your name on the visitor list, then it would be a breeze."

That was a good thought. I ran my palm along the steering wheel, struggling to keep my optimism in check. The approved visitor list was on their computer. Grandfather could hack into it and add me. It was a great suggestion. Except Grandfather was back at Moonhill. And I didn't want to wait. I wanted to do it now. On top of that, I didn't want him to ask why seeing her now was so important to me.

Screw it. "There's an easy solution," I said, winging down the side street. "I won't try to get in by pretending to be a visitor."

"What are you thinking—a nurse or intern instead?"

"Something like that." It was a total bluff. I had no idea what I was going to do. "*Zero. Zip. Zilch. Nada,*" as Dad liked to say.

A half second later, we pulled into Beach Rose House's parking lot. The facility itself was small and somewhat modern. It actually looked like a grade school with fancy landscaping.

"Wait here. I won't be gone long," I said.

Selena reached for her door latch. "You want help?"

"No, really. I'm going to just say hi. I'll be right back."

I jumped out of the car before she could insist on coming, and strode across the parking lot toward the front door. But I hadn't even gotten to the sidewalk, when a woman in a turquoise nurse's top came out, wiped something off the door's glass, and then retreated back inside. It was the woman who'd been on duty at the reception counter when Chase and I had visited. Damn it. Of all the people I didn't want to run into, she was at the top of my list.

To my left, rose bushes and hedges screened a tall stockade fence that enclosed the facility's side yard. No getting in that way.

I veered to the right, toward where a service driveway wound around toward the back of the building. Partway up the drive, the chain-link gate that was supposed to close it off stood open. Okay. Last time I was here Chase's mom had given me her room number. There had to be numbers on the doors and maps to the rooms or signs in the main hallways. All I had to do was find an entrance and get inside without setting off an alarm.

I marched like I knew where I was going, through the gate and around the corner to the back of the building. The stench of rotting garbage hit my nose, followed by the clank and grind of a rubbish truck hoisting a Dumpster into the air.

The rubbish man nodded a hello. I smiled back and prayed that I'd find a way into the building and soon. It was kind of hard to keep looking purposeful without a destination in sight. Plus, it was likely the rubbish man had opened the gate so he could drive in. What if he also had a key—and locked it when he left? Sure I could hop the gate, but there was no discreet way to do that.

A whiff of cafeteria food and cigarette smoke mixed with the garbage. Glancing toward where the smell was emanating from, I spotted a loading dock just beyond the Dumpsters. A skinny guy in a cook's apron crouched on the dock next to a door, a cigarette in his hand and a can of Red Bull on the concrete beside him. This looked promising.

I sucked in a breath, raised my shoulders, and strolled toward him, hips swaying, boobs pushed out.

His gaze swept over me and he grinned approvingly.

I sashayed up a set of stairs to the dock. "Hey, I was wondering if you could help me. I pushed the buzzer by the front door, but no one answered. Can I get to the kitchen through here? I've got an interview . . ." The rubbish truck's hydraulics whined as it lowered the Dumpster, drowning out my voice.

The cook guy shouted something about food service manager, down the hall, and things looking up. I didn't hear any more and I chose to ignore his hand gliding across my butt when he opened the door and let me in. Asshole.

The door slammed shut behind me. I took a quick glance around to make sure he hadn't followed, then jogged past the kitchen's open doorway and down the hallway toward a set of swinging double doors with windows set into them. The windows were meshed with wire, but they still gave an okay view of the cafeteria on the other side of the doors.

It had to be almost two o'clock, but the place wasn't totally deserted. A few nurses and what looked like office workers sat together at some of the tables eating. At the other tables sat a mix of patients and people who were probably visitors. Near a window, a thin, dark haired, middle-aged woman sat alone, nibbling on a sandwich. Chase's mother. I was sure of it.

I stepped back and scanned the cafeteria again. Yesterday, when the plumbers had arrived at Newt's house, I'd learned how quickly something that appeared to be easy could turn sour.

Not giving myself time to second-guess, I pushed the swinging door open and walked into the cafeteria.

Instantly, my gaze caught a flash of turquoise as a woman swished in on the far side of the room and headed for the food service window. It was the woman from the reception counter again. How could she be everywhere?

I bowed my head and wandered toward Chase's mother, letting my hair screen my face. As long as I didn't look at the turquoise-topped woman, I'd be all set.

An orderly in a bright-white uniform stepped in front of

me, blocking my path. The name tag on his mountainous chest read: SVEN.

He glared down at me. "Looking for someone?"

My pulse went crazy, hammering so fast it made my voice tremble. "I—I was just . . . I came to have lunch with my aunt. She—she disappeared on me." I looked past him, then waved at Chase's mom as if I'd just spotted her. "There she is now."

She blinked like she had no idea who I was. And I realized I'd made an awful mistake. Sure she'd been fine the last time, but that didn't mean she'd be all right this time. This was a permanent care facility. People weren't committed to this place for no reason.

Slowly, she tucked the remains of her sandwich down the front of her bejeweled cardigan. Then she smiled at me and lifted her hand in a shaky wave.

I whooshed past Sven and toward her, arriving just as she wobbled to her feet. I offered her my arm and she clutched it for support. "So wonderful to see you," she murmured.

I kissed her cheek and whispered, "Is there a place we can talk? Privately."

She nodded. "My room."

Her bony fingers dug into my arm, steering me toward the hallway on the far side of the room, a dozen or more tables away. One step at a time, we shuffled toward it.

I turned my face away when we came to a table where the turquoise-topped woman was crouched, talking to—Was it Sven? I held my breath as we passed, preparing for the blast of a whistle or a shout of "*Intruder!*" from the woman. Had they seen us? Were they talking about us?

A sick feeling twisted in my stomach. But I didn't dare take a second look.

Chase's mother quickened her pace. We went past the last table and were almost to the hallway, when she stopped in her tracks and gripped my arm with both hands.

"How is my little Chase doing?" she asked softly.

"Ah—" I glanced around, fearful of being caught. "Where's your room? We should go there."

She released me and pulled out the remains of her sandwich. Taking off the top slice of bread, she turned it over and then put it back on. "My room has a view of the garden," she said. "It's so lovely." She took a bite of the sandwich, looked at me, and smiled sweetly. "There are roses. Blue ones and green ones."

Sweat beaded on my temples. She definitely wasn't all there. Still, I'd come too far to not at least try to get my answers.

Chair legs scraped and a group of nurses got to their feet. Trays in hand, they headed for the dirty-dish window. The other employees, visitors, and patients followed suit. Soon they'd all be flooding our way, the turquoise-topped nurse and Sven included.

"We need to get going," I whispered to Chase's mother. "Is there someplace closer where we can talk?"

She giggled. "I knit mittens for Chase. Blue and green. His favorites."

I swallowed back a lump in my throat. This was horrible. She'd seemed so with it the last time.

A terrifying possibility crept into my mind and my breath faltered. What if the turquoise-topped woman had told Chase's stepfather about my last visit? What if he'd figured out it had been Chase with me? He hated Chase and would do anything to keep him away. Could that include bribing a doctor into messing with her prescriptions—to make them screw up her mind, so she wouldn't be lucid enough to talk to Chase?

I glanced at the crowd clustered around the dirty-dish window, then back at the hallway a few feet ahead of us: a sanitary tunnel of white tile and closed doors. Partway down the hallway there was an extra-wide door with a handicap bathroom sign on it. A single stall.

Before Chase's mom could object, I whipped my arm around her waist and propelled her down the hallway and into the bathroom. I locked the door behind us. Perfect. Just the two of us. Alone.

She swept to the sink and washed her hands, then held them under the air-dryer. "It feels like butterflies are dancing on my skin," she said.

A newborn headache throbbed behind my eyes. Why had I ever thought coming here was a good idea? *For Chase,* my heart whispered the answer.

The air-dryer shut off. She let out a long breath and turned toward me. Her posture. Her expression. Everything about her now appeared shockingly sane.

She smoothed down the sleeve of her cardigan. "Now, tell me why Chase isn't with you."

For a heartbeat, I couldn't react. She even sounded fine.

A memory flashed into my mind and I scuffed backward, retreating from her until my back pressed against the door. I'd witnessed abrupt changes in personality like this before, when my dad had been possessed by the genie Culus. Most of the time his symptoms mimicked dementia, but once in a while he'd act chillingly sane. But it couldn't be. Not again. Chase's mother couldn't be possessed.

As if she could read my mind, Chase's mother reached into her sweater sleeve, pulled out a balled-up tissue, and opened it, revealing an assortment of pills. She tossed them in the toilet and flushed. "It's rather satisfying to watch my husband's money go down the drain."

I laughed as much from relief as anything else. I couldn't believe it. I'd been right about her husband bribing the doctors to mess with her medicine. But I'd been very wrong about how brilliant she was.

"Chase is in trouble," I said, stepping closer to her.

She stiffened. "Is it Malphic?"

"Yes, partly. Chase is trapped in the djinn realm again."

Her gaze met mine, eyes unflinching. "What can I do?"

"I need to know what it was like when Malphic came to you in your sleep. How real it felt." It sounded rudely blunt and surreal, as if it had come from someone else's mouth instead of mine.

She lowered her eyes for a second. When she looked back up, understanding shadowed her expression. She knew why I'd asked. "There are experiences that are soul-crushing. They feel unreal at first. Then they grow into an addictive pleasure, followed by endless loneliness."

"Yes, go on." I nodded encouragingly, not wanting to break her train of thought.

"The first time Malphic came, my husband was in one of his moods. The stock market wasn't doing well. I'd put too much sugar in his coffee. Folded his socks wrong, something, nothing, everything was wrong . . . It was raining outside. But there was this place in the garden, a hidden spot beneath the lilacs' branches. I crawled under there. Can you believe it? A grown woman hiding under a bush like a child, when I could have simply taken the car keys and left?"

I nodded. From what Chase had told me about his abusive stepfather, it made perfect sense.

"I kept hoping I'd hear my husband drive off. But he didn't, so I stayed under there for hours. The rain soaked through my clothes. I was so cold, shivering and shivering. Then suddenly the air warmed and a glow like a million blue fireflies surrounded me, swirling and caressing my body, flowing over and into me. The sensation was titillating and consuming, a feeling of ecstasy that left me on the border of tears and oblivion. I was certain I'd fallen asleep and had an amazing dream." Her cheeks went red, but her voice became taut. "My husband had a lot of girlfriends. He'd started bringing them home. I wanted revenge so badly."

"It's understandable," I said, barely able to whisper.

For a moment she hugged herself, rocking back and forth as if gathering her nerve before continuing. "One day, the doorbell rang. I answered, and Malphic was standing there on my doorstep. He told me he wanted to be with me. He told me I had to leave a door or window open, so he could come to me in the night. I thought I'd lost my mind and that he was a side effect of the insanity. Until that day . . ." Her voice trailed off as she turned away, her back now to me. "Malphic was still inside me when I felt it, the instant Chase was conceived."

This time my face heated. I swallowed dryly. Hearing the most intimate details of my boyfriend's conception wasn't exactly comfortable. Still, the blue fireflies, the warmth, the addictive bliss were all familiar to me, from when Chase and I had made love—and from last night on the clifftop, when we'd been together in what might not have been a dream after all.

I brushed my hands down her arms. "Did he keep visiting you?"

"He did. But I don't think he realized I knew about the pregnancy, at least that soon. Sometimes, when he thought I was asleep, he'd slip into my room and touch my stomach. I caught a glimpse of him once at one of my husband's company parties, watching me through the terrace doors."

Footsteps stopped in the hallway right outside the bathroom and we both went silent.

"She's not in her room," a man's voice said.

"She was in the cafeteria a few minutes ago," another man answered. Sven, maybe.

Chase's mom moved close to me, her voice a fast whisper. "My husband didn't come to the hospital when Chase was born. But Malphic was there." Her mouth tightened. "I'll never forgive him for taking Chase from me or for any of the barbarous things he did to him. But I know with all my heart, Malphic loves Chase."

The footsteps moved on, hurrying toward the cafeteria. It was only a matter of time before they decided to search in here. Once they discovered us, I'd get thrown out. But what would they do to her? She could flush pills, but she was no match for someone like Sven armed with a straightjacket—or a needle and syringe.

I leveled my eyes with hers. "You have to leave with me. It's not safe for you here."

She shook her head. "I can't. My husband would find me, and there are places a lot worse than this."

"My family's estate is like a fortress—"

She cut me off. "No, I'll find my own way out of this, legal and permanent." She nodded crisply at the door's lock. "Open it. I'll create a distraction. When the coast is clear, run."

My muscles tightened, not wanting to do as she asked.

"Open it now," she insisted.

Swallowing hard, I turned the lock. I reached for the door latch, but hesitated. There was one more question I had to ask. If I didn't, I might regret it forever.

I swiveled toward her. "Why you? Why do you think Malphic chose you?"

She smiled. "I've had a lot of time to think about that." She tilted her head as if weighing whether she should tell me or not. She licked her lips. "Malphic told me a story once. My husband had gone away for the weekend and Malphic and I spent every second together. We sat in the garden, drinking wine he'd brought. Musty, but it was wonderful. The way he told the story it sounded like an entry in *Tales of the Arabian Nights,* a sultan's chief warrior, a powerful princess, war and forbidden romance." She gazed off into space.

"But the story was real?"

"Yes, I'd heard it before from my mother and grand-mother. Way back—so long ago that the girl's name has been forgotten—one of my ancestors had a baby, conceived in the middle of a battle, a love child born from a star-crossed union between a Malmuk warrior and a daughter of Genghis Khan. That's why Malphic chose me—because of my ancestors. Why else would he have made a point of telling me that exact story?"

I could only stare at her. Chase had told me Malphic honored triumph above anything else. The bloodline of two powerful human warriors, a lineage worthy of joining with his.

She touched my hand. "I'm certain it's true. I devoted years to double-checking my family's genealogy. There is no doubt, I am a direct descendant of Genghis Khan."

CHAPTER 9

Powered soft and light, foxglove dust
fills the night. Dust to nose and dust to mouth,
steals the breath and stills the heart.

—Night Death Spell: attributed to
Malphic, Warlord of Blackspire

To say Selena's parents weren't pleased with her makeover would be an understatement. In fact, I used the excuse of needing to find Grandfather to escape before the blame could shift in my direction. It turned out, Grandfather and Dad were in the billiards room playing a game and having a before-dinner brandy.

The balls clanked as Dad made a shot. He set his stick down and picked up his snifter off the bar. "I hear Selena underwent quite the transformation?"

"How did you know about that?" The only people Selena and I had seen since we got home were her parents. I rolled my eyes. Of course. "Zachary told you, didn't he?"

Grandfather sunk the last ball. "I believe he was trying out his new telescope when you two pulled in. Razored sides, is it? Her father must be livid."

"I think she looks great." I folded my arms across my chest. "She deserves to go on the rescue mission tomorrow. Seriously, Newt probably wouldn't even recognize her."

He chuckled. "We'll see. The mission's about rescuing Lotli, not Selena's pride."

Dad raised his snifter to me. "By the way, Annie, you look quite lovely."

"Thanks." I settled onto a barstool and caught Grandfather's gaze. It was him, not Dad, who had the money and pull with the old boy network.

He tilted his head. "Something on your mind?"

"I wanted to ask you something." I continued quickly before I could lose my nerve. "After we had our hair done, I went to see Chase's mother."

His eyebrows arched. "And exactly how did you manage that?"

"I kind of—" My face heated. "Let's just say I got in."

Dad groaned. "Why do I feel like I'm somehow responsible for this?"

"Because she's just like you?" Grandfather chuckled again.

I sat back on the stool. "Grandfather, we—you've got to do something. We can't leave Chase's mother there . . ." I explained about the overmedicating and Chase's stepfather. "Chase has done a lot for our family. The least we can do is get his mother out of there—and get rid of her husband."

Grandfather glanced at Dad. "What do you suppose she means by 'get rid of'?"

"I'm not joking," I said. "This is serious."

"I realize that, dear. Don't worry. I'll have a talk with our lawyer. I think in this case divorce is more prudent than cement boots and a short ocean cruise, wouldn't you agree?"

"Of course—though a really nasty curse wouldn't be bad." I winked, indicating I was joking, at least kind of.

The comfort of knowing Chase's mom would be okay energized me all the way through dinner. When the whole family went to the library to look at satellite images of the King's

Pine Yacht Club and discuss tomorrow's rescue mission, all the stress and aches in my muscles started to catch up with me again. And by ten o'clock, I was a mindless zombie. So, I said good night and went up to my room.

No sooner had I shut my door than a yowl came from the hallway outside. Houdini. Sometimes it felt like he knew what I was doing every second of the day. He'd probably been taking lessons from Zachary.

I let him in and he wound around my legs while I changed into my nightshirt. Bored with me, he moved on to the open window and started sharpening his claws on the screen.

"Stop that," I shouted at him. "If you can't behave, I won't let you sleep on my pillow."

He gave me the stink eye and went right back to sharpening.

I started across the room to swat his butt, but he zinged under the bed.

"Think you're smarter than me," I said, shoving the screen up. A fleeting stab of worry went through me, fear that he might jump out of the now totally open half of the window. More likely he'd drive me nuts chasing moths or mosquitoes, anything that flittered in.

I crawled into bed. The breeze coming through the window fluttered the curtains. Houdini jumped up and took over the pillow next to mine, his purr loud and steady. As I drifted off, Chase's mother's words floated into my head, *"He told me I had to leave a door or window open, so he could come to me in the night."*

I jolted awake. *Chase.* Cats were known for their ability to sense otherworldly presences. Had Houdini scratched at the screen in an attempt to tell me Chase was there? *No.* That didn't make sense. Chase wasn't a full-blooded genie. Full-bloods could only enter a house or a room through unlocked entrances or with the owner's permission. Though perhaps the rules were different now that Chase was able to transform into an ethereal form, if he really had come to me.

A wave of longing for Chase roiled inside me. I ran a finger along my lips, imagining his lips on mine. An ache built in my chest. I wanted to be with him, so bad—

I clenched my teeth, driving off the thought. If he was trying to reach out to me, I couldn't encourage it. I couldn't do anything that might bring on the change. We needed to get him back home, then Grandfather, Kate, and everyone could help him cope with it or maybe even stop it altogether.

Struggling not to think about Chase, I stared at the ceiling, the moonlight sending shadows dancing across its pale surface. Shadows. Darkness. Blood. His skin had been slick with it.

Fear, sadness, and utter helplessness overtook me, drowned me in their dark tidal force. Shivering, I rolled onto my side and pulled my knees to my chest. I filled my mind with the satellite images of the King's Pine Yacht Club. I pictured Selena's new pixie cut, the pink bow ties, the tuxes, Lotli, Newt, Myles, Dad. Step by step, I went back through tomorrow's rescue plans. In the morning we'd pick up a rental van and the clothes . . . I even wondered about Taj. It was interesting that he was visiting Maine on the same weekend that the Sons were gathering.

Finally, my mind surrendered and I drifted into sleep.

I woke to the press of lips against mine. The whole room sparkled with diamond-cut shards of blue light. I reached up, cupping the glimmering image of Chase's face, bringing his lips back to mine. I opened my mouth, ecstasy, a slow dance of warm breath and tongues. His chest pressed against my breasts, and electric streaks of pleasure sizzled and seethed inside me, settling into a warm pulse between my thighs.

My fingertips moved up his stomach, exploring, enjoying

the warmth and silky skin, hard ropes of muscles. No blood. Not a trace. A rough scar. Had it been there before?

My eyes met his in a silent question.

His fingers barred my lips. Saying it wasn't important. That we didn't have much time.

Somewhere deep within the fog of sleep, I asked him why? Why didn't we have time? Another voice whispered inside me. *Hush. Don't worry. This isn't real. Just a dream. Enjoy.*

His fingers swept down my shoulders, trailing tingles in their wake. His tongue circled my nipple. A nibble. A suck. I arched. *Chase.* The ache inside me exploded into reckless need. I pulled his head against me. My body thrummed—

"No!" I screamed, shoving him back. "We can't. You can't. Go away, now!" My voice was husky with emotion. Tears burned in my eyes. I had to stop him. He'd change. Go berserk. I had to sacrifice tonight or risk losing him forever. If this was even real.

The blue diamond light shattered. A chill settled over me.

I sat upright in bed.

The room was filled with nothing, except darkness and empty moonlight.

CHAPTER 10

Connect the dots across the world and migration
routes appear. Routes that mirror the lines of
Ophiuchus. This is no coincidence. This
is the treasure map to prolonged existence.

—Discovery, Mystery, and Truth
www.SerpentWrestler.com

King's Pine Yacht Club was essentially a large boathouse and historic inn that sat on the shore of a sheltered bay. According to Olya's last-minute round of scrying, at some point during the night the magic fence had been moved out of the boathouse. It now shielded something on the inn's second floor. This meant that the wedding reception, the Sons of Ophiuchus meeting, and Lotli all were in the same building. However, since the wedding was on the beach at five and the meeting wasn't until six-thirty, we did have a window when anyone who might recognize us would be away from the inn, at least for a while.

It seemed like the perfect timing. Except midafternoon an unexpected storm blew in and Selena found out from Newt that the ceremony location had changed to the inn's veranda, much closer to Lotli's location than Dad and I would have preferred. It didn't seem to faze Selena, though. All she cared about was that she'd been allowed to come with us.

Promptly at four-fifty we pulled into the inn's parking lot in our rented van. The place was a mess, rain still slicing down. Fog had rolled in off the ocean, cloaking everything in a thick, wet haze. It was hard to even see the other cars, let alone the inn's front door.

Dad got out. Fighting the rain, he opened a giant umbrella and held it for Selena and me as we dashed around the puddles to the back of the van and retrieved two giant cellophane-wrapped gift baskets. One was packed with miniature cheesecakes, coffeecakes, and pink macaroons. The other was weighed down with little bottles of champagne, juice, and sodas. The baskets were Tibbs and his mother Laura's contribution to our plan. They'd come up with the idea of us pretending to be delivery people, bearing custom treats for the after-reception partiers. The plan was for us to stride in the front door of the inn. Once inside, we'd ditch the baskets on the gift table and blend in with the employees and vendors.

Dad closed the van doors, but as we turned to start for the inn, Selena raised her hand to stop us. "We've got trouble," she whispered.

A black limousine was pulling up to the curb. The groom and his ushers most likely—aka the groom, plus Newt and Myles.

Dad gestured for us to retreat. "Back in the van, quick."

I took a fresh grip on my basket and squinted against the rain. On one end of the inn there was a glassed-in porch. No doubt there was a side door there. But there was a white picket fence between it and us. My gaze went to the other end of the inn. Despite the haze, I could make out what appeared to be the shape of a Dumpster. Perfect! The delivery entry had worked yesterday, so why not today?

"Come on," I said to Dad. "I've got an idea."

Like I was swaggering into a high-end auction with a million dollars in my pocket instead of slogging through pouring rain, I strode away from the van, past the fog-shrouded limo and the front walk, and down a short service road.

Next to me, Selena matched my stride, rain and muddy water slinging up onto her raspberry-pink spikes, her new pixie-cut tossing with each step. Dad followed, the perfect tuxedoed gentleman, holding the umbrella over the baskets and us.

"You better be sure about this," he said.

"Don't worry. I am." I led them past the Dumpster and up a ramp to the service entry. I shouldered it open and stepped into a kitchen—

And came to a screeching halt.

The room was steamy hot and loud: a madhouse, people running everywhere with trays of hors d'oeuvres or pitchers of iced water, pots banged, a dishwasher growled, someone swore.

"You there!" A man in chef's whites pointed a spoon at us. He clapped it down on an empty spot on a counter. "Put those here."

I raised my chin and met his beady eyes. "We can't. We're supposed to"—my mind staggered, struggling to come up with an excuse. We couldn't leave the baskets in the kitchen. We needed to get farther into the inn where we could blend in. I glanced over my shoulder at Dad. He was still outside, wrestling with the umbrella. The rain had barely touched me or Selena. But he looked like a drowned rat, if wet rats dressed in tuxes and had shoulder-holster-shaped lumps on their sides. Mortified, I wheeled back and flashed a smile at the chef. "We were told to leave them—"

He cut me off. "I'll make sure the wedding coordinator gets them."

"We can't just leave them," Selena chimed in. "This isn't grocery-store champagne, you know. Those tiny bottles cost fifty bucks each."

A woman rushed up to the chef, her voice bordering on

hysteria. "The cake. The florist bumped the table. It slid. Oh
my God. When the bride sees it."

"That"—the chef snarled—"is not my fucking problem.
Tell the wedding coordinator. She hired the hoity-toity cake-
maker. She can deal with it."

I leaned toward Selena. "This isn't working," I whispered.

She nodded. "We should just ask him where the meeting
room is."

I blinked at her. She was right. I raised my voice louder
than the chef. "Excuse me. We don't have all day."

He pivoted, glaring at me like a deranged rhinoceros.

I glared back. "The baskets aren't for the wedding. They're
for a meeting at six-thirty. We were told to deliver them upstairs."

His expression dropped. "Oh." He gave Selena and me another once-over and then glanced out the door toward Dad.

I held my breath, hoping we'd pass whatever inspection he
was currently doing in his head.

Finally, he pointed the spoon out the door and motioned
to the right. "Take the deck stairs. At the top there's sliding
glass doors. They should be unlocked. Straight ahead is a hallway. That meeting's scheduled for the Commodore Boardroom. Leave them on the sideboard."

"Thank you," I said.

Dad left his umbrella beside the kitchen door, his hand
resting inside his jacket as we set off with the baskets up a set
of roofed stairs to the enclosed deck. From there, we went
through the sliding glass doors and into a dimly lit reception
hall.

The room had an overpowering new-carpet smell. And it
was eerily quiet, so much so that for a heartbeat I wondered if
there was a soundproofing spell on it, like the one I'd encoun-
tered in Malphic's harem.

"Wait here," Dad said. He crept toward an open set of double doors that led into a hallway.

The loud ding of an elevator chime broke the silence.

Adrenaline shot into my veins. I scanned the room for a place to hide. Tables. Chairs. Plastic trees. A folding screen stood in one corner.

"Pssst," I said to get Dad and Selena's attention. I gestured at the screen and we all sprinted for it, the thud of our steps quiet, but still too loud in the silent room.

"You think they heard us?" Selena whispered, as we scrunched into a narrow space between the back of the screen and a stack of extra chairs.

Dad shook his head. "I don't think so."

The whine of a vacuum cleaner started up in the hallway, growing louder as it moved back and forth, down the hall closer and closer toward our room. Shit. The last thing we needed was to be discovered by a cleaning crew, or spend what little time we had holed up in a corner. But we couldn't exactly snoop around while a bunch of employees were watching either.

"We can't just wait for them to finish," I said, leaning close to Dad.

Selena crowded in. "I could scry now to save time."

I let go of my basket with one hand and clamped her wrist, stopping her from reaching for the mirrored compact she used for scrying. "We're probably still outside the fence. You'd get hurt."

"It's better than doing nothing."

"Shush." Dad lowered his voice even more. "Be patient. Annie's right. The only reason they'd have for moving Lotli from the boathouse to up here is if they want her at their meeting. I'm willing to bet the fence is around the Commodore Boardroom and maybe a private room attached to it."

The vacuum cleaner's whine became deafeningly loud,

moving in the hallway right in front of our room. Sweat trickled down my sides. The basket seemed to get heavier and heavier, as I waited and waited for the sound to pass. But it didn't. For a long moment it approached and retreated. Approached and retreated—

The whine stopped.

A clatter of wheels and a man's tuneless whistle moved away from our room. The elevator dinged. Then silence.

Dad stepped toward the edge of the screen. "Wait here. I'll double-check."

He snuck across the dark room to a doorway and then motioned for us to join him. When we got there, he nodded across the hallway to a carved-oak door. Above it, COMMODORE was etched into a brass plaque. The inn might have been historic, but my eyes went right to the latch on the door. It was modern with a slot for a keycard in it.

"Let's hope it's not locked," I said, though it didn't seem like the chef would send us to a room we couldn't get into.

Turned out, he hadn't. Still, I let out a relieved breath once we were all inside the boardroom with the door closed behind us.

It was a narrow room. Straight ahead of us, an exquisite Federal-style table and chairs occupied the center of the room. Little more than a yard beyond it was a wall of sheer glass. A glimpse of the bay appeared and vanished in the deluge of rain and mist.

A sense of vertigo washed over me. I took a breath and looked away from the view. To my left was a built-in bar and leather-topped stools. Behind me sat a sideboard as valuable as the table. Above it hung oil paintings of clipper ships and race horses.

"Without a keycard we can't lock the door, so we need to work fast," Dad whispered. He made straight for another door on the other end of the room. "Bathroom," he announced, stepping inside.

Selena and I set our baskets on the bar. I tried a nonde-script door next to it. A coat closet, half-full of trench coats and jackets. I moved them aside. No hidden doorway or secret room appeared to exist.

The sound of organ music echoed up from the floor below.

"Shit," Selena said. "It sounds like they've moved the wedding inside."

Thump. A dull noise sounded right outside the boardroom door.

"Watch where you're going," a man said sharply.

"Sorry. I thought I left the door open," another man answered.

Crap. They were coming in here!

I raced for the coat closet and yanked the door open. Dad got there a heartbeat later. Selena was—

I glanced behind me and let out a panicked yelp. Where the hell was she?

Fast as I could, I surveyed the room. She was at the bar, fussing with the cellophane wrap on one of the gift baskets.

"Selena," I whispered, my voice rising with hysteria. "Get in here, now!"

She snatched something from the basket, then flew toward the closet. We all piled inside and I shut the door, just as the door to the hallway opened.

My heart banged against my rib cage. I slid off my spikes and wriggled noiselessly between the coats, positioning myself against the back wall between Dad and Selena. The closet reeked of wet coats and stale cigar smoke. It was also dark. Pitch-black, except for a wedge of light slicing in along the bottom of the door. Black as the space under a bed. Black as death.

Clutching the mud-splattered shoes against my chest, I swallowed my fear. This wasn't the time to lose my cool. Besides, I'd made peace with darkness. It was my friend, especially right now.

One of the men's voices came from inside the room. "Put the pitcher and glasses on the table."

"They aren't having a bartender?" the other guy said.

"No, this is strictly a closed-door meeting."

"What's with all the hush-hush stuff, anyway?"

"Don't worry about it."

Footsteps scuffed toward the closet, or maybe they were headed for the bar. I held my breath and looked at Dad. He stood, gun in hand.

One silent second passed. Then another.

Pfffffst! The hissing noise fizzed out from Selena's corner of the closet.

I froze, every muscle in my body bowstring-tight and ready.

"What was that?" one of the guys said.

The closet door flew open, light spraying through the line of coats. Selena stood flat against the back wall, her eyes wide, and an open can of cola in her hand. Why hadn't she done that before?

"Quit screwing around," the other guy said. "It's just the damn rats again. You'd think with all the money this place makes, the owners could afford a decent exterminator."

The light vanished as the guy shut the door.

I shot a glare at Selena. She grimaced apologetically, then cautiously settled down cross-legged on the floor. In the wedge of light, I saw her take her mirrored compact out and rest it on her knee. She poured a little cola on the mirror, so she could use it to scry, and set the soda can on the floor.

Dad's hand brushed my shoulder. "What's she doing?"

"Scrying," I said, totally hushed. As dark as it was, I couldn't imagine how she intended to do it. But scrying did seem to involve *seeing* with the mind as much as the eyes. We undoubtedly were inside the fence by now.

THUNK. The sound echoed outward from right in front of me: a wet coat slipping off its hanger and hitting the floor. My heart sank. We were screwed.

"Rats, my ass," the guy said. The door flung open, coats shoved aside.

Dad was ready, his gun pointed at the guy's chest. "Move a muscle and you're both dead," he said, hard as stone.

The guy's hands went up. He backed out of the closet.

Dad followed him. "You," he said to a bigger guy standing near the table with his hands out in surrender, "lock the door. Don't try anything or I'll shoot you both."

Ignoring the panic inside me, I dropped my shoes beside the closet and went to stand behind Dad, shoulders squared.

"Take anything you want," the big guy said, edging to the doors. Of the two guys, the calmness of his voice and the steadiness of his hands told me he was the one we had to watch. "There's silverware in the sideboard. It's real. Take it." With one hand, he pulled out a keycard, slid it in the door's lock, and withdrew it. Then he moved slowly back toward us and his buddy, his arms away from his sides.

Dad yanked off his tie and held it out to me. "Gag this one first." He gestured to the smaller guy directly in front of him. "We need some rope or duct tape." He glanced to where Selena stood just inside the closet.

In a flash, the bigger guy rushed at Dad.

I dove forward, grabbed a bar stool, and swung it at the guy with all my strength. CRACK! The stool caught him in the chest. He stumbled backward, then swiveled toward me, his arm cranking back, his fist aimed at my head. I ducked, snatched a piece of broken stool off the floor, and slammed it into his groin. He dropped and curled up, groaning on the floor. "Bitch. Goddamn, crazy bitch."

I stared down at him, stunned. I'd hit him. I'd taken him down. I'd probably broken his ribs. Not to mention his nuts. I could have killed him. Holy crap.

Dad chuckled. "At least you didn't use one of the expensive chairs."

"I guess," I said, my voice weak. Sure, I'd knifed a genie before, more than one. But we'd been battling for our lives then. This guy was technically innocent. We'd broken in. Held him at gunpoint.

Selena appeared with duct tape and a cord she'd found behind the bar. "Do you think anyone heard?"

"They'd be here by now if they had," Dad said. "But we don't have any time to waste."

CHAPTER 11

On the eve of castration I watched the moon,
dreaming of scrolls and tablets at my fingertips
instead of a sword in my hand. Fear not sacrifice.
Fear not reaching for impossible dreams.

—Jaquith, Son of Malphic and High Eunuch

It took forever to locate in which pocket the big guy had hidden his security keycard and to get them tied up in the closet. When we were done, I turned to Selena. "Did you finish scrying?"

Her chin dipped, embarrassment written on her face. But she recovered in a flash. Her gaze met mine. Her voice pitched lower, steady and determined. "Yes, we're inside the fence. Lotli's in this room, somewhere. I'm a hundred percent certain."

"All righty, then," Dad said. "Let's get cracking and find her. Selena, use your senses, see if you can home in on Lotli's magic. Annie, scan the walls for anything that could activate a hidden door. I'll check the floor for levers. It could be a button or something ornamental."

Starting next to the bathroom, I scanned clockwise around the room, looking at everything. Light switches. The wall paper . . . Back at Moonhill, some of the mirrors served as secret doorways. The Sons of Ophiuchus might easily have developed similar devices.

My gaze stopped on one of the paintings over the sideboard. A clipper ship. White sails. Full moon. Six stars, forming an irregular hexagon.

"Selena," I said sharply.

She frowned. "What? I can't focus with you talking at me."

"Does this look like the constellation Ophiuchus?" I pointed to the stars in the painting.

She dashed over. "Yes! Exactly, though I think the constellation actually has a few more stars."

I tugged on the frame. It didn't come away from the wall. I yanked on one side. Nothing. I yanked on the other side. There was resistance, then a click and the side pulled away from the wall—like a medicine cabinet door opening. Behind it was a hand-size metal panel with a keypad set into it. Three rows of numbers across. Four rows down. The bottom row had symbols on either side of a zero, like a phone.

"Shit," I said, glancing back at Dad. "What do we do now?"

He studied the keypad. "We're going to have to be careful. With this kind of lock, we'll only get three tries before it shuts down and sets off an alarm."

"That's not good." Selena stepped closer. "There has to be a million possible number combinations."

I nibbled my bottom lip. "We could try words. On old-fashioned phones there are letters that correspond to each number, right?"

"Good thinking," Dad said, resting his hand on my shoulder. "It'll be a simple word, something easy to remember. Why don't you try *Sons*?"

My face went hot from embarrassment and I grimaced. "You'll have to do it. I can't remember what those kind of phone keypads look like, which letters go with what numbers."

"Don't worry. I'll tell you." He went on, his voice slow and steady. "7-6-6-7—that will be S-O-N-S."

I took a deep breath and punched in the numbers. Nothing happened. Not even an electronic buzz.

"Try *Wrestler*," Selena suggested. "The Sons are guys—and that's a guy word."

Dad said the numbers slowly, allowing me time to press each key before he went on to the next. "9-7-3-7-8-5-3-7."

Nothing again.

I wiped my hand over my head. And though I wasn't a follower of the Goddess like Kate and Olya were, I mumbled a prayer, "Please, Hecate, Protector of the Gateways, guide my hand."

"Serpent," Dad announced. His voice grew taut as he gave me the first number. "7—"

I raised my hand to press the key. But just as I was about to punch in the number, my thoughts went back to the painting. The constellation Ophiuchus represented by six stars. An irregular hexagon. The tension in my gut told me I was on to something. But if my hunch was wrong, the keypad would lock down, sending off an alarm. Still, I had to chance it.

Blocking out Dad's voice, I pushed 2-4-9-0 in consecutive order. The only keys that formed a lopsided hexagon that resembled the one in the painting.

The lock hummed.

I held my breath, excitement jumping inside me as the panel holding the keypad rose. But my joy was short-lived, replaced by despair when I saw what had been revealed.

"Ohmigod." Selena gasped. "It's a retinal scan."

"Perfect." Dad sanded his hands together in glee. "Now, Annie, if you'll give me room, I'll do this next step."

"What are you talking about?" I said.

He stashed his gun and took what appeared to be a pudding cup from his pants pocket. "You didn't expect your grandfather to send us without a few tricks up our sleeves, did you?" He unscrewed the top on the container and pulled out an eyeball. A real eyeball.

"I can't believe I didn't see that coming," Selena said calmly.

I cringed. "I sure didn't. How . . . Whose is it?"

"Jeffrey White's," Dad announced, holding the eyeball up to the scanner.

The wall next to the sideboard began to inch open, but I couldn't look away from the eyeball. "How did you get—"

Dad dropped the eye back into the container. "Don't worry. It's a reproduction. Pig gelatin granules, an image of our good Jeffrey White's retina acquired from a friendly—albeit money hungry—ophthalmologist combined with your grandfather's hocus-pocus. The 3D printer did the rest."

"No shit," I said.

Applause rose from the floor below. My pulse leapt. It could only mean that the bride and groom had kissed. The ceremony was over.

I rushed for the still-opening doorway and shimmied through the gap sideways. Dad and Selena followed right behind me. Once we were all through, I glanced around trying to take everything in as fast as possible. The room we were in was dimly lit. A tiny office, narrow and windowless. Bookcases. A treadmill. An antique globe. A mahogany desk. A roll of duct tape, thin knives, gigantic needles and syringes. A pair of handcuffs lay on a metal tray. I went cold all over. That didn't look good, not at all.

A muffled cry came from behind us. I whirled around. Lotli was slumped in a large metal chair. Both her wrists were handcuffed to the chair's arms. Duct tape wrapped her legs and spanned her mouth. Something vomit-yellow stained the front of her peasant blouse, and her purple wrap pants had a rip up the side. She raised her face, her thick dark hair hanging lank.

Dad took out his gun and handed it to Selena. "Watch the doorway. You know how to shoot, right?"

She grinned. "It's a Glock. 9mm. I was weaned on these."

While Dad fished a lock-picking kit out of his jacket, I peeled the tape off Lotli's mouth, trying hard not to yank her lip ring out.

"Please," she whimpered. "Get us out of here."

Dad went to work on the handcuffs. I snagged a knife from the tray on the desk and started cutting the duct tape off her ankles. I couldn't help but think of the night I'd found her in the car trunk with tape around her ankles, just like this.

A minute later, she was free. She wobbled to her feet and swayed.

I caught her by the elbow. "Are you all right?"

Slipping free from my grip, she nodded. "We will be fine. But our flute, we need our flute."

"Do you know where it is?" Dad asked.

"Jeffrey White. He put it in his jacket pocket. An hour ago, no longer. He said he was going downstairs." She clenched her hands and pulled her arms tight against her chest, shuddering. "He is your height, bald."

Dad nodded curtly. "I've seen him on TV."

"We do not like him." She staggered toward the doorway. When she reached Selena, her knees began to buckle. "Oh, our head. So dizzy."

Selena hooked her arm around Lotli's waist. "It's not far. We'll do it together."

"Thank you." Lotli looped both arms around Selena's neck and leaned against her.

Selena bit her bottom lip, sagging under Lotli's weight as they hobbled through the doorway into the boardroom. Actually, Selena looked a bit pale and shaky herself. She wasn't admitting it, but I couldn't help wondering if the scrying she'd done in the closet or the closeness of the magic fence was affecting her. She looked like she might barf.

"Let me have that," I said, taking the gun from Selena's hand. I would have offered to help with Lotli, but Lotli was already starting to look better. Once we got across the hallway and outside the fence, they'd probably both be fine.

Music rose from below us. A fast throb and a muted announcement like a DJ might make. Most likely, cocktail hour had begun.

I sprinted ahead and slid the keycard I'd taken off the guy into the lock. Once everyone else arrived, I opened the door partway.

"Wait," Dad said. "I'm going first. I'll check the elevators to make sure no one's coming this way. If there is, I'll come right back. If you don't see me in a minute, that means the coast is clear. Head straight across the hallway and to the van as fast as you can. I'm going downstairs to do some pickpocketing."

"Dad, you're—" I waved my hand, indicating his still rain-soaked clothes and hair. "You'll stand out like a sore thumb."

"Don't worry about it. I doubt I'll be the only one." He touched Lotli's chin, bringing her head up. "Don't you worry either, kiddo. We'll make them pay for this."

She nodded and smiled. But I scowled. I didn't like the sound of his promise. I didn't like the sounds of the pickpocketing. Dad was shrewd, but he wasn't a thief, and I didn't believe for a second that the wedding guests would be soaking wet. Still, I didn't protest as he slipped out the door, quietly shutting it behind him. We didn't have a choice. Jeffrey White had the flute. And without it, Lotli couldn't open the veil between realms.

I looked at Selena and Lotli. "Ready to go?"

Selena glanced at my feet. "Aren't you forgetting something?"

My shoes. Shit. I set off for where I'd tossed them by the

bar. I put the gun down and wiggled my feet into the spikes. My eyes went to the closet. We'd tied the men up and gagged them, so it made sense they weren't making any noise. But I couldn't help hoping they were okay, especially the guy I'd hit.

I clenched my teeth. Why was I worrying about him? The guy had attacked Dad. What else could I have done?

Shoving that thought aside, I jogged back to Selena and Lotli. "Ready?"

They both nodded. With the gun firmly in hand and them behind me, I slowly pushed the door open—

And came face-to-face with Newt. Myles stood an arm's length behind him.

My mind went blank, my body numb with the shock.

In his tux and raspberry-pink bow tie, Newt looked even taller, blonder, and yacht-club athletic than usual. Myles still reminded me of a pasty-pale slug. How had they and Dad missed one another? Different elevators. Different staircases. It didn't matter.

Myles's lips curled into a snarl. "What the fuck are you doing here?"

Newt gawked at Selena. "Is that you? You look—different. Your hair . . . it's—"

Clenching my jaw, I squared my shoulders and raised the gun. My legs quaked with fear and sweat slid down my spine. But I put on my best poker face, praying they wouldn't see through my false bravado.

Selena shoved Lotli behind her and stepped up next to me. "My hair? You love it, don't you?"

Newt nodded like a marionette, unable to do anything else. "Totally stunning."

Myles smacked him in the bicep. "Fuck, Newt. What's wrong with you? They aren't here to party." He nodded sharply at the gun in my hand.

I took off the safety and leveled it on the two of them. "Get inside," I said, stepping backward into the boardroom. Selena and Lotli followed my cue and moved back as well.

Newt and Myles raised their hands and did as I commanded. But, as I locked the door behind them, Newt edged closer to Selena, his voice cooing. "Sweetheart, don't let her do this." He jutted his chin to where Lotli had slumped onto a bar stool. "You need to stay away from her. She's dangerous."

Selena glared at him. "Screw you, Newt Harrison—if that's even really your name. Now move it." She pointed toward the secret room and doorway we'd left open. It was exactly where I'd thought of taking them as well.

Newt lowered his arms, holding them out as if to say he meant no harm. "Selena, trust me. I only want what's best for you." His voice deepened into a low threat. "I don't want to hurt you or your friends. But if I have to—"

I elbowed Selena. "Why don't you take the gun? You're a better shot than I am."

Newt paled and Myles's arms shot up higher. Clearly, they were familiar with her weapon prowess. Luckily, they hadn't known my lack of experience.

"Wait here," I said, glancing back at Lotli. She'd slouched over the bar, head buried in her folded arms. We needed to get her to the van, and fast.

Selena, on the other hand, appeared to have recovered her strength and was totally focused. It was as if the anger in her system had nullified the fence's magic or whatever had been getting to her before. She was now the ultimate pixie-haired Bond girl, gun ready, muscles flexed, and every movement confident as we herded Newt and Myles into the secret room.

She made Myles handcuff Newt to the chair. Then I handcuffed Myles to the treadmill.

I stepped back and grinned. "It was nice of the Sons to provide such a well-equipped holding cell. I especially like the accessories. They look exquisitely sharp." I tilted my head toward the needles and knives on the desk. Not that I planned on doing anything, but after everything Newt and Myles had done they deserved at least a moment of mental torture.

Myles pulled against the handcuffs, steel rattling. "You bitches are going to regret this."

"Shut up, Myles," Newt said. His gaze went to Selena, his voice syrupy. "Nothing's going to happen to you, darling. But you need to let us go right now, sweetheart baby."

I pivoted toward Selena. "Do you mind getting me the duct tape? This room might be soundproof, but I'm sick of listening to them."

Ignoring me, Selena shoved the gun into her waistband and whipped out a pocket-size bottle of pepper spray from her jacket. She strode right up to Newt, her expression transforming into a mask of dark amusement. "This is going to be fun, *sweetheart baby*."

His mouth fell open. "What are you doing? I love you."

"Not for long." She sprayed him directly in the eyes.

He screamed in agony, squirming against his bonds. His eyes slammed shut, tears weeping from between his lashes. Blood trickled from his nose. He gasped, made a gurgling noise, and then his head flopped forward as though he'd blacked out.

A whiff of the spray drifted my way, not caustic like pepper spray. The scent of violets. In a flash, memories flooded back to me: fifteen years ago, Kate's fingers on my face, massaging oil onto my eyelids. And only a few weeks ago, me doing the same thing to Culus, the genie who'd possessed Dad. Violet-scented oil intended to wipe out memories. But Selena's spray contained more than just violet oil, a hint of something sweeter.

Selena closed her eyes and raised her hand. "Queen Bee, take these memories, take me from his eyes," she chanted. "Petals to lids. Petals to eyes—"

"What—what are you doing?" Myles's voice quaked. "Stop it."

Selena opened her eyes and knifed him with an evil pixie grin. "Don't tell me you aren't a fan of *A Midsummer Night's Dream*? It's my favorite."

He scuffed backward against the treadmill as far as the handcuffs allowed. "You're crazy. Both of you are crazy!"

My breath caught in my throat. I wasn't that sure he was wrong.

"Watch and learn." Selena flipped her compact open. Holding it out, she grasped Newt's hair and yanked his limp head up, face-to-face with the mirror. "What thou see when you awake."

I gasped. Selena was reciting from *A Midsummer Night's Dream*. Fairy magic. Flower petals. Eyelids. Titania falling in love with the donkey. I knew what she was up to. She was going to free herself from the curse by transferring Newt's love onto someone else. Oh my God. The mirror. She intended on making him fall hopelessly in love with himself.

Her voice lifted. "What you see when you wake, do it for your true love take." She let go of his hair. His head flopped back down and then raised slowly, his gaze inching upward toward the mirror.

"No!" Myles shrieked.

Newt's head stopped traveling upward and swiveled toward his brother. His lips parted. His eyes glistened. "Myles?" he said, sugar-sweet.

CHAPTER 12

At the molecular level, a solid body and smokeless
fire are more similar than one might imagine.

—Hector Freemont

We weren't even a mile down the road when Selena spilled the full truth to Dad about what had happened to Newt. It wasn't like she had a choice about telling this time. After all, Dad had returned from successfully swiping the flute in time to see Newt ogling Myles and get the gist of what had transpired. Plus, testing the truth out on him was a good way to prepare for the reaction we'd get at home.

Stone-faced, Dad took his gaze off the road and glanced in the rearview at Selena. "His brother? You tried to transfer the curse and Newt looked at his brother?"

"I feel really bad about it," she said with the conviction of a wet sponge. "I mean, Newt did always love himself a lot. That would have been perfect. Of course, the best thing would have been to remove the curse entirely—which I couldn't do. Seriously, I swear, I'll never do another irreversible curse again, never ever."

The corners of Dad's mouth twitched, his serious expression weakening. Finally, he couldn't hold it in any longer and he burst out laughing. "I can't begin to imagine. In love with his brother?" He stepped on the gas, the rental van growling its way through the wispy fog. "One thing's sure, it's going to take the Sons a while to get that mess straightened out."

We were all laughing now, as much out of relief as anything else. It went without saying that we were lucky to have escaped. And equally lucky that Lotli appeared to be mostly dehydrated and exhausted, not tortured or subjected to mind-altering drugs in an attempt to get her to spill secrets.

Clutching her flute, Lotli snuggled into the old jacket Dad had loaned her. "We are so grateful to you all," she said.

Dad ran his hand over his head, smoothing a few stray hairs back over a balding spot. "Unfortunately this isn't the last we'll see of the Sons."

"That's for sure," Selena murmured.

As Lotli dozed off, Dad and Selena retreated into their own thoughts. I lowered the side window just enough to catch a slight breeze, the scent of damp pine trees and ocean. Here and there, glimpses of shoreline and water broke through the mist.

We drove over a drawbridge, the bridge's metal grates humming beneath the van's tires. When we reached the far side, the mist lifted a little, revealing a small building surrounded by sand and picnic tables. The plywood around its entry was painted to look like a pile of rocks, dotted with cartoonish seagulls and puffins eating ice-cream cones and burgers.

A lump formed in my throat, deep sadness welling in my chest as we passed by. It was Mr. Puffin's Snack Bar, one of Chase's favorite places to eat. It was definitely kid-oriented and not all that close to Moonhill, but he loved their fries and burgers, and absolutely adored their ice cream. I'd always get a chocolate Cree-me. He'd order a deluxe hot fudge sundae with the works. But before he'd take a bite, he'd snatch the cherry off the top and toss it to me.

Tears prickled in my eyes. Smiling slightly, I fogged a tiny patch of the side window with my breath and traced the outline of a cherry on the cool glass, turning it into a heart. I loved so many things about Chase. But there was no arguing the fact that he had unusual table manners. Well, truthfully, they were horrible.

He ate fast with little regard as to whether his hands, shirt-sleeves, or a jackknife got involved. And he ate anything, gulping down microwaved hot dogs with the same gusto as he devoured Laura's special roast beef, stuffed with mushrooms and feta cheese. He acted like peanut butter was manna from God. And nothing, absolutely nothing could hold him back when it came to slurping down a glass of cold milk.

I twisted in my seat, catching a final glimpse of Mr. Puffin's as it faded behind us. Whenever I watched Chase eat, I inevitably was left wondering how many days he'd gone hungry as a boy in the djinn realm, how many nights he'd lain awake in the barracks, his stomach cramping.

I squeezed my eyes shut. Was he hungry right now?

When we got to Moonhill, Dad carried Lotli into the library's sunroom and set her on the daybed. It wasn't a normal guest room, but Lotli had chosen it when she first arrived at Moonhill.

Anger bristled inside me as I recalled that afternoon when we'd gone to the campsite and returned with her. Lotli had been offered a bedroom next to mine, but claimed it was too ostentatious. She needed a smaller, more natural space. She'd suggested the stone cottage where Chase lived by himself. It didn't take much imagination to figure out what she really wanted—namely Chase.

I dug my fingernails into my palms, ending that poisonous train of thought. Why was I even thinking about that? Lotli had risked her life by going into the realm with us to try to save my mother. And she was going to help us again. That day when she'd first arrived, she hadn't realized I was interested in Chase.

"Thank you for letting us wear this," Lotli said, handing the jacket back to Dad. "And thank you again for getting our flute. It means everything to us."

Selena draped an afghan over Lotli's shoulders. "Do you remember anything about the kidnapping?"

She shook her head. "Not much. We remember escaping from the realm. We came in here to change our clothes. They surprised us from behind, put a rag over our mouth and nose. The smell was so strong. Everything went black. When we woke up, we were in the boathouse. That is all we remember." She glanced at me. "What happened to you and Chase?"

I folded my arms across my chest, hands tucked under my armpits. I didn't like thinking about this, but she had a right to know everything. I told her in detail about how, after I'd tricked her into leaving the realm without me, I'd dressed as a dancer and gone back to the full moon festival. I started to tell her about watching Chase being forced to fight, but I couldn't keep my voice steady. So I summarized the rest: about me turning ethereal, being put into a decanter and thrown back through the veil, and landing on the outcrop of rocks.

Lotli pulled the afghan close around her. "We feel so horrible about everything."

I eyed her. She was shivering like she was chilled to the bone. "You probably should take a hot bath and get into some clean clothes," I suggested.

"I've got some new pajamas you can have," Selena said. She grimaced. "Annie and I really should have thought to pick up some clothes for you while we were at the camper."

"That would have been smart," Dad said.

Lotli stiffened. "You went to our camper?"

I nodded. "We were hoping that—" I felt myself pale. "Shit. We forgot to tell you about Zea."

"Zea?" Lotli's dark eyes widened.

"Don't worry," Dad said gently. "He's gone missing, but we're certain he's okay."

Selena jumped in. "I scried for him. He's not that far from the campsite, a couple of towns away at the most. It felt like he was drifting."

"Drifting?" Lotli rubbed her lips, then smiled. "Zea has a friend with a houseboat. He goes there sometimes when we are away. You sensed the movement of waves."

Selena nodded. "That's exactly what it felt like. This friend is someone Zea can trust, right?"

Lotli didn't answer. Her gaze swung away from Selena, searching the room. "Are you saying all our clothes are gone? Everything?"

"They went missing when you did," I said. "We assumed Newt or whoever took you grabbed all your stuff as well."

She rocked forward, pressing her hands over her eyes. "Our backpack. We remember now. They had it."

"They didn't get everything," Selena said quietly. "Zachary found your talisman bag under the bed."

She looked up. "He did? Where is it?"

"Mom made him put it under your pillow—for when you got back."

Leaving the afghan behind, she scooted to the head of the daybed, retrieved the tiny bag, and pressed it against her chest. "We are so grateful to have this." She closed her eyes, her gratitude palpable. "Clothes can be replaced, but this was our grandmother's and our great-grandmother's before that."

Dad cleared his throat. "If you ladies will excuse me, I'm going to go update Kate before dinner."

After Lotli thanked him for the millionth time, Dad took off and a second later, Olya and Zachary showed up. I stayed for another minute, then made my escape. It was time to get out of my tux and spikes and into something more comfortable. Also, I suspected Dad and Kate weren't just going to discuss what happened at the yacht club. Now that Lotli was back, they'd finalize the plans for going to the realm. I had to make sure they included me.

I padded away from the sunroom and through the library, the rhythm of my spikes muted by the Persian carpets. Once I reached the marble-floored hallway, it was harder to hide the sound of my steps. I momentarily considered taking off my shoes to silence my footfalls. It wasn't a bad idea, but it would look a bit too obvious.

I slowed, creeping along. Dad most likely had headed straight for Kate's office. But I needed to give him a few minutes to get there and get settled, otherwise I wouldn't be able to eavesdrop for a moment before I went into the office. That was, if the door to her office was open.

I passed a painting of a brooding pirate and paused to take a look at a display of shrunken heads. The heads' eyes and mouths were sewn shut. They kind of reminded me of old, leathery persimmons. I shuddered and turned down the west wing hallway.

A figure stepped out from behind a pillar, dark against the backdrop of a bright window.

I yelped and scuffed backward, my heart racing. It wasn't as big as a shadow-genie, but still—

The person folded their arms across their chest, foot tapping. I knew that foot tap. Dad.

"And exactly where are you going?" he said.

I smiled weakly.

He stepped toward me, the darkness leaving his face. "You weren't planning on showing up at Kate's office, were you?"

I shoved my hands in my hip pockets and shrugged. But it was silly for me to pretend innocence. Any skill I had at reading body language I had learned from him. "It's just . . . I've been to the realm. I could draw a map of Malphic's fortress for you."

"And you will. Right now, be patient. Let me do the planning alone, like we agreed."

"I won't say anything to piss Kate off. Promise." I really didn't get why he was being so stubborn. "We need to go to the realm as soon as we can. Chase doesn't have that long."

Dad unfolded his arms. "I'll see you at dinner," he said firmly. He swiveled away.

Anger flashed through me. "Dad, I need to know what's going on."

He turned back and smiled. "I suggest you go to bed right after supper. Get some extra rest tonight."

My anger drained, replaced by a flicker of hope. "What are you saying?"

"It looks to me like Lotli should be fine by morning. I'm going to tell Kate that I think we should go to the realm tomorrow evening." He raised a finger to his lips. "Just between us for now, okay?"

It was hard not saying anything through dinner and dessert. But I stuck to my word, kept my lips sealed and didn't butt into any of the conversations, not that Dad, Grandfather, or Kate said much about the upcoming mission to the realm. Mostly everyone talked about what happened at the yacht club. Oddly enough, when Selena told her parents about the curse and Newt, they didn't rag on her. A nice change that left me smiling. However, I was certain they wouldn't be so easygoing once they discovered she intended to go on the mission.

After dinner, I took a hot bath, then planted myself in bed. Dinner had been late, so in reality it wasn't *that* early, maybe nine-thirty.

I stretched out on my right side, one arm under a pillow,

the other under the covers, my standard go-to-sleep position. I closed my eyes and let my mind drift, thinking about how this time tomorrow we'd be sneaking through Malphic's fortress. It was an eerie, dangerous place filled with torch-lit corridors and exotic scents. Sheer curtains fluttered in open windows, dyed violet and green by the nighttime auroras. All the doorways were curtained, too. And there were magic carpets. The carpets didn't fly like in human stories. They hung on the fortress's walls. If you stepped into one, you'd come out somewhere else. But you never could be sure where, since Malphic's magi continually switched the locations they connected.

A twinge of pain spread up my arm, pinching my neck. Of course my bruised muscles would start aching now, after not being so bad all day. I rolled over onto my other side, once again thinking about the djinn realm and what had brought us to a place where we needed Lotli so badly.

A decade ago, Grandfather had acquired an artifact known as the Lamp of Methuselah. It contained oil with magical properties. Normally, human bodies transformed from solid to ethereal when they went through the veil and entered the djinn realm. But coating a person in the oil made their body ethereal in the mortal world and solid in the djinn realm. It had the exact opposite effect on genies. However, the oil had two problems: First, it only lasted from sunset to sunrise; and second, its strong cabbage-and-wet-sheep scent. Five years ago, when Kate and Uncle David had used the oil and gone through the weak point in Moonhill's gallery in an attempt to rescue Mother, it was the smell that had alerted the genies. Kate, David, and Chase had gotten back to Moonhill, but Malphic had sealed the veil with a swift and powerful warding spell before Mother could get through. Since then, both our family and Malphic had tried to keep the weak point warded. But—just as Malphic had found ways to neutralize our wards and get into Moonhill—we'd found our own way to break his wards and get into his fortress, namely Lotli and her flute-magic. Sure, even without her flute-magic we could use the oil to turn our bodies ethereal and get through a broken or un-warded weak point in the veil. We didn't even have to worry about the oil's smell since Kate had found a way to make it scent-free. But Malphic's magic was more powerful than ours. The second he caught wind that we'd trespassed, he'd repair his wards. Lotli was the only way we could escape anytime we wanted. I sighed. It was a case of the lesser of two evils. We were either dependent on Lotli for safety's sake or easy prey for Malphic.

I opened my eyes and gazed across the bedroom. On my dresser were the fingerless mitts Chase had knitted for me to wear into the realm so the genies wouldn't notice my girly hands.

A sad feeling gathered in my stomach, spreading out, tug-ging at my heart. *Chase.* I curled up into a ball, the cold sheets twisting around me. I needed to sleep. I had to.

But it would never happen with my head whirring like this.

I wrestled my way free from the sheets and got out of bed. The floor chilled my feet as I wandered to the window. The sky was cloudless, scattered with stars and a barely waning moon. Beneath the dark outlines of the pine trees, mist hung in the glistening wet gardens. Normally there would have been at least a few fireflies or the glow of a garden light to break up the shadows. But there were none. There were no other sparks of brightness either. *Chase.*

I rested my forehead against the window glass, tears hot behind my eyelids.

Two figures appeared in the misty garden. Olya and Uncle David. Holding hands, heads close together, talking as they drifted through the stripes of haze and light cast out from the windows, through the shadow of trees, statues, and flower spires.

I drew a shuddering breath, the aching loneliness inside me a million times more intense than anything my muscles could create.

Turning from the window, I stumbled blindly across my room. I threw on my robe, found my lock-picking tools and a mini flashlight, and fled into the hallway. I couldn't encourage Chase to come to me. I couldn't really be with him. But I could go up to the widow's walk. It was the last place we'd made love. Being there would make me feel closer to him, help me relax, maybe even sleep.

The hallway was as dark as the gardens. I turned on my flashlight. Its beam brightened the carpet, crimson except for a thin spiderweb of dark designs. It wasn't far to the alcove and the door that hid the attic stairs. But tonight the walk felt endless, the parade of closed doors on either side of the hall seeming to stretch forever.

When I reached the attic door, I put the flashlight between my teeth. With its beam trained on the keyhole, I pulled out my lock-picking tools. Almost instantly, I realized my effort was unnecessary. The door was ajar.

A sudden chill brushed the back of my neck, making every hair on my head stand on end. Whipping the flashlight out of my mouth, I wheeled around. I'd felt this same way every time I'd stood in this spot. But supposedly Moonhill wasn't haunted and—

I let the flashlight's beam wash across the floor, looking for catlike shapes. One time when I'd felt the chill and seen a tapestry move, Houdini had proven to be at fault.

Not finding him, I moved the beam upward to the tapestry. It lay motionless, its image of a shepherd herding his flock toward a blood-red sunrise grayed by dim light.

My pulse slowed, thumping as loud and steady as a kettle drum. Though the tapestry in no way resembled the bold patterned magic carpets in the djinn realm, my thoughts of them were too recent for my mind to not try and draw a connection.

Something whisked my ankle. I jumped and whirled around, my heartbeat soaring. Until I spotted Houdini fleeing into the darkness.

"Quit that," I called after him.

He yowled and trotted back. Kate was right, he was a total brat.

His tail curled around my legs as I opened the attic door. I glanced upward. The stairwell was pitch-black. Not even a single thread of light filtered down from the attic. Clearly no one was up there.

I followed Houdini to the attic and started up the narrow staircase to the walk. Brightness seeped in through its windows, fading before it reached more than a yard into the darkness. When I got to the top, I stepped out on the widow's walk deck and froze. I wasn't alone.

On the far end of the deck the eerie glow of a camping lantern brightened the outlines of Grandpa, Zachary, and Tibbs. Their backs were to me and they were fixated on something in the air beyond the railing.

Grandpa swiveled partway to the left and I spotted a wireless control in his hands, an ultramodern contrast to his dapper tweed jacket and bow tie.

Tibbs craned farther outward over the railing. "I thought it was going to hit the roof for sure that time. You said it can disable a car engine at what—a quarter mile?"

"Easily. They'll be armed with darts tipped with frog venom. That should knock out any intruder for a good hour or two." Grandfather chuckled. "I don't think Selena will be fond of that."

They all pivoted, watching as what looked like a supersize bat whizzed up from below, swooped over my head, and back down toward the garden.

"Annie!" Zachary said. "Did you see Grandpa's drone? It's so cool."

I walked over to them and smiled at Grandfather. "I thought you hated being watched?"

"Different times call for different measures. Right, Tibbs?"

Tibbs nodded. "It'll make my job easier." His gaze met Grandfather's. "You're thinking a couple dozen with different flight routes?"

"I'm going to leave that up to you." Grandpa handed him the control. "For now, why don't you and Zach test this one a bit more thoroughly? I want to spend a moment with my granddaughter." His smile transformed into a serious expression.

I hugged myself. Why did he want to talk to me alone? This abrupt increase in electronic security made me think Chase was on his mind. With his enhanced half-genie senses and stealth mode, Chase was the linchpin of Moonhill's security. Without him, these new electronic measures would be mandatory. Did Grandfather think I didn't realize how likely it was that Chase wouldn't make it back from the realm unscathed?

Grandfather rested his hand on the back of my shoulder and walked me around to the other side of the deck. He strolled along like there was nothing special on his mind. But the tautness of his sinewy arm echoed my worries and the quiver in my stomach told me I should have stayed in bed.

When we got to the farthest railing, he pulled me closer and said, "Earlier this evening, Kate and David argued against you going to the realm. I sided with your father and in the end we won. After all, besides Lotli, you're the one who's been inside the fortress most recently. You know where the harem is and what your mother looks like."

"Thank you," I said, but I wasn't as overjoyed as I might have been. There was an almost too-gentle pitch to his voice that warned there was more to come. I gritted my teeth, preparing myself.

Grandfather stepped away from our embrace and took me lightly by the shoulders, his eyes looking directly into mine. "You also are the only one of us who your father will listen to. And I'm worried about him."

I looked at him in surprise. This was definitely not the way I envisioned the conversation going. My throat squeezed and I couldn't think of a thing to say.

"I'm going to channel your aunt Kate for a moment and be blunt. I'm not concerned about your father going. But I am worried about what might happen once you get there."

My mind raced. "What are you talking about?"

"Your father, Annie . . . I know he loves your mother. But ever since he was a little boy, he's had a hard time with forgiveness."

He was right there. Except—"He's not that way anymore. What happened while he was possessed by Culus, then spending time with you and David in the mountains—he's changed."

"Maybe his attitude toward the family has. But watch him. I'm not sure how deep his hatred for Malphic goes. The urge for revenge can make a person do foolish things, take unnecessary risks."

I ran my hand down my neck, my trembling fingers closing around the signet ring that hung at my throat. The ring Grandfather had given me, the ring that by all rights should have been Dad's if the tangle of lies and hatred hadn't driven a wedge between him and the family for so many years. And I thought about other people Dad had held grudges against, about his patient but inevitable retaliation. Grandfather was right.

In the distance, the stars glistened. Zachary said something I couldn't quite hear. The ocean beat a slow rhythm I could feel as much as hear. I lifted my gaze to Grandfather's. "Don't worry. I'll keep an eye on him."

Grandfather kissed my forehead, a warm touch. "Good. I don't want to lose any of you."

CHAPTER 13

Everything changes, even stars and sea glass.

—Anonymous

The next morning, I smelled the mouthwatering aroma of the Belgian waffles and hot maple syrup even before I walked into the dining room, but my stomach squeezed and my appetite plummeted when I heard raised voices coming from inside.

"Even if the girl is feeling fine, you can't go this soon," Kate said resolutely. "There are details to work out."

"We'll lose the element of the surprise if we wait," Dad replied.

I stepped over the threshold and into the room.

Everyone was already there: Grandfather at the head of the table, Kate on his right with Uncle David on his left. Dad sat at the other end in what I imagined had once been Grandmother's place. Lotli and Selena sat next to Dad. Olya, Zachary, and the Professor occupied the various middle seats.

Kate raised an eyebrow at Dad. "And where do you plan on crossing the veil? If you think Malphic hasn't fortified the wards on his side of the gallery gateway, then you're crazier than I thought." Her gaze shifted to Lotli. "Even if your flute-magic can break the new wards, he'll have posted guards."

Dad shook out his linen napkin with a sharp snap. "That, my dear sister, would be why we won't be using that gateway."

Zachary bounced in his seat, arm waving. "I know. I know. The Pirate's Coffin. That's where Annie ended up when she was thrown from the realm! There were loads of shipwrecks there, too, lots of people died—even great-great-great-grandma Stephanie."

The Professor set his coffee cup down. "Brilliant idea. It has to be a major weak point in the veil."

"Exactly," Dad said.

I smiled good morning to them all and wandered toward the buffet to fix my breakfast. I figured it was only a matter of time before Dad realized the huge flaw in his plan. I flopped a couple waffles onto my plate and drizzled syrup over them. I poured a coffee. When I started toward an empty chair next to Dad, he was still talking about the Coffin. As much as I didn't want to contradict him, I couldn't stay silent any longer.

"In theory that may sound great," I said, settling into the chair. "But I fell out of the sky and into the Coffin. The weak point is somewhere in midair—above the Coffin."

Zachary bounced again. "You could parasail into it!"

Olya clamped her fingers on his arm, holding him down. "That is enough, Zach. Let the adults talk."

"It's a good idea," he grumbled.

"Grandpa?" Selena's voice was more subdued than usual. "Wouldn't there be a weak point where Grandma died?"

He paused for a moment, smiling wistfully. "Her passing certainly left a hole in all our lives and hearts. But I imagine the one in the veil is long healed."

Lotli nodded. "That is true. Unless the death was tragic, then the weak point remains. But crossing at a point like that comes with the risk of ending up in the wrong place, like heaven or hell instead of the djinn realm."

She went on about how the only thing more difficult, time-consuming, and potentially impossible would be to attempt to rip a gateway in an undamaged place in the veil. As I listened to her, a thought nipped at the back of my mind. My mother and I had been playing hide-and-seek in the gallery when Malphic came through the veil and kidnapped her. She'd been trying to end their affair at that time, so it didn't make sense for her to be playing with me in a place where she knew her ex-lover could appear. That meant he must have used a different weak point when he'd visited her previously. Not Pirate's Coffin, it had to be inside Moonhill, where he wouldn't have to get through locked doors or closed windows.

A chill sank into my bones. Holy crap. I should have listened to my gut—and Houdini.

"Lotli?" I said, so hushed that everyone turned to look at me. "Cold spots indicate a tear in the veil, right?"

"Yes, many people believe it is an indication of a spirit. But you are correct. It is the icy gasp of the wounded veil, not a ghost or a sign of what lies beyond it. Why do you ask us this?"

"There is a cold spot at the bottom of the attic stairs. At least, I'm fairly certain of it. It's right near where a tapestry hangs on the wall. Whenever Houdini gets near that place, he yowls and acts up. I think he's been trying to warn me." The bitter taste of nausea crawled up my throat. This was making more terrifying sense by the second. "I think Malphic might have replaced the original tapestry with one of his magic carpets to create a gateway, so he could insinuate himself into my mother's life."

Everyone started talking at once. "I should have sensed it," Olya said.

"That's all right, dear," David consoled her. "It's not like you were the only one. We all missed it."

My mind whirled, connecting more pieces. The cold spot. The tapestry. Malphic. My mother. My gut screamed that the tapestry was what Grandmother had discovered, the final straw that had made her come to me and ask if I'd seen someone visiting Mother at night. If only I hadn't lied to her.

Something bumped my sneaker. Dad's shoe. I glanced at him. "It wasn't your fault," he said below everyone else's chatter.

I nodded, not that surprised that he'd known what I'd been thinking about the lie and Grandmother's death. I took in his kind face and tired eyes, and an overwhelming urge to protect him took root in my heart. Then Grandfather's words from our talk last night on the widow's walk, about Dad's vengeful streak, flitted into my mind. I nudged Dad's shoe and met his eyes, trying to telegraph my message. *We all need to forget and move on.*

"Lotli"—Grandfather's booming voice silenced everyone— "since you're the expert here, what do you suggest we do?"

She sat back in her chair, surveying us all. "We could play our flute just long enough to crack open the veil and sense what lies beyond this cold spot, then let it close. That would tell us if Annie is right."

"Perfect," Grandfather announced with finality. "Once everyone's done eating, we'll take a look at the disguises Kate has picked for the mission; then we'll check out this cold spot. If it isn't what we think, we'll have to find a way to make the Pirate's Coffin work." He picked up his coffee cup, cradling it between both hands. "For the life of me, I can't imagine how we'd hoist the three of you up and through some undeterminable spot in midair."

Three? That wasn't right. Four of us were going. Me, Dad, Lotli—and Selena.

I glanced across the table at her. Since our trip to the hair salon, she'd made it clear nothing was going to hold her back. Dad had bragged last night about what a good job she did at the yacht club. Lotli had said the same thing. In front of everyone.

Avoiding my eyes, Selena set her fork on her untouched

plate of waffles and pushed her chair back from the table. "If everyone will excuse me, I've got stuff to do."

"Wait," I said, jumping to my feet. This wasn't fair. "Selena's going. She proved yesterday that she's—"

Selena cut me off. "Annie, stop it."

"I'm not going to. You deserve to go."

"I don't want to," she said, raising her chin in a stubborn gesture that reminded me very much of Kate—and me. Totally a Freemont move. But it was total bullshit.

I toughened my voice. "Selena, come on. You know that's not how you feel."

David leaned back in his chair, a particularly smug look settling over his face.

Asshole. What had he said to Selena to make her change her mind?

Selena shot a glare at him and I was stunned to see the smug look drop from his face. What was going on?

Selena rose to her feet. Her gaze met mine. Her voice became soft. "I appreciate you standing up for me. Really, I do. But I didn't change my mind because someone told me I couldn't go. I'm not going because I'm needed here."

I blinked at her, totally lost for words.

"We have no way of knowing when the Sons will retaliate—today, a year from now—but we know they will. I want to make sure we're ready." She took a deep breath, her eyes pleading with me to understand. "I'm responsible for Newt discovering Lotli—for starting this whole Sons of Ophiuchus mess."

"Selena, you're not the only one who's—"

She held up her hand to silence me. "The other truth is—you three will have less to worry about without me. Here, there's a lot I can do. I can ensure that you have a safe place to come back to."

She was right about both things.

Abruptly, the familiar rebelliousness flashed into her eyes. "But," she said, "before I do anything else, I'm going to brew up a few surprises for you to use in the realm. Maybe some special ointments—or a spray."

"Selena," her mother said warningly.

I smiled at Selena and she gave me a sly wink.

Maybe some things about her had changed, but not every-thing.

CHAPTER 14

We snared the griffon by shadow-glow,
under a waning moon and shooting stars.
We drilled his wing bone with a copper
awl, and blessed it in a wormwood fire.

—As told to Lotli by her mother's grandmother

Not long after breakfast, I walked back to my room with the coarse brown robe and drab woman-warrior tunic that Kate had picked out for me to wear to the realm. It was strange how heavy a bundle of clothes could feel. A mix of apprehension and excitement jittered inside me. In less than ten hours, I'd be wearing the cloak, its hood pulled in close around my face. The oil would be poured over me; then I'd step out of this world and feel the stones of Malphic's fortress beneath my boots. Soon, I'd see Chase. Know for certain if he'd resisted the change or lost the battle. Know if he was still alive. But meanwhile, there was something I had to do.

I set the bundle on my bed, snagged my flashlight, and went back out into the hallway. I didn't turn toward the alcove where Dad, Kate, Grandfather, and Lotli were meeting to test the cold spot. Instead, I sprinted in the opposite direction, toward the kitchen elevator.

I lengthened my strides, hurrying down the hallway. The whole idea that Dad's desire for revenge might make him do something reckless was beyond worrisome. So I'd come up with a countermeasure, something I could trade for Dad if he got himself in trouble. There was a poison ring down in one of Moonhill's secret treasuries. It was the ring that the genie Culus had used to weasel his way into Dad's life. It was also the ring Grandfather had eventually trapped him in. Culus was Malphic's son and a full-blooded genie.

Granted, Chase and Grandfather claimed that Malphic would have no interest in a son who had been defeated by humans and imprisoned. Malphic valued victors above all others. But the things Chase's mom had told me about Malphic made me wonder if Grandfather and Chase were wrong. If Malphic loved Chase before he was born and as a child, before he proved himself as a warrior and man, then perhaps Malphic harbored similar feelings toward Culus.

I turned down a dead-end hallway, loped to the elevator, and pushed the down button. As a rule, I didn't like elevators. But it was the fastest way to get downstairs without running into anyone. Once I reached the kitchen, all I had to do was get to Kate's office. I knew which treasury the ring was in and I could find my way to it, as long as I used her office as my starting point.

The elevator dinged, its doors whooshing open.

Lotli stood there illuminated by the elevator's bright stainless-steel and mirrored interior, her dark hair pulled back in a fishtail braid, a muslin top and loose wrap pants, arms banded with copper cuffs, her neck weighted down with a collection of necklaces, feathers, and symbols, her talisman pouch. I wasn't sure who she'd borrowed all the jewelry from, but she looked more than ready to tackle opening the veil.

I swallowed hard. "I'm surprised to see you here. I thought you were in the alcove with everyone else."

"We are on our way there. You are not going?" She craned

her neck and tilted it to one side, an odd gesture that reminded me of an egret readying to spear a fish.

I tucked my hands in my pockets so she couldn't see I was nervous, and faked a smile. "I'm going down to the kitchen to fix some baggies of salt for us to take to the realm." It was the same excuse I'd given Dad for not wanting to see what happened with the cold spot.

Lotli's eyes darkened with doubt. "Really?"

"It saved our ass last time." That was the truth. Salt was one of the best defenses against genies.

The elevator pinged and the door began to slide shut.

I pressed my hand against its edge, holding it open so Lotli could get out. "I hope I'm right about the cold spot," I said, waiting for her to leave.

She wet her lips with her tongue, a slow and deliberate motion that made the hairs on the back of my neck prickle. Then in a flash, she seized my wrist and yanked me into the elevator.

The door whooshed shut.

I flew toward the elevator buttons. Lotli blocked my way, a smirk slipping across her face. I squared my shoulders and lifted my chin. This was my family's home. Not hers. How dare she try to intimidate me.

She brushed a finger across the flute tucked into her waistline. Her flute. Her weapon. As powerful as any sorcerer's staff or genie's muscle and magic. More deadly than Chase's knives.

"We have been wanting to talk to you," she said. The chill in her voice sent goose bumps across my skin. And my gaze detected something I'd never noticed before. As always, her complexion was richly tanned, a tone that gave the impression that she possessed Native American blood. But beneath that tan pulsed blue veins as visible as if her skin were as thin and pale as the shell on a hummingbird's egg. My mind flashed back to the hummingbird egg pendant she'd given me and the grenade-like energy that had exploded out from it when I'd gotten angry in the realm and smashed it against the ground. That's what this was like, pent-up power throbbing just below the surface of her skin.

I backed away from her, my heart pounding a million miles per hour.

She slid her flute from her waistband, stroking it slowly as she slithered toward me. "We'll keep this simple. You have something we want."

I took another step backward, my spine now against the elevator wall. "What are you talking about?"

"Chase."

Anger flashed through me. "Well, I'm sorry about that. But he's a man, not something I can give or take away from you."

Her head lulled back. "You did not ask us if we were willing to go to the realm this time. We did not offer to go either."

"You never said you wouldn't. We assumed."

"We could leave. We could vanish anytime we desire. What would you do then? What would become of your mother?" She toyed with the blue and green streamers of Chase's yarn that hung from her flute, letting the beads and charms that were attached to them trail between her fingers. "Would your father go after her without me and become trapped? What about your lover? Would he die in the Red Desert, berserk and alone?"

"You wouldn't dare," I snarled.

"We won't. If . . ." She raised the flute to her mouth and caressed its tip with her tongue. She lowered it, saliva now shining on her lips. "We will go with you to the realm. We will help you—if you forsake Chase."

If it hadn't been for the flute, I'd have grabbed her, wrapped my fingers around her neck, and squeezed until the last breath left her lungs. I planted my feet firmly and narrowed my eyes.

"You know I would never abandon him. Why the hell would you want to leave him there?"

"We both know that is not what we mean. We want you to withdraw your love. We will go with you, help your mother and lover escape. In exchange, we want a free path to his heart. All that is required is your promise and three hairs from your head to seal the agreement."

I gaped at her, fury boiling inside me. Who the hell did she think she was? "No, I'd never do that to him."

"He claims to love you. If he truly does, then he will not trade you for us. Are you scared to take that chance?"

Of course not, I wanted to scream. I knew he loved me. She did, too. She'd been there the last time I'd spoken with Chase, that moment of anger and passion in the dark corridor of Malphic's fortress when he'd declared his love for me in front of her.

She rolled her shoulders. "Maybe you need more enticement. If you refuse, we will open a hellmouth in the middle of Moonhill and let the demons out to feast on your family. We are certain the Devil would not complain."

Inside, terror gripped me. But she wasn't going to trick me with empty threats. I lightened my voice and scoffed. "You're full of shit."

"You do not think we have that sort of power? You think helping people cross into death or the djinn realm is all we are capable of?"

Before I could answer, she put her flute to her lips and blew.

A screech filled the elevator, the sound jackknifing higher by the second. The metal walls shuddered. Mirrors shook. I clamped my hands over my ears as the sound morphed into the yowl of wounded animals, cycloning toward glass-shattering levels.

My eyes widened as cracks branched across the mirrors. Oh my God. I couldn't risk her destroying them. They were entries to Moonhill's secret hallways and treasuries. I couldn't let her see that. But I couldn't forsake Chase either.

Beneath my feet, the floor quaked and bowed. With an echoing boom, it thrust upward in the middle, sending me flying into a wall. Pain shot through my body. I grabbed the safety railing, clinging to it for dear life, as the elevator shimmied and shuddered. Suddenly the floor sucked downward, a black hole opened at its center, and widened by the second. Blistering-hot steam and sulfur fumes hissed out from it. Holy shit. A hellmouth.

Through the haze, I glimpsed Lotli, standing firm on the other side of the hole, her flute raised upward. Her gaze caught mine. She gave another quick trill, then stopped playing.

The elevator stilled. The hole closed, the floor shifting silently back to normal. The cracks vanished from the mirrors.

Utterly drained, I stood there in the swirling fumes, paralyzed and soaked with sweat.

Lotli sheathed her flute in the folds of her waistband and smiled at me. "We will give you time to decide." Her eyes narrowed. "Say one word about this or our offer and we will vanish—after we make the hellmouth permanent. You will seal your family's extinction and hurry your mother's death. And Chase, we can see him, dressed in blood and sweat, Malphic's living weapon—or dead, his body thrown out into the desert to rot."

She pressed an elevator button. The door swished open and she was gone, taking the last of the steam and stench with her.

CHAPTER 15

Jingle, jingle, jingle. What is the cost?
A hair from my lady's head. And
a promise from her heart.

—Disturbing Nursery Rhymes
www.DarkCradleTime.com

In a daze of bewilderment and rising panic, I rode the elevator down to the kitchen. I had to tell Dad and Grandpa and Kate what had happened. There was no other choice. But I couldn't do it in front of Lotli, and they were together in the widow's walk hallway testing the cold spot right now.

The elevator door whooshed open and I stumbled out into the sunny kitchen. The aroma of homemade bread and roasting chicken filled my nose. It felt absurdly normal in the light of what I'd just experienced.

"Annie?" Laura's voice said. "Are you all right?" She stood on the other side of the kitchen's work counter, her barnboard weathered face reflected a dozen times in the copper pots hanging from the overhead rack. She wiped her hands on her apron and started toward me without mentioning anything about ear-shattering sounds or an earthquake coming from the elevator shaft. Clearly, Lotli had somehow managed to keep everything contained.

I held up my hands to keep her at a distance. "I'm fine. I just—I hate elevators." She was *like* family, but she wasn't family. Definitely not the first person I should discuss things with. "Mostly I'm just crazy busy," I added, sidestepping toward the hallway door.

"I imagine so. Can I help with anything?"

My brain staggered, my thoughts jumbling until I couldn't think of a thing to say. I shook myself free. What was I doing? Sure, I was terrified. Sure, I was confused. Anyone would be. But, damn it, I needed to pull myself together. *Focus. First things first.* That's what Chase would tell me to do.

I pushed my shoulders back and took a steadying breath. No matter what ended up happening with Lotli, I still needed to get the poison ring and this still was the best time to do that. "Actually, you can help me," I said to Laura. "Would you mind putting some salt into baggies for me? About a half cup in each bag. A dozen should be enough."

She smiled. "No problem. I can do that in two shakes of a lamb's tail."

"Thank you. I'll be back to get them."

I fled the kitchen before she could ask where I was going. But my worries and fears dogged me. Why had we ever let Lotli into our lives?

A sinking feeling settled into my stomach. *Mother. Chase.*

I hurried through the front foyer and past the dining room. When I reached the library, my ear caught the muffled sound of the Professor and Zachary discussing something. But they didn't hear me. And in no time at all, I was down the west wing hallway and in Kate's office.

As I'd hoped, no one was there, except for an assortment of cats. A pair of Siamese and a couple of others swished their tails and followed me into the office bathroom.

Across from the toilet a full-length mirror took up most of the wall. For a moment, my mind went back to the mirrors in the elevator. The shaking and crackling sounds. It was just freaking luck that they hadn't revealed their secrets to Lotli. That would have made things even worse, if that was possible.

I breathed on the mirror, fogging up the glass, then gathered my nerve and stepped forward. Grandpa had entered my DNA into the Moonhill's security system, so technically there wasn't any reason for it not to work.

Walking through the mirror was like walking through a wall of super-cooled, burbling Jell-O. Next thing I knew, I was on the other side, and standing in what resembled a torchlit hallway in a medieval castle, except a massive Easter Island–type statue glared at me from the far wall and the torches were glowing crystals.

Something short and furry ghosted past my ankle. But this time I didn't jump.

"Good kitty," I said as Houdini made another circle around my legs. In truth, I was glad for the company, though I couldn't begin to imagine how he'd gotten through the DNA scan.

I glanced down the hallway. So far everything appeared the same as the last time.

In passing, Grandpa had joked about how he'd enshrined the poison ring in the display case that used to hold the Lamp of Methuselah. There was a certain ironic justice to that, since Culus originally stowed himself in the ring in order to gain access to Moonhill and steal the lamp. It was also lucky for me, since I'd seen the case where the lamp was stored.

I started down the hallway, keeping an eye on the bees carved into the walls. They marked the way to the treasury I wanted. When I came to where an enormous Aztec calendar stone interrupted the bees for a few yards, I stopped long enough to brush my fingers across the ferocious face chiseled into its center. My dad was responsible for the stone being here, but deep inside I couldn't help wondering if it really belonged back in its homeland. It was a national treasure and—

"What the hell is that?" I said to Houdini, bending closer to the stone.

I rubbed my eyes and took another look. Above the face was the likeness of a pyramid, its peak decorated with an irregular hexagon of dots.

My mouth dropped open. Oh my God. Not just any hexagon. It was the constellation Ophiuchus, just like the painting at the yacht club, like Newt's tattoo. I'd never even heard of the constellation before and now it was everywhere. That wasn't exactly comforting.

I studied the face again. Something about it bothered me, too, maybe its feathered headdress or eyes. Or maybe it was the hands chiseled into the stone on either side of it, hands that clutched bloody hearts.

I forced myself to look away from the calendar stone. I was letting myself get distracted. I'd come here to get the ring and that's what I needed to do.

With renewed resolve, I began jogging down the shadowy hallway. I approached the spot where Chase had taken my hand and first told me that he was half genie. My dream was to have him back home, sane, and in my arms again. But the truth was, even if he wasn't sane or mine, I couldn't leave him in the realm—any more than Dad or I could forget Mother. And the only safe way to rescue them was with Lotli and her flute-magic. If I said a word, that wouldn't happen. In fact, even worse things would happen than I'd previously feared.

My mind flailed. What had seemed so obvious was now impossible to decide. I slowed and picked up Houdini. Holding him against my chest, I veered down a narrow passage. Rolled-up carpets and packing crates littered the floor. Hundreds of skulls with symbols painted on them leered out from niches in the walls. Their vacant eyes watched as I passed. Their dark mouths seemed to chant a single question: "*What do you have to fear? What do you have to fear, if he loves you?*"

Houdini dug his claws into my shirt and stared up at my face as if he agreed.

Sweat dampened my sides. I had nothing to fear. All Lotli wanted was for me to give her a chance to win his heart. The second all of us were back safely in our world, I'd tell the truth. Chase loved me. It would be okay. Going along with her would put an end to the threat of her unleashing demons and the denizens of hell on my family.

I picked up my pace, striding away from the skulls. Ahead loomed the archway carved with warding symbols that marked the entry to the treasury. I set Houdini down and strode under it and into the small, circular room with a high-arched ceiling. On the far side of the room another entryway gaped. Twin mirrors hung on either side of it. Brightly lit display cases with black stone bases sat everywhere. One case contained a beagle-size scorpion with glistening eyes. Another held a glowing orange crystal. Everything looked exactly as I remembered, except the globe-like case in the center of the room now held a poison ring instead of the terra-cotta Lamp of Methuselah.

I jogged to the case, took off the necklace that held my signet ring, and pressed the ring's carved stone against a dime-size indentation on the case's base. The glass case unfurled, like a time-lapsed video of an opening tulip. I snatched the poison ring and tucked it into my bra. It would be safe and secure there. I'd never even have to take it out when I changed to go to the realm. When I returned, I'd simply sneak the poison ring back into the case—that was, if luck was with us and I didn't need it.

I wiped my hands down my pants legs and took a breath. Then I headed for the twin mirrors. I didn't dare go back the way I came. Kate might be in her office by now. But I didn't know where either of these mirrors would take me.

Houdini dashed to the left-hand mirror and began rubbing

his face against it. All right, I hadn't caught on to a lot of things he'd tried to point out before. But I'd learned my lesson.

Still, worry fluttered in my stomach. How could he know what was beyond it? Plus, it could be just something he wanted, like a pit full of rats or cockroaches.

Cringing at that possibility, I picked him up and fogged the mirror. "I hope like hell you aren't screwing with me," I said, stepping into the glass.

I came out into the secret hallway across from Moonhill's armory where all the antique weapons and costumes were stored. Perfect.

Houdini struggled against my grip, but I held him tight and made for an obsidian-framed mirror only a short distance away. I'd been through it several times before.

As I expected, that mirror took me into Moonhill's ultra-modern and closet-like arsenal. Above my head, giant ghillie suits and netting hung, illuminated by blindly bright security lights. Racks of guns and boxes of ammunition covered every wall, binoculars, game cameras, bullet-proof vests. Camouflage rifles with huge scopes, weird, lethal-looking thingamabobs.

I set Houdini on the floor and beelined for the secret door on the far end. On the other side of it was Tibbs's windowless office in the garage. Perfect once more, since Tibbs was no doubt off setting up new security measures along Moonhill's borders or up on the widow's walk working on the drones' flight patterns.

I pushed my hand against the door. Without a sound, it swung open. Houdini streaked out, his tail brushing my legs as he zinged past. I followed him and stopped midstride.

Selena was lounging on the corner of Tibbs's desk. Lounging wasn't exactly the right word. She was dressed in cargo pants and a black cami top, and I suspected she'd just stretched out when she spotted me in an attempt to hide something behind her back. Tibbs sat in the desk chair. Even with his cap pulled down over his eyes, he couldn't hide the flush creeping up across his face and tipping his ears.

Selena grinned at me, looking more than a little sheepish. "Should we ask what you were doing?"

"Should I ask you?" I said teasingly.

She giggled, her grin transforming into a wicked smile as she sat up, revealing an array of vials, granules, and one of Grandfather's drones. "Tibbs and I are working on some extra-special security ideas."

There were other things on the desk as well: a couple of modern handguns, grenades, and a gorgeous antique pistol with an etched handle and multiple brass barrels. Truthfully, I suspected whatever they were doing was something Grandfather would be delighted with, not upset. But Selena helping with the drones was another story. The drones would put an end to her sneaking off the estate at night. Even with Newt out of the picture, it didn't seem like she'd totally give up partying.

I caught Tibbs's gaze and his flush deepened. Okay. There was something else going on here. Something he was particularly uncomfortable about. I bit my tongue to keep from smirking. Tibbs's interest in Selena wasn't exactly a secret. Had I walked in on him making his move on her? I totally approved. Still, weren't they a little busy for that right now?

"I thought you were making some stuff for us to take to the realm—ointments, sprays?" I said.

"I was, and we did. You'll see later." Selena frowned. "But, seriously, is there something you need our help with?"

A knot tightened in my chest. *Lotli.* I could tell them. They could keep a secret. Heck, Chase was Tibbs's best friend. *Chase.* But it made so much more sense to trust that he loved me. Keep this simple. Between just Lotli and me. If I was going to tell anyone, it should be Dad. He was the one going to the realm with me.

I stilled my body—hands, legs, face—forcing myself to keep

outwardly calm, like I was at an auction about to bid and didn't want anyone to know. "Thanks," I said, "but I already dealt with it. I was down in the armory, returning part of the disguise Kate picked out for me." I grimaced and continued my lie. "It was this huge leather corset thing."

Selena laughed. "Kate probably meant to keep it for herself."

"Yeah, probably," I said.

"You're going as a warrior?" Tibbs asked, clearly surprised.

"No. Well, kind of. Kate thought all of us should wear hooded eunuch robes with warrior outfits underneath. Two disguises in one." That wasn't a lie, except the basic women-warrior tunics for Lotli and me were anything but showy.

"Sounds smart." He picked up the antique pistol, turning it over in his hand. His gaze met mine. "This one's black powder. One of a set of two dueling pistols. It can take almost any kind of shot, lead, pieces of glass, pebbles—even something like cherry pits."

His less than subtle suggestion set off a dangerous giddiness inside me and made my fingers itch to take the gun. According to myths—and Chase—the only way to kill a full-blooded genie was to hit them super hard with a fruit pit. I tucked my hands in my pockets and repeated the warning Chase had given me when I'd made a similar suggestion. "Unfortunately, human inventions don't work in the realm. When they do, they're unpredictable, more dangerous than useful."

Tibbs nudged the gun farther away as if trying to distance himself from the idea. "Sorry. I didn't know that."

"Don't worry about it," I said.

He glanced at Selena. She looked back at him, her expression unreadable. For a long moment an awkward silence filled the office.

Finally, I cleared my throat. "I should let you guys get back to work."

"You can stay. We weren't doing anything special, really," Selena said.

I waved her off. "Thanks, but I've got to find Dad."

Wondering what the two of them had really been up to, I hurried out of the office and through the garage. But I didn't head for the house to find Dad. I took the path that went to the family graveyard instead.

Houdini zinged ahead, vanishing into thickets and bounding out again. Under my sneakers, the damp ground squelched. Still, it didn't take long to hike up to the fancy iron gate that barred the graveyard's entry.

Beyond the gate, black sheep grazed amongst the gravestones and hydrangea trees rustled in the breeze.

The gate creaked as I opened it and latched it behind me. As I walked toward the closest obelisk, the sheep raised their heads, watching closely. When I'd first come to Moonhill, my connection to my family and ancestors had begun to sink in here.

I walked deeper into the lines of crowded graves, moving toward the mausoleum at the top of the hill. So many of my ancestors had been brave, done amazing things. What advice would they give me about Lotli if they could speak?

I stepped off the worn path, went down a line of newer gravestones, stopping in front of a glistening white one. Etched into it were seagulls circling between swirling clouds at the top and the likeness of a family of seals on the bottom. In the middle were mine and my father's names and birthdates, and a space where the date of our deaths would be added when the time came. My mother's name was there as well.

Closing my eyes, I prayed that I'd hear my ancestors' answer in the breeze or rustle of the trees. If I listened hard enough. If I—

A growl came from deep in Houdini's throat.

"That is a rather unpleasant greeting," Lotli's voice said.

My eyes flashed open. I wheeled to face her. She was strolling past Houdini and down the line of newer gravestones toward me, hips swaying.

I frowned. "I thought you were testing the cold spot?"

"We have done that already. You were wrong about the tapestry. It is normal." She pressed her lips into a self-satisfied smile, holding back the rest for a long moment. "The weak point is in front of it. It does open into the djinn realm and is securely warded on their side."

I countered her smugness with sarcasm. "Wards that I'm willing to bet you could easily break—*if* you chose to."

She dipped her head. "Yes, *if* you choose to forsake—"

"I'm quite familiar with your so-called offer. But you didn't give me much time to think."

"Sunset is not far away. We have things to do if we are going to the realm. If not . . ." She licked her lips. "We are not sure if an elevator is the best place for a hellmouth. Perhaps your father's room would be better."

Every muscle in my body tightened, readying to lunge at her. But something had just occurred to me and it helped me to hold back. There was one obvious detail she had neglected to mention, something that might just get me out of this. "Are you forgetting that my family has a contract with Zea? As I recall, it states that you'll work for us until the next full moon. We could easily find him and tell him what you've been up to."

She blinked and a tendon in her neck flinched. Then a nasty smile tweaked the corner of her mouth. Her hand slithered to her waistband and she drew her flute. She stroked her fingers down its length. "Yes, ten thousand dollars and we are yours for one lunar cycle. Are you not ashamed of using me like that? Chase was. He thought it sounded like slavery." She stopped stroking and smiled. "Yes, Chase, he is the matter at hand."

I grasped at another straw. "This whole thing doesn't make sense. Why would you want a guy who doesn't love you?"

"Hmmm. Let us see—" She lifted a finger, bringing it down on the flute as she ticked off her list. "Pure muscle. Pure heart. Schooled by the djinn in the art of lovemaking."

"Shut up," I screeched. My hands shook from fury. White-hot anger roared into my veins. But my eyes homed in on her flute. I couldn't be stupid. I had to keep my head.

"It's your choice. All the promise required is a word from your lips and a few hairs from your head," she cooed. "Forsake Chase. Or risk your entire family." Her gaze sliced toward Houdini. "We are willing to bet the demons would like the taste of him. Maybe we should split him open and drop him in a hellmouth right now."

"Leave him out of this," I snarled.

Her eyes knifed back to me. "That depends on your answer. What will it be?"

CHAPTER 16

*One carving on the temple unmistakably pointed
to the race of nomads we'd previously uncovered
traces of in Greece, the mountains of Slovenia,
and Mongolia. It was fascinating to discover them
here, in Mesoamerica alongside Huitzilopochtli.*

—Jeffrey White
Sons of Ophiuchus: Annual Address

I found Dad and Grandfather in the billiards room, talking
and having a midafternoon brandy. They paused to greet me
as I walked across the room to them.

"What are you guys up to?" I attempted to sound casual.
But between what had happened in the elevator and my en-
counter with Lotli in the graveyard, I was pretty shaken. However, I wasn't defeated. I'd learned to come out on top at
auctions by doing the unexpected, and that was exactly what I
intended to do now, no matter how difficult telling the truth
was going to be.

Dad's eyebrows lowered as if he sensed the turmoil inside
me. He polished off the last of his brandy and got to his feet.
"Don't get comfortable, Annie. I wanted to go over that map of
the fortress again, in detail." He swiveled toward Grandfather.
"You don't mind if we desert you?"

"Not at all. I was contemplating taking a short siesta. It's going to be a long night, especially for you two."

"Sounds like a good idea. I might just have to grab forty winks myself." Dad took me by the elbow, snugged me close, and paraded out of the room. It wasn't until we got to the top of the main staircase that he drew me into a shadowy alcove and let go of my arm.

"What's going on?" he said in a gentle whisper.

I sucked in a deep breath, gathering my courage. "It's Lotli. I don't trust her."

"I don't either," he said without hesitating. "I don't think anyone in this house does. She's powerful, manipulative."

"You can say that again."

He folded his arms across his chest and raised an eyebrow. "Is there something else?"

That's when I noticed a hand-size bulge at Dad's beltline. It was the right size to be a gun, but it was covered by his shirt, so I couldn't be positive. Even if it was, it wasn't his usual gun or it would have been in the shoulder holster he was wearing. My mind flashed back to a little while ago in the garage, to Tibbs flushing like he was uncomfortable about something and later offering me the black powder gun, the one leftover from a set of two dueling pistols.

I let my eyes linger on the shape for an overtly long moment and then met Dad's gaze, waiting for him to confess.

He looked past me and went back to talking about Lotli. "We're only assuming it's her ability to help people cross into death that interested the Sons of Ophiuchus."

Anger heated my face. "That's a black powder pistol, isn't it? I hope you're not planning on taking it to the realm."

One of his hands moved, his fingers scratching his elbow three times. That was Dad's one and only tell. He was preparing to lie. But why not tell me?

Revenge, Grandfather's fear whispered in my ear.

"Did you get it from Tibbs?"

Dad laughed. "Nothing gets past you, does it?" He patted my arm. "Don't worry, Tibbs just texted me about the unreliability issue. I was planning on giving it back to him when I got the chance."

"Good." I glanced down at the floor, the crimson carpet burnished black by shadows. As much as I wanted to, I couldn't put off telling him what had happened any longer. I needed his advice. "Ah—speaking of Lotli . . ."

My voice trailed off as his hand started for his elbow again, but quickly retreated to his pants pocket. Damn it. He was either lying about giving the gun back or preparing to lie again about . . . Holy freak shows.

"Lotli didn't say or do—she didn't threaten you, did she?" I said.

His hand came out of his pocket, flagging away my comment. "Of course not. And whether we trust her or not isn't the point. We need her. Without her magic, this whole mission would be too risky to attempt."

But you'd still go, risk or not—and even without telling me, I thought.

I brushed my hair back from my face, my fingertips sweeping the tiny sore spot near my temple. "*Three hairs. Root and all,*" Lotli had insisted. Three hairs and a promise I'd hated to make.

Dad wrapped his arms around me, hugging me tight. "Don't look so worried. She's got her flute and magic. But you and I have each other. Besides, I imagine she wants to get this over with and get back to her old life as badly as we do."

A heavy feeling settled in the pit of my stomach. Why for all that was sane and sensible had I given in and made such a ridiculous deal with Lotli?

★ ★ ★

Dad and I parted ways, he headed toward his room to take a nap and I took off for mine. As I walked, I went back through what had happened in the graveyard, trying to discover if I could have done anything differently. One detail that had gotten past me at the time, now stood out. When I'd asked Lotli about the contract Zea had with our family, she'd blinked and a tendon in her neck had flinched as if my words had hit a nerve with her. Then she'd cleverly redirected the conversation, talking about how we were using her and making me angry with innuendos about Chase. Lotli deserved bonus points for that move. If she'd let me keep thinking about the contract for even a second longer, I'd have realized why my mention of it made her uneasy, and I would never have sworn to forsake Chase. The contract might have been between us and Zea, but Lotli was sworn to do as Zea commanded. Lotli had lied in the elevator. She couldn't possibly vanish and not go to the realm with us, any more than she could desert us there.

I opened the door to my room, feeling less depressed and certain not telling Dad about the agreement had been a good choice. He had enough to worry about, and this was something I could deal with myself in the long run. We'd only be in the djinn realm for a few hours. The second we got back, I'd break my promise and tell Chase—and everyone—what was going on. What harm could come from letting Lotli flirt with Chase unhampered for such a short time? It wasn't like we were going to a party where she could haul him off into a dark corner and put a love spell on him.

I rubbed a chill from my arms. Even if she did, that was something Selena and her mom could counteract—just like a hellmouth. There wasn't a cure for berserk or dead, and I needed Lotli to get Chase and Mom out of there and all of us back safely.

Out of the corner of my eye, I glimpsed a small black gift bag sitting in the middle of my bed. The last time I'd received one of these, I'd freaked. Black is the color of death, the color of darkness, and all kinds of nasty things. Not the color I'd choose for a gift. But this time, I knew who it was from: Selena. She'd even warned me she was going to whip up something.

I opened the bag and pulled out a tissue-wrapped bundle. Inside were a braided bracelet made out of what appeared to be Kate's special willow and a small gift box.

Smiling, I slid the bracelet on. Convenient for relieving pain, and decorative.

I took the lid off the gift box. Nested inside folds of black satin lay a tiny decorated egg pendant on a silver chain.

I flung the box onto the bed. A hummingbird egg? Why the hell would Selena give me that?

My entire body simmered with anger. What was she thinking? The designs painted on its shell were different, but for all practical purposes it was exactly like the so-called friendship gift Lotli had given me, the exploding egg.

I picked the necklace up by the clasp, watching as the egg swayed back and forth like a hypnotist's watch. It was pretty, mesmerizing swirls of color with a teardrop-shaped piece of sea glass dangling down from it. The thing was heavy, too, almost like it was weighted.

The door to the hallway scraped open. "So, what do you think?" Selena's voice asked.

I whipped around and glared at her. "You do know what this is, right?"

She hustled over and took the necklace, grinning as if it were the best thing in the world. "I thought you'd wonder about that. It was my idea. Mom made it. Seriously, you need it—and the bracelet."

Her light tone dampened my anger. "I absolutely love the bracelet, and I'm guessing it's for first aid. But, honestly, I have no idea what the egg's for." *Please, let it be anything besides friendship.*

"It's a pendulum." She grinned. "You can use it to find things."

I frowned, unsure what she meant.

"Things like Chase and your mom. You won't know where they are, and according to you the fortress is massive."

Excitement fluttered in my stomach. "You're talking about scrying?"

"More like dowsing. People use it to detect the presence of ghosts or spirits in buildings. It's used in medicine to locate problem areas. It's easier to learn than scrying. I'll show you."

Selena pulled scrap paper from her jeans pocket and laid it on the bed. It was a simple floor plan of Moonhill divided into quadrants.

I glanced from the egg to the map and back again. I intellectually grasped that the same type of egg could be used for different magic purposes. I wasn't worried that Selena or her mom would be out to get me. Still, I couldn't help worrying. "You're sure it won't do anything unexpected—like explode?"

"Mom feels really bad about that. She swears the symbols were nothing harmful and it was empty when she tested it."

"I believe that. It's just—" I touched my throat, letting my fingers slide down to where Lotli's egg had hung. "Do you really think the energy it absorbed was from me?"

"Some of it, but most was probably sucked out of the atmosphere. I imagine that realm is supercharged."

I nodded. Even I'd sensed that.

Another possibility flickered in my mind. When I'd been in the realm the last time, I'd discovered that my mother had the ability to maintain a solid body for brief amounts of time. This was unique since humans normally were ethereal in the djinn realm like genies were in our world. It undoubtedly indicated that my mother had an above-average amount of energy.

If I'd inherited any kind of unique ability from my mother, then Lotli giving me the egg would make more sense. But I didn't have a gift. I hadn't even pretended like I did. On top of that, Lotli hadn't learned about my mother's ability until long after she'd given me the egg. So why give it to me? What was Lotli up to?

I gave the egg another once-over. "If I hadn't broken the egg, what do you think Lotli was going to do? Ask for it back and then use it to bomb Bar Harbor or something?"

Selena shrugged. "Who knows? While you're gone, Mom's going to work on locating Zea. Our guess is that he'll be able to answer those questions. Maybe Lotli lied—maybe he made the egg pendant and she didn't know what it was for."

I wasn't so sure about that. It didn't seem as if a detail like that would slip past Lotli. But clearly she wasn't above lying. I bit down on a smile. Speaking of lies, this was the perfect time to get a little more reassurance that my hunch about her last one was true. "What sort of bond do you think Lotli has with Zea? I mean, what guarantees that she'll do as he asks? Is there a code of honor between shaman and apprentices, or a binding spell?"

"I imagine she dribbled her blood onto some sacred object and vowed—you know, a blood oath." Selena took hold of the pendant's clasp. "Now watch how I do this. And don't worry. You don't need any kind of special talent or powers. It's a basic technique."

Shoving my thoughts of Lotli aside, I concentrated on Selena. "You're going to swing it and focus, right?"

"Focus, but don't swing it. It's designed to work with your energy." She held the egg pendant over the map. It dangled for a second, then began to slowly circle. "Ask it simple questions to start with." She wet her lips. "What direction do I go to find Annie? Right? Left?"

The pendant swung until it reached the place on the map

that indicated my room. Then it spun in a tightening spiral. It was cool as heck.

"Now it's your turn," she said, handing me the pendant.

I palmed the egg for a second and my mind went back to the hellmouth opening up beneath my feet. "Selena?" I swallowed dryly, the rest of what I wanted to say sticking in my throat. "Maybe I can do this. But I'm scared of Lotli. I was the first time we went to the realm, and now—She terrifies me."

"Keep an eye on her flute. Take it by force if you have to. Without it she may have little or no ability."

"*May* have? That's not exactly comforting."

"She can't be that powerful. She's like me—still in training. Otherwise, why would she be with Zea? The powerful kind of witches and shaman you have to worry about don't show off by doing things like making smoke move to their music in the middle of a town park. Remember Zea? How quiet he was? You could feel the power radiating off of him."

"Yeah, I guess." I took a deep breath. Opening the veil seemed pretty powerful to me. And there was the hellmouth. Except Laura had been directly below us in the kitchen and she hadn't noticed anything. Had I been mistaken? Had it been a clever illusion, perhaps enhanced by her ability to open the veil? Maybe.

Selena tapped a finger against the side of her head. "Magic is partly about focus and accessing energy, about self-control. But it mostly involves discovering spells and remembering words. You've got the Freemont smarts—and that is more vital than any so-called special gift."

I smiled, feeling even better. But that feeling almost instantly subsided. Dad and I had met a Santeria priest in New Orleans. He was all about glitter and show—much more so than Lotli—and the rumors said he could kill people with a doll and a simple prayer, or make a woman miscarry by merely looking at her stomach. Selena might be right that magic was more about learning and remembering than what you were born with. But she was wrong about the glitz. Sometimes the show was real.

It took me a couple of tries, but Selena was right. If I focused and asked the pendant questions as hard as I could, the pendant answered every time. The trick was asking the right thing. And by the time Selena left my room, I had no qualms about wearing the new necklace to the realm. In fact, I wondered how I'd ever hoped to find Chase or Mother without it.

I glanced at the clock on my bedside stand. Grandfather and Dad's idea about a nap wasn't bad. I had time.

Chase drifted into my mind and excitement fluttered in my chest. I'd promised to forsake him when we went to the realm. But I hadn't said anything about before. It was a seriously bad idea to do something that might get his adrenaline or hormones flowing, but it couldn't hurt to reassure him that we were coming soon.

I slid the window screen up, then stripped down to my shirt and panties, and crawled into bed. The crisp cotton sheets were cool against my skin. I closed my eyes, concentrating on Chase. I scrunched a pillow against my chest, imagining each detail, his smell, the taste of his skin, enough to let him feel my need. Not enough to turn him on, at least not very much.

My breathing slowed. I could feel each muscle relaxing. Legs. Arms. Neck. Relaxing. Drifting. Nothing except him in my mind as I sank into a dream.

We stand in a garden, mist and the scent of rosemary swirling around us. His hand cups my chin, lifting my face. His eyes are sad, and shrouded by my sleep state and the haze.

"Annie," he says, hushed as the breeze.

I press my fingers against his jawline, rough and dark with stubble. And my body awakens, pulse quickening, desire threading through me. I want him. He takes a shallow breath and I know he feels the same. But this won't work. It's wrong. Not why I called him. It's dangerous for him.

Words form in my heart. I need to explain. To tell him we're coming. To say I'd never forsake him, for real. I step back and cold air settles between us.

Suddenly the ground beneath my feet shudders and bursts upward, tossing me aside. A fissure cracks open. Steam hisses out, cutting the mist and separating him from me.

Chase is a long ways off now. He's on the horizon silhouetted by a bonfire. Lotli's there, too, playing her flute. Her music is fluid like moonlight, like a waterfall, a distant caterwaul raking chills up my spine. He moves with her music, the gold flashes of his scimitar brightening and darkening her face, his leather armor as blood red as the night sky.

The rhythm of a pendulum begins to mark the seconds, echoing in my head. Tick-tock. Tick-tock. Tick-tock.

Lotli glides toward me, until she's right on the other side of the steaming fissure. Her eyes are on mine, as black as death. Her fingernails count off the loops of blue and green yarn wrapped around her flute. Tick-tock. One. Tick-tock. Two. Tick-tock. Three . . . She reaches six, touching a loop of my hair instead of yarn—

And the pendulum explodes like a grenade. White light blazes out from it. Orange flashes. Red flashes. Shards of eggshell knife outward, flying at me, as sharp as glass spears or razorblades.

I woke with a start. The sheets soaked with sweat, the nightmare hot and vivid in my mind. But I also felt clearheaded. More so than I'd been in ages.

Climbing out of bed, I went to my desk and got a pen. Then I began carefully drawing on my palm. First a large rectangle, then a smaller horseshoe shape to the right of it, a row of dots, a winding line that reached up the inside of my wrist.

I'd never bragged to Lotli about having abilities. That was

because I didn't have any. But she hadn't known what I had or didn't have when she gave me the egg. However, she did see the energy blast when the egg exploded and I'd seen the shock on her face. The force of the explosion had surprised her. Sure, I hadn't done anything to stop her from opening the hell-mouth, or when she'd taken my hairs and wrapped them around her flute next to Chase's yarn. But the glorious truth was: She didn't know what I might be capable of—any more than I could be certain of her level of abilities.

I went to my dresser and slid on my fingerless mitts, tug-ging them up until the drawing on my hand was mostly cov-ered. Better for Lotli to just catch a glimpse and wonder what the mysterious lines were for than having her see their entirety and fully grasp their much more mundane purpose. Like Se-lena said, the quiet ones were the ones to watch out for. Hope-fully Lotli believed that, too.

CHAPTER 17

I am not Ophelia. And neither madness nor
love shall take me there. I am determination.
I am as a morning star, baptized in the dark
waters of night, I rise again, wielding
the strength of my own skin.

—Journal of Stephanie Freemont, 31 October 1795

Dad gave me a kiss on the cheek. "I'm proud of you,
kiddo," he whispered.

"Back at you," I said.

It was a few minutes before sunset and we were waiting in
the dimly lit alcove by the widow's walk staircase. Everyone
was there to see us off—even Houdini, wriggling to get free
from Zachary's grip. The last thing we needed was to have him
follow us into the realm.

I slid my fingers down the dagger hanging at my loosely
belted waistline and then reached into my robe's secret pockets, checking that I had my bags of salt and mini flashlight. This
was so different than the last time when Lotli, Chase, and I had
snuck into the realm behind the older generation's backs. It
was different, too, with all of us dressed in brown eunuch
robes, our faces already sheltered by deep hoods. The flute in
Lotli's hand was a reminder of her power and the spell that
bound me to keep my promise. But seeing her in the plain

robe with charcoal striping her face bothered me far less than the belly dancer costume she'd worn on our previous trip.

I touched my throat, pausing when I reached the egg pendant mixed in with a conglomeration of other necklaces and chains. Genies loved their jewelry, so I'd figured a whole bunch tucked into my robe would draw attention away from the egg and look more normal than just one or two. Of course, the poison ring was totally invisible, hidden away in my bra.

Out of the corner of my eye, I glimpsed Lotli stealing a look at the pendant. Her gaze darted to my wrist, where a couple of my penned lines were barely noticeable. I narrowed my eyes and gave her a sly smile just to let her know she'd been caught, then pulled my hood closer around my face.

A searing pain knifed through my guts, sharp and unrelenting as if someone were raking my intestines with red-hot claws. I hunched forward as one excruciating contraction surged into the next. I gritted my teeth and forced myself to straighten up.

I sliced a look at Lotli. With a sly smile that mimicked the one I'd given her a second ago, she plucked at her flute, one fingernail jabbing at the section wrapped with my hair.

Another wave of pain knifed inside me, stopping as she lifted her finger. She might have sworn an oath to Zea that made it impossible for her to not do as he commanded, but clearly that didn't prevent her from torturing me. Still, I wasn't done yet. It was time to take my pretense at having abilities a bit further, and get more reassurance while I was at it.

Keeping my face expressionless, I casually drew my dagger and held it out toward Lotli, handle first. "Before we leave, there is one thing we neglected to do last time. You forgot to swear a blood oath to not desert us in the realm."

Her eyes went dark. "We could not have left the realm last time without you or Chase, if you had not tricked us into doing so."

I stepped even closer to her, all but forcing the dagger into her grip. "Cut yourself. Swear a blood oath on your flute."

"This is unnecessary," she said. But she took the dagger and pricked the end of her thumb. A drop of blood rose. She smeared it the length of her flute, gaze hard on mine. "We swear on our grandmother and great-grandmother's souls that we will not break our sacred vow to you and your family—as long as all promises to us remain unbroken."

I did not take my gaze off hers. Her straight shoulders, solid voice and flared nostrils, every inch of her said she was ir- ritated but had sworn with full honesty and believed the oath had power over her. I bit back a smile, though in truth it had been created out of nothing more than momentary inspiration on my part.

Grandfather cleared his throat. "That was a nice touch," he said. "However, it's time. Who wants to go first?"

Plastering on a smile, Lotli turned away from me. "We are ready." She lowered her head so he could pour the Methuselah oil over it.

He tipped the lamp. The oil shimmered against the dull brown of her hood. She raised her arms and the oil swept up- ward, coating her arms, hands, and each fingertip. There was no smell or blackness, or oily excesses puddling on the floor. No sound. Not even the breath of everyone watching. Even Houdini watched in silence as she transformed from solid into a ghostly gray shadow.

My insides quivered with a mix of nerves and excitement. I stepped toward Grandfather and bowed my head, waiting for the writhing sensation of the oil to coat me, and prayed: "*Hecate, Queen of the Sky, Protector of the Gateways of earth, heaven, and sea. Watch over us, protect us on this journey. And bring us all home again.*"

CHAPTER 18

*According to legend, the Lamp of Methuselah contains
oil that will turn a human body ethereal, allowing one to
pass through unwarded weak points in the veil. Once on the
other side, the body will again become solid. We'll know
if this is true come sunset, when Kate and I attempt to cross.*

—Journal of David Freemont, March 9th

I held my breath as the oil coated me. Shivers followed in its
wake, icing my skin until I trembled. A second later, that
sensation faded and only an almost undetectable resistance to
my skin remained, like my body had been sealed in an ultra-
thin coat of varnish.

Our plan was simple. Find my mother first, most likely in
the harem. She'd be able to take us to Chase. Then we'd all escape back to Moonhill.

I opened my eyes and slanted a quick look at Lotli's shadowy form. Once we got back, I'd scream at the top of my
lungs about the deal she'd forced me to make. But for now we
were a team.

A vibrating sensation crept over my body and I closed my
eyes again, waiting for tingles that would signal I was becoming as ethereal as Lotli. I was beyond ready for this. Still, after
all the waiting, time seemed to be flying by now, the chance to
back out a fading memory.

"I'll go first." Dad stepped between me and the space in front of the tapestry. His body shimmered, shedding the last of its solidness as he became ethereal. "Ready, girls?"

Dread and an odd sense of inevitability settled in the pit of my stomach. It felt as if I'd been moving toward this moment my entire life. I took a shaky breath. "I'm ready."

"Ready," Lotli echoed, only inches behind me.

Time hung in the air, the moment as frozen as a photograph. Selena had her hands cupped together, fear written in her eyes. Uncle David stood behind Olya, holding her tight. Houdini watched me from Zachary's arms. The Professor had his phone raised above his head, recording the event. Kate lifted her chin and gave me an approving nod.

"We'll wait right here until you return," Grandfather said.

The first notes Lotli played whistled gently, like a shepherdess soothing her flock, rising and falling. My throat dried as I waited. The soft notes became insistent, fiercer, harder, shriller. The air trembled with the eerie sound. Pressure built in my ears and I retreated farther into my hood. There was no ward on this side to block us, just whatever spells Malphic had in place on the other side.

Cold exploded outward, rushing toward us. The flute's music whistled higher. Houdini yowled, but his cries faded under the ringing pressure singing in my ears. Ahead, between us and the tapestry, the air unzipped, like a tent flap ripping open with sparks of electricity crackling all around it. Beyond the opening, gray mist swirled and eerie orange light whickered.

Dad stepped forward. The flute music lowered a staccato march, suddenly shrieking upward again, a piercing wail. The sound vibrated inside me, even the marrow in my bones shook.

This was it. I swallowed hard, and followed Dad.

Electricity sizzled all around me. The air became stifling, oppressive and hot. It pressed against us, an unyielding tide fighting to shove us back. Dad lowered his head like a bull and pressed on. Pressure squealed in my head, almost too much to bear. But I stuck close to Dad. One step. Another step. Lotli's music reverberated behind me—

My ears popped. The resistance vanished and my muscles once again took on solid weight as I lurched into a small chamber, its curved walls brightened by flickering torchlight.

Dad's hand steered me to one side, preventing me from stumbling over a low stand with an unlit hookah resting on top of it. Next to it sat a pile of embroidered floor cushions. Adrenaline thumped into my blood. This was great. There wouldn't be a sitting area like this arranged directly in front of a weak point if it was actively being used.

I swiveled, guiding Lotli into the room like Dad had done for me—

A masculine snarl reverberated behind us.

I swung around. A man-shaped black shadow leapt out from nowhere, the dark blade of his scimitar glinting. A shadow-genie!

My head whirled, my heartbeat crashing in my ears.

Dad sprung forward. The scimitar slashed toward him. Dad ducked and came up, his fisted hand slamming into the shadow-genie's stomach. The lung-searing stench of bleach flooded the room. The shadow howled and stumbled backward. Dad rammed his fist into its rib cage. That's when I noticed a short white rod in Dad's hand. He yanked the rod upward and the shadow writhed, crumpling to the floor, shrieking and wheezing as oily black liquid boiled from the frothing wound.

Fear jolted through me. Someone had to have heard the shadow's screams. We had to get out of here. I swung around, studying the entire room. No windows. No doors. Silk draped the ceiling. Carpets covered the curved walls. Carpets. But where did they lead?

"The shadow!" Lotli screeched.

It was on all fours, staggering to his feet. His jaw hung open. Black goo oozed from a gaping hole in its chest. Dad hauled his arm back, slamming the rod into the shadow's eye. But whatever he was using for a weapon disintegrated on impact, crumbling into melting sludge.

The shadow stumbled toward Dad, teeth bared. I pulled a bag of salt from my pocket, my fingers fumbling with the ziplock as I yanked it open. Grabbing a handful of salt, I threw it at the shadow's face. Crystals rained down, hissing like acid against the shadow's body. Shrieking wildly, it spun like a cyclone. Then it splattered down on top of a floor cushion in an oily black mass, dead-still, for now.

"Hurry," Dad commanded. "Lotli, open the veil. Annie, help me shove him through."

Flute music filled the room, an erratic whistle. The barely closed veil crackled open. I grabbed one side of the floor cushion. Dad took the other. My neck muscles pinched from the effort as we heaved it back, then shoved it forward, shooting the cushion and shadow through the slit in the veil, like mafia henchmen heaving a body in the East River.

Dad chuckled. "Bet that will surprise your aunt Kate."

I stared at him incredulously. How could he laugh? "Yeah, and in about two seconds this place will be full of other guards."

He raised a finger and cocked his head as if listening. "Do you hear *anything?* Anything at all—such as sounds from outside of here?"

Lotli blinked. "We hear nothing."

I smiled. "It's soundproof, like Malphic's harem. Noise barely travels inside and can't escape or get into here." My fears returned. "That doesn't mean other guards won't show up. That one probably has a partner."

Lotli stepped toward the center of the room. "This is not a

safe place. Malphic works magic here." She scuffed a sheepskin rug aside with her foot, uncovering symbols chiseled into the stones and stained with dark-red splatter.

I shuddered. Blood? Brain matter? I really didn't want to think what the stains were from, but I couldn't help it. They weren't the only creepy things either. On a stone table, a jar filled with yellow liquid and bird embryos sat next to a bowl of half-burnt charcoal, and an uncoiled scroll. A brass face mask with thumbscrews on the sides and spikes around the eye sockets waited on a side table. Shelves and crannies overflowed with books bound in leather, some clasped with jewels, others with glowing seals. A carpet hanging on the wall behind the stone table depicted a warrior standing on a clifftop. Blood covered his torso. His lower half was a dark tornado of shadows and symbols. In one hand he held a raised scimitar, lightning rose from his other. At his waist, a knife with a moonstone glistened. A knife whose handle held the branding iron, the one that had marked Chase's collarbone. A knife like the one Chase had taken from Malphic five years ago when he escaped the realm with David and Kate's help. No question about it, this room was Malphic's inner sanctum.

Dad strode to the wall, resting his hand on the nearest carpet. "Like it or not, there's only one way out of here. But who the hell knows which one? What do you think, Lotli?"

She tucked her hands into the folds of her robe. "We cannot say. This magic is not within our understanding."

"Don't worry. I've got this one," I said confidently. I stripped off my mitt and tucked it into my strap-like belt, then took off the egg necklace. The only way to keep a leg up on Lotli was to not let any hint of insecurity leak through.

"Annie—?" Dad started.

I cut him off, hoping he'd manage to cover his confusion and give me a chance. "Don't worry. The magic in here won't affect me."

Holding the end of the chain, I let the egg dangle just above the drawing on my palm, boxes and lines representing the layout of the fortress. I drew in a deep breath and let it out slowly. *Please, please, let this work.*

Nothing happened, except for desperation and fear blooming inside me. Any second, Lotli would start laughing for sure.

I set my jaw and focused again, blocking out all other thoughts. A tingling sensation sparked in my chest, branched outward, sweeping toward my arm, and down to where my fingers and thumb held the chain.

"Show me where we are," I said.

The egg swung slowly until it hung directly above the far side of the horseshoe-shaped arena. It began to circle right where my drawing ended. Shit. We were in the part of the fortress I hadn't seen last time.

Lotli bent close, watching the circling egg. "Ask it how we can get out of here."

"Show me a doorway," I said. But the ache in my chest told me my heart longed to ask a different question. *Where is Chase? Help me find him?*

"You probably should be more specific," Dad whispered.

I nodded and took another breath. "Where is a doorway that leads to what lies just beyond these walls?"

The tightness in my chest intensified. I lowered my palm and held the pendulum out in front of me, letting it swing as I walked forward: left, right, left, right, forward, back . . . changing direction when I went the wrong way, like the ticks of a metal detector homing in on a buried coin.

The egg stopped swinging and began to circle in front of a slender carpet decorated with a knife embraced by a long-stemmed white rose with clawlike thorns. I'd seen the design before over the door to the harem: the insignia of Malphic and Sovereign Mistress Vephra.

"This one," I said.

"Good choice." Dad nodded to a sheathed sword, leather gloves, and a long scarf hanging on a rack beside the carpet. Genies wore scarves like that because the realm's salty air weakened them slightly. Most of the time, they just kept them looped around their necks. But when they wanted extra strength, they'd use the scarf to shield their mouth and nose from the air. It was the sort of personal item Malphic might want quick access to.

"If this is Malphic's inner sanctum, I'm willing to bet this carpet might not change as often as the public ones," I said.

"We think so as well." Lotli started toward the carpet.

But before she beat me to it, I leaned forward. The carpet's threads diffused into colored mist, and static shocks snapped against my skin as my face pressed through it. Beyond the carpet a narrow enclosed stairwell led steeply downward toward an opening illuminated by an eerie lime-green and orange glow, most likely nighttime darkness and firelight mixed with the realm's ever-present auroras. The air echoed with the distant clank of metal against metal and lots of masculine grunts and groans. *Chase.* Maybe the pendulum had answered both of my questions.

I glanced over my shoulder at Lotli and Dad. "It's a stairwell. There are men sparring, I think. But I can't see anyone."

"Chase," Lotli cooed. Her hood might have shielded her face, but I knew there was a nasty glint in her eyes.

I bit my tongue, refusing to be baited into her trap. Instead I fixed my gaze on Dad and asked a question that was eating at me. "What did you stab the shadow with?"

He gave me a wink. "Remember the story about your great uncle Harmon and the Canary Islands sirens?"

"A salt shank?" I said, gaping at him. Harmon had escaped from the sirens by using a knife made out of salt. Kind of like how modern prisoners make shanks in jail by melting Jolly

Ranchers. But when had Dad had time to make one? And, if he had, then why hadn't he made them for all of us?

He tucked his hands into his pockets, his body going a bit too still. "Unfortunately I only had time to whip up one."

I felt my face pale. He was lying for the second time today. My gut told me so. The way he was controlling his body language said it as well. But what was he hiding? It was possible that he'd swiped the shank from Moonhill's treasury, instead of making it as he'd claimed. But I couldn't imagine why he'd bother to lie about that. However, it made perfect sense for him to not want me to know he had another shank stashed if he intended to use it for a very dangerous and specific purpose. Something he didn't want me involved in. *Revenge.*

CHAPTER 19

Perhaps it was the way Chase didn't flinch when
Malphic held the branding iron against his skin,
or the way he protected the younger boys. But
that child was different. I believe Malphic saw it, too.

—Susan Woodford Freemont

We slipped through the carpet and crept down the enclosed stairwell, our boots shushing against the stone treads. All around us, animal skulls studded the walls, their dark eyes and fanged jaws lit by glowing oil lamps. As we neared the stairwell's mouth, the clang of metal and grunts grew louder, and the tang of the realm's harsh air and bonfires filled my nose.

When I reached the last step, I held out my arm to stop Dad and Lotli. Cautiously, I walked out of the stairway's protection and onto a broad landing that overlooked what couldn't have been anything other than a training yard. Torches and fire pits flashed light across a maze of crowded fighting rings, some raised and others nothing more than worn spots in the dirt. Low, barrack-like buildings enclosed what I could see of the yard. Everywhere, dozens of boys—shirtless, skinny, and dirty with long, scraggly hair and sunburned skin—wrestled, boxed, or sparred with staffs and swords. Men and older teenagers shouted at them, jeering and giving sharp commands. Servants and eunuchs scurried through the haze of smoke and eerie light.

Chase had told me the daylight hours in the realm were too hot even for the genies' fiery nature to do anything except rest. At night, their natural heat mixed with adrenaline, amplifying their abilities, as well as those of the half-genie slaves. Still, it was surreal to witness, bizarre and barbaric, like Attila the Hun might step out at any moment and announce a challenge.

But it is real, I reminded myself. It was also where Chase had grown up. This was his childhood. Kidnapped. Branded as a slave. Fighting to survive.

A deep sadness pressed against my chest. One time, Tibbs had talked to me about Chase's life before he escaped and came to Moonhill.

Tibbs's hands had stilled. *"He fakes it real good, but Chase doesn't get the same stuff we do, inside jokes about old TV shows or movies. He didn't listen to the same music we did, snap selfies, or do any of the stuff normal kids did. He grew up training and watching friends die because they weren't good enough. He grew up protecting people."*

That day, what Tibbs said only partly sunk in. But I hadn't seen this yet.

"Impressive," Lotli said, coming up beside me. "Yes, very much."

Dad rested a hand on my shoulder. "I doubt Chase is down there, but you should try your egg to be sure, before we take off to find your mother."

Lotli tsked. "No need for magic tricks. You may not see him. But we feel his presence."

"Of course you do," I said tartly.

She wet her lips. "We are surprised you don't."

Heat roared through my body, my anger a million hot spikes. I gritted my teeth. *Evil bitch.*

Dad squeezed my shoulder. "You all right?"

"Fine," I snapped. "Let's get going."

His grip tightened. "First, I need both of you to promise you'll let me do all the talking from here on out. We don't need your womanly voices giving us away, eunuch doesn't necessarily equal feminine. Agreed?"

"We agree," Lotli whispered demurely.

"Yeah," I said, wriggling from his grip.

He raised a finger, signaling he wasn't done. "If we get separated or something worse happens, come back here. With its wards broken, the inner sanctum weak point is our best chance for escape. Understand?"

I nodded that I did. But there were a lot of *ifs* involved with escaping here or anywhere for that matter. *If* Malphic or his magi didn't notice the broken wards and restore them. *If* we weren't detected and lived to make it back to here . . . *Ifs* and more *ifs* that none of us could afford to think about at this point.

I strode away from Dad and Lotli toward a set of wide stairs that led down to ground level and the entry to the training yard. But I forced myself to stop and let them catch up. I couldn't let my worries, or my temper for that matter, make me stupid. I was better than that. I had to be.

Together, we headed down. As Dad had pointed out, Lotli and I needed to be careful about talking, but that wasn't the only thing. Olya had padded the shoulders of our robes. Our boots had thick soles and heels to make us taller. Of course our eyes were shadowed with kohl. Still I came across as a particularly small guy, and Lotli looked more like a boy. All we could do was hope we'd fade into the background of eunuchs and servants in general.

"Looks like your pendulum was right," Dad said, nodding at a colonnade to our left and in the opposite direction than the training yard. It was clear now that we'd descended from a squatty tower that sat atop the colonnade. Just beyond it was the horseshoe-shaped arena where I'd broken the egg and Chase had been forced to fight. Past that, the ornate spires and domed rooftops of Malphic's main palace rose, ghostly light glowing behind its curtained windows. As the egg had indicated on my palm, we were outside the part of the fortress I was familiar with.

"Chase is that way." Lotli jutted her hood toward the yard.

I resisted the urge to remind her that we'd planned to get Mother first. The truth was, both my heart and pulse were screaming to find Chase.

Dad put a finger to his lips and bowed his head as a group of servants carrying bottles of wine and bowls of shriveled mushrooms and half-rotted apples hurried past us into the training yard. Once they were a few footsteps ahead, he whispered, "Since we're so close, we should at least locate Chase." Then he took off, leading us into the yard, like we were just another group of servants.

Two brown-robed eunuchs rushed by us, their arms weighted down with blood-splattered clothing. When we passed a group of buckets filled with water, Dad snatched one by the handle. Good idea. It would make it look like we were on our way to do something specific. I grabbed another with a rag draped over its side.

Lotli's hood brushed against mine. "A slop bucket. Suits you," she snickered, too low to travel beyond my ear. Her voice took on a dangerous edge. "Remember. He belongs to me. . . ."

As her voice trailed off, a shooting pain slammed into my belly, agony ricocheting through my guts and down my legs. I hunched over, my fingers tightening around the bucket handle as I rode out the spasms. I wanted so badly to swing the bucket at her head. Drop her in her tracks. But I couldn't call attention to us, or we'd all be dead. Not just me or her. But Dad, Mother, and Chase as well.

"Forsake," she whispered. And the pain vanished, totally and in an instant.

"Screw you," I spat. But she knew I would do as promised. She knew I didn't have a choice.

I lengthened my strides, leaving her behind, moving ahead of Dad as well, past teams of naked boys wrestling on the ground. Bruises mottled their faces and bodies. Some had fresh gaping wounds. Others' knuckles were wrapped in cloth, dirty and bloodied. All had brands on their collarbones, the youngest ones still pink, the older ones scarred over. Slave brands like Chase's. I longed to locate him, and get this over with. But in a way, I hoped he wasn't here. Finding him after Mother would give Lotli less time to screw with his head. I didn't want to confuse him. I didn't want him to think I didn't care.

A dull headache throbbed at the front of my skull, and anger, frustration, longing, desperation—every emotion in the book—boiled inside me.

On a stone platform, a pair of teenage girls punched and kicked a boy whose hands were tied behind his back. Blood ran from his nostrils and speckled his ripped tunic. Shadow-genies and werewolf-like lealaps circled around cheering. Nearby, a man reprimanded a boy. The marks on the man's body glowed like blue fire. Scars cross-thatched his face. The lower half of his body whirlwinded into a cyclone, and he slammed his fist into the boy's neck. The boy dropped to the ground, vomiting. "Defend yourself, little bastard, or I'll kill you," the man snarled.

Dad started toward them. Holding tight to my bucket, I snagged his arm with my free hand and turned both of us away from the sight. But I could still hear the squelch of the man's fist hitting flesh, hear the retching and smell blood and vomit—

My body went numb. I stopped walking and stared. On the farthest end of the yard near what most likely was the fortress's massive outer wall, a blue glow burst upward from a large well or cistern. At least that's how it appeared. It was hard to tell through the crowd and haze.

Adrenaline coursed into my veins. Could it be? Was it Chase's aura?

I let go of Dad and hurried toward the well, the water in my pail sloshing. In a second, Dad and Lotli caught up with me. This time it was Dad snagging my arm to hold me back. "Be careful," he whispered.

Sweat drizzled down my face, stinging my eyes. "It's him. I know it."

"Yes, it is," Lotli purred.

We weaved through the crowd. Once we got closer, I could see the well was about twenty feet across with a waist-high stone wall surrounding it and an iron grate overtop. The blue light flared up though the grate's bars, strobing like heat lightning.

A group of teenage boys in short, grubby tunics banged on the bars.

"Kill him!" one of them shouted.

Another shook his fists. "Use your knife! Gut him."

Two women my age with swords strapped to their backs gazed downward, whispering to each other. I wormed my way in next to them and caught a few words.

"Satan's balls, he's as crazy as a stallion," one of them said.

The other one giggled. "I'd ride him—even if he goes berserk."

I set my bucket down and leaned over. In effect the grate was the top of a tall, narrow cage. Twenty or maybe thirty feet down, two shirtless men were fighting. Swirls of glowing marks covered their skin, brightening and dimming like heartbeats. Dirt and blood caked their arms and shoulders. The larger man leapt onto the cage's bars, his long black braid snaking out behind him as he screamed like a banshee and cartwheeled back down, dagger glinting in his hand. The other man growled and spun, flowing white pants flaring, fist catching the larger man off guard. My heart screamed that he was Chase, but I couldn't see him well enough to be sure.

A flash of firelight struck his face, and I was certain. Chase. Eyes wild. Blood trailing from his nose and mouth.

Lotli's fingernails dug into my wrist. "Hurry. We must help him."

She let go of me, snatched my bucket, and fled away from the hole. Dad gave me a puzzled look, but I didn't take the time to answer. I gathered up the hem of my robe and sprinted after her. No matter how much I hated her, I knew hate wasn't what she felt for Chase. She was up to something. Something that would help him.

CHAPTER 20

We are the Hexad. The banished ones.
The song of the stars. We whistle to the
wind with our grandmother's bones
and drink the hummingbird's power.

—"Song of the Hexad"

Lotli skirted around a line of punching bags and vanished through an arched doorway set into the fortress's outer wall. Of course. It made perfect sense. There had to be a way down to the bottom of the fight cage, and this door was the closest one to the grate.

With Dad inches behind, I went under the archway and into a stifling-hot room that buzzed with flies and smelled like rancid milk. There were lines of wooden tables and benches. A boy slumped at one of them, sleeping with his head buried in his arms.

Lotli was a few feet away, desperately scanning the room, the bucket clutched against her stomach. I squared my shoulders and started searching. There were no other slaves or genies in the room. Narrow windows. Two other doors. The shape of a half wall struck me. It was the top of a stairwell.

I fast-walked toward it, dirt crunching under my boots. I was about to start down, when gravelly voices echoed up from below and three beefy men dressed in midnight-black leather tunics came into view, shoulder to shoulder, marching up the stairs toward me. Shit. I knew those uniforms, midnight-black with silver bracers, lots of tattoos, and scarves looped around their necks. These weren't just any genies. They were members of Malphic's guard.

I stepped to one side and cupped my mitt-covered hands behind my back, staring at the floor while I waited for them to reach the top. I could only guess it was the respectful thing to do. It seemed wiser than trying to plow through their ranks. I could only hope Dad and Lotli had done the same thing.

Cold sweat iced my body as they slowly moved upward. I wished they would hurry. We needed to get to Chase. On top of that, it would be a miracle if none of them picked up on the fact that we weren't eunuchs they'd seen before.

"Glad my watch is over," a guard with a rough voice said. "I don't want to be around when that one snaps."

I scuffed backward, my chills transformed into sheer terror. He sounded like the Hulk, a guard I'd run into the last time we were here. He would have forced himself on me if I hadn't threatened him with a knife and said I was a gift for the Sovereign Mistress's pleasure.

Careful to keep my hood close around my face, I glanced at him. His skin was a deep russet and he had a curly black beard. Definitely not the Hulk. He'd been clean-shaven, except for a narrow strip of beard.

Curly Beard stopped on the top step and swiveled toward the other guards. "Malphic's going to regret not gelding that bastard."

The tallest guard snorted. "If he lives."

REACH FOR YOU   165

Curly folded his arms across his chest. "Fuck. You remember what he did to Malphic? Beat the hell out of him and claimed his knife as a prize. He was a snot-ass kid then—not a berserker."

"Death Warrior," the third guard corrected.

"I don't care what anyone calls them," the tall guard scoffed. "This guy isn't going to make it that far. Did you see his eyes? He won't make it through another fight."

I could barely breathe. They were talking about Chase. I shifted my weight from one leg to the other. How long were they going to stand there bullshitting and blocking the stairway? Couldn't they see we were waiting?

Finally, their conversation died. They came up the last step and marched past us without a single glance.

I darted down the stairs, Dad and Lotli trailing. With each step, the light from above faded, darkness growing deeper. The air filled with the sharp reek of body odor and urine.

Dad coughed. Lotli gagged. But none of us slowed and none of us asked the obvious and terrifying question: Why wasn't there any sound coming from below? When we'd looked through the grate, there'd been lots of noise. This place wasn't soundproof like the harem and Malphic's inner sanctum.

The pungent smell of blood mixed with the other stenches. A moment later, we rounded a curve and the stairway opened up to a view of the grim chamber below, washed in torchlight and a macabre blue haze. The chamber was laid out like a wheel. Black carpets hung on the curved outer wall interspersed with dark-mouthed tunnels. In the center of the room, the grated fighting cage rose from floor to ceiling.

Chase crouched in the cage, his face pressed against the bars. A long chain went from a post in the middle of the cage to the shackle on his left ankle. His fisted hand clenched the knife he'd taken from Malphic in that infamous fight. So much dirt and blood caked his face and body that it was impossible at this distance to tell if he was hurt and how badly—or if the blood belonged to someone else.

A brown-robed eunuch and two guards hunched over a figure that lay outside of the bars. The other fighter. He was motionless, his mouth slack open, blood oozing from it and both his eyes. I glimpsed a coil of intestine protruding from his stomach. I turned away, swallowing hard to keep from vomiting. I succeeded at that, but the acrid taste of bile flavored my mouth.

One of the guards straightened up and thrust his thumb in Chase's direction. "Tend to him," he said to the eunuch. "We'll get the next contender."

The eunuch rose to his full height, matching the guard's posture. "He needs more than tending. He needs rest and food."

"Malphic's orders. This one keeps fighting." The guard glared at the eunuch for a long moment, before he and the other guard seized the dead fighter by the wrists and dragged him across the room and into a tunnel, leaving a slick trail of blood in their wake.

Something thumped into my leg. Lotli's bucket.

I turned to glare at her. *Why the hell had she done that?* Then I realized I'd stared longer than was wise, considering that the guards could see us. Dad was still doing the same thing a few steps above.

"He's even sexier like that," Lotli whispered.

Anger roared into every part of my being. I hauled my arm back and slapped her across the face. Unfortunately, her hood got in my way, taking the force out of the blow.

Lotli quietly set the bucket down. Her hand snaked into the folds of her robe.

Her flute. I clenched my teeth, bracing myself for the pain, preparing to not cry out. . . . An ear-splitting howl erupted from Chase. He dropped his knife and collapsed to the ground, whimpering. *Oh God.* My hair wasn't the only thing wrapped around Lotli's flute. Chase's yarn was on there as well.

The eunuch squatted up close to the bars, right in front of Chase. "Give into it. Let the change take you. It'll be over then."

"No," Chase groaned.

Rage fisted my hands. My nostrils flared and I struggled against an urge to shove my knife into Lotli's ice-cold heart. Chase might have been changing and hurting in a million ways, but what he was feeling this instant had nothing to do with that and everything to do with her.

Lotli tilted her head, dark eyes sparking at me. "Last warning," she said, barely above a breath.

I ground my teeth, but lowered my eyes. I wanted to kill her. Kill her dead. Wrap her in duct tape and send her back to the Sons of Ophiuchus.

Dad's boots shushed against the stairs as he came down to us. He nodded at the scene below. "Any suggestions?"

But his words were lost on Lotli. She was already slithering down the rest of the stairwell, bucket clutched in both hands. She crept across the room to the cage. Sinking down, next to the eunuch, she retrieved the rag from her bucket, reached through the bars, and dabbed wetness against Chase's neck.

The eunuch rose from his crouch, studying her as if trying to figure out what she was doing—or who she was. Suddenly he whirled and looked directly at where Dad and I still stood on the stairs.

Without missing a beat, Dad set down his pail and strode downward like a lord descending into his own grand ballroom. His right hand reached into the folds of his robe as if going for his salt or shank. "Time for your break, boy."

I ran after Dad and grabbed his forearm. "No," I said forcefully.

His arm relaxed. "I suppose you're right."

The eunuch's gaze darted from us to Lotli and back. He raised his arms out from his body to show he wasn't going to reach for a weapon. "How about if I leave? Get dinner. Take a piss."

"Make it a long one," Dad suggested.

The eunuch hushed his voice. "You should wait. He's got one more fight. After that, he'll be put in a cell." He nodded at the sparks crackling across the cage's open doorway. "That's warded. There's no way you—or I—can get in or get him out." He turned on his heel and started toward the stairwell, but swiveled back. "Stay strong. Stay proud. Stay free."

"Same to you," I said in the deepest tone I could muster.

He nodded and took off up the stairs.

"What was that about?" Dad said.

"It's some kind of rebel motto. Chase's half brother Jaquith said it when he was helping us escape the last time," I said. That was questionably true. Jaquith had said that, but I wasn't sure if my breaking the egg was solely responsible for our escape going horribly wrong or if Jaquith had double-crossed us and was partially at fault.

Chase grabbed the bars and pulled himself to his knees, face pressed against the metal. His face was dark with beard stubble. One of his eyes was bruised and swollen shut, blood crusting along the lid. His nose lay flat. His lips split open. Bruises. Blood. So much blood.

"Here," Lotli said, pressing the damp rag to his lips. "This will help."

He lolled away from her hand, a faint blue aura oozing from his marks as his unfocused eyes strained to look my way.

My chest squeezed. My heart, my soul, every part of me longed to comfort him, to hold the cloth to his lips, to charge through the sparking cage doorway and get him out of there.

I clamped my eyes shut and planted my feet, struggling against the urge to race to him. If I made one wrong move, Lotli would reach for her flute. And it wouldn't be me who felt its sting. It would be him, and it would be worse this time.

Lotli dampened the rag with fresh water, touched it to his swollen eye, and cooed, "Don't worry about her. She does not like what you are becoming. We will not desert you like she will. The blood, the death, it does not bother us."

Dad crouched down, up close to the bars. "Chase," he said firmly. "Was the eunuch right—will they put you in a cell later?"

Hope fluttered in my stomach. I pulled my hands up into my robe's sleeves, scrunching the fabric tightly. I couldn't do or say anything to help Chase, but Dad could. *Please, Dad. Let him know I care.*

Chase gazed blindly at Dad. "Later good." His head moved, eyes searching again, finding mine. His lips parted and he rasped, "Annie, I lov—"

Lotli sliced a look at me.

I wheeled away, turning my back on Chase's needy eyes. For a heartbeat, I held my breath, unable to do what I had to. Then I fled.

CHAPTER 21

The Moon. The Ace of Swords . . .

—Tarot cards drawn for Annie Freemont

I fled across the training yard, the thump of fists and weapons, the jeers of the onlookers, the screams, the shouts, all blurring into a dizzying roar. I ran under the colonnade and down into the empty arena. Not a single torch marked the way, only the light from the aurora and the waning moon.

My sides ached from running. I could hardly breathe. I stopped and hunched over, clasping my hands behind my neck. *Chase.* His last words rang in my head. I could see the anguish in his eyes. His ruined nose. The bruises. The blood. The blue of his aura oozing from the marks drawn on his skin.

Last year, I'd taken an ethics class with some of my homeschool friends. The instructor had asked us if we could kill. I'd said no. But I'd attacked the shadow-genies and Culus to save my dad when he was possessed. I'd attacked the guy at the yacht club. And now I was certain. I could kill. Lotli.

"Annie." Dad sprinted up next to me, his breath ragged. "What's going on?"

"We need to find Mom," I said brusquely.

I clenched my teeth against the pain in my side, straightened up, and started walking again, heading for a tunnel entry on the other end of the arena. I knew where it went. I knew its tricks: deadly glass rosebushes that could block off retreat, magic carpets that could lead to anywhere. But the tunnel was also one of the fortress's main arteries and was regularly used without dire consequences.

I lengthened my strides. In the distance a bell began to toll, marking the hour or the changing of the guard, I didn't know which and didn't care.

Dad grabbed me by the arms, jerking me to a standstill. "Stop this. What was that bullshit Lotli said about you not liking what Chase is becoming? What did she do to you?"

"She didn't do anything," I snapped.

"We're not going anywhere until you tell me the truth."

I yanked free. "We have to get Mother."

"Did she threaten you?"

"No, she told me she'd vanish. Without her, we'll never get Mother or Chase." I ground my teeth. "Is that enough for you, or do you want to stand here all day?"

I clenched my hands, my pulse ratcheting so high my head felt like it might burst. Just as I was about to scream from utter anguish and frustration, I realized my feet were planted next to the arena platform where Lotli had performed in front of Malphic and everyone. Where she'd played her flute and made Chase act like her sex-starved puppet. I stood on exactly the same spot where I'd smashed the hummingbird egg. The spot where I'd caused our last mission to fall apart.

Dad lowered his voice, a demanding growl. "What else?"

I shook my head, readying to repeat my denial, but I couldn't. Last time, I'd let Lotli drive me into being stupid. I couldn't—*no*—I wouldn't let her do that again. Besides, Dad loved me. I loved him. Until recently, we'd never kept anything from each other. Together we were stronger, smarter.

Cold hard determination lifted my chin. No more craziness. No more lies. *Focus, work as a team,* that's what Chase would say—and do. I met Dad's eyes. "I agreed to forsake Chase. . . ."

I gave him an abbreviated rundown. I even told him how Lotli had opened a hellmouth in the elevator. "I don't know if it was real or an illusion. But I know Lotli is way more powerful than she's letting on. If we're lucky, Kate and Olya will find out exactly how much from Zea. But we have to play by her rules for now, even if it hurts."

Dad crossed his arms; then he unfolded them. He gave a resigned sigh. "I don't like the idea. But I suppose you're right." His gaze darted back toward the colonnade. "Chase and Lotli are expecting us to get your mom, then meet up with them once he's put in the cell after—" His voice dropped off abruptly. The detail he'd avoided mentioning hung in the air between us. The fight. Chase had to survive one more, both physically and mentally. Then he'd be alone with her.

I bit my tongue, struggling to shove thoughts of what could happen from my mind, the fight, the change, Lotli. "This way," I said, taking off at a fast walk.

Dad caught up with me, his hand swept my arm. "Annie, remember, if something does happen between them, it doesn't matter. Sex isn't everything."

I hurried my steps, jogging out of the moonlight and into the eerie brightness of the tunnel's flickering torches. My brain knew it was true. But my heart rebelled against the possibility. Of course sex mattered. Or at least it had to a little.

The march of footsteps came from ahead of us, followed by the distant outline of a swiftly approaching guard. We slowed our steps and bowed our heads submissively. The guard passed without a glance.

Once his footsteps faded Dad continued, his voice a cautious whisper, "I'm serious. Lotli and Chase. Your mother. Malphic. What happened or happens between them. That doesn't matter."

"Don't tell me you wouldn't like to see Malphic dead," I muttered before I could stop myself.

He shrugged. "Maybe. Okay, I did for a long time. But in the scope of things that could happen, Chase and Lotli . . . it doesn't matter." He patted his chest. "What's in here matters, right?"

"I guess." But mostly I didn't want to talk or even think about it.

We came to where the tunnel intersected another. I turned right. My muscles were tense, my insides on fire from so many emotions going every which way.

Dad leaned in close to me and chuckled. "To tell you the truth, I wish Malphic's nuts would shrivel up and drop off."

I let out a long breath, my tension melting away. "I wish all her hair would fall out—and her teeth."

Dad gave my hand a squeeze. "That's my girl. Now let's get this done."

In silence we hurried on toward the portico and main palace, the swish of our robes loud in the empty tunnel. On either side of us, frescos of glowing genies battling with humans, shadows, and wolfmen that were transforming into whirlwinds decorated the walls. Swords. Knives. Rods. Whips. Hatchets. Blood. Guts. The deeper we went into the tunnel, the more alive the frescos seemed in the gloom and torchlight.

Finally, I slowed. "It's awful quiet around here."

Dad nodded. "Where do you think Malphic is?"

"Too close," I said as two guards and a man in flowing black robes appeared in the tunnel ahead of us.

CHAPTER 22

When we headed into the arena to spar or fight,
I used to calm myself instead of getting hyped up
like most of the slaves . . . I'd walk down that tunnel
and pretend I was walking down my parents' driveway,
the trees' canopy overhead, my mother holding my hand.

—Chase Abrams

The genie in a flowing black robe and his retinue of guards strode straight down the tunnel toward us. The robed genie was too short to be Malphic. But that didn't mean he wasn't dangerous.

Dad dipped his head and stepped close to the tunnel wall.

I fell in behind him, glancing up from lowered lids.

"I'm hungry enough to eat a goat's asshole," the guy in the robe said to the bulkier guard.

The guard grunted. "That would be better than the shit they fed us this morning."

A lump knotted in my throat. My legs trembled. The march of their boots and the rustle of their leather armor and the robe's swish seemed deafening as they passed. But they were moving on. And that's what mattered.

The footsteps stopped, replaced by the scrape of boots doing an about-face.

A voice boomed. "You there, eunuch. Halt!"

The air went out of my lungs. I slowly turned to face them. I was dead. So dead.

I peeked up subserviently through the keyhole frame of my hood. The bulkier guard was striding back toward us. But he wasn't aiming for me!

In two strides, the guard swaggered up to within inches of Dad and glowered down. "I don't recognize you."

The guard had a shaven head, and a narrow strip of dark beard—Fuck! The Hulk.

I glanced at the other guard. He was taller and loaded with scars, tattoos, and gold piercings. His sleek ponytail was pulled up high on his head. Crap. I knew him, too. The last time I was here, we'd outsmarted him.

The Hulk took another step and yanked Dad's hood back.

Shock rocked me to the core. I bit my lip, holding in a gasp. The man beneath the hood was Dad. But not the Dad I knew. His mop of graying brown hair was gone; his head was now shaven and smudged with tribal swaths of red and black. A gruesome scar that I'd never noticed through his hair puckered and zigzagged across his skull and ended in a large dent. He'd told me about a car accident he'd been in as a teenager, but I'd never dreamed he'd been quite so disfigured. He looked forbidding, powerful—and crazy, like . . . Well, like he belonged in the realm.

Dad smoothed his hood back even farther, exposing his entire head and neck. He folded his arms across his chest, casually scratching his elbow. "Now do you recognize me?"

Pride replaced my terror. Dad was amazing. And if he could fake it like a pro, then so could I. After all, I'd learned from the best. Namely, him. I pulled my shoulders back, stepped forward, and grunted. "We're lookin' for Jaquith."

Hulk ignored me and gave Dad another once-over. No recognition showed in his eyes. He harrumphed. "They should have taken your head with your nuts."

The black-robed genie stepped toward us. "I think Jaquith's in the magi's study," he said to me. His gaze shifted to the Hulk. "Are you done screwing around? I'm starved."

The Hulk shot Dad another glare. His top lip curled in disgust. "You smell horrible."

"Been inspecting the kitchen." Dad grinned.

Hulk rolled his eyes. "No wonder you stink." He spun around and marched off down the tunnel, his buddies going with him.

Dad dropped his voice to a hush. "You don't really think we should find Jaquith, do you?"

"Of course not. But he's the head eunuch. We're eunuchs. It made sense for us to be looking for him."

Smiling, Dad pulled his hood up. "Well, it was a marvelous bit of fast thinking on your part."

"Kind of like your hair?" I whispered.

He cuffed me in the shoulder. "Don't go getting any ideas. Leave the hair loss to Lotli."

As we started walking again, a new level of worry began prickling under my skin. We'd been incredibly lucky so far, but the chance of that continuing was getting slimmer with each step.

We came out of the tunnel and strode into the open air of a raised portico. The faint scent of musk wafted out of the palace's arched doorway, only a few yards to our left. On the other side of us, stone terraces and walks dropped down into torchlit gardens. Way below that, I could make out the glow of buildings and the awnings of perhaps a bazaar, and the dark line of the outer wall, then the endless darkness of the Red Desert beyond that. The moon was halfway across the sky. Almost midnight. At best, there was another five hours until sunrise.

Without a word, we rushed through the arched doorway

and into the palace. As we started down the hallway, an oily orange aroma joined the heavier musk scent—and my prickle of worry transformed into a full-blown sense of fear. There were no guards stationed along the hallway or at any of the doorways. None at all. There weren't any servants or other eunuchs, not even distant voices.

We went by the weaving room, where I'd seen the ropes of silkworms and looms that made the magic carpets, where Jaquith had confronted me and I'd learned he was Chase's half brother. It was also silent, except for the murmur of moth wings and the rustle of hatching cocoons.

"It's too quiet," I whispered to Dad.

He nodded, but tilted his head to indicate we should keep going.

I led the way to the reception hall. I'd first seen Mother there, amongst a crowd of Malphic's party guests. It was so different this time, just an empty gold and white box with pillars and doors on all sides. I curled my hands up into my sleeves, rubbing a chill from my arms. Something strange was going on here.

With all my senses on high alert, I gestured toward a curtained doorway on the other side of the room and hushed my voice even further. "The harem's through there."

Dad rested a hand on my shoulder. "Like Old Samuel always said, 'The straight path is the wisest.'"

Yeah, right, I thought. Our crazy ancestor, Samuel, had a lot of wise advice, according to Dad. He also was known for making some very stupid mistakes.

I pressed my fingers against my chest to make sure the poison ring was still in my bra, my little safety measure. Then, shoulder to shoulder with Dad, I tiptoed to the doorway and slipped into the harem, the curtains rippling silently shut behind us.

The harem's mirror-tiled walls glistened like ice, so did the long silver banners that draped from the ceiling. But the room was hot, more like an airless tomb than a frozen cathedral.

We headed for the center of the room, where an island of gold furniture and potted palms gathered around a flaming pit. Though I knew a soundproofing spell hung over the room, it was strange to feel the fire's warmth before I got close enough to hear its crackle.

My eyes zeroed in on a large cabinet with glass doors, and a barely controllable desire for vengeance hummed into my blood. Behind the doors were rows and rows of bottles, prison cells for Malphic's concubines, prisoners like my mother.

I touched Dad's sleeve. His face was hidden by his hood, and his posture revealed nothing. But his rage hung in the air, palpable and even hotter than mine, mingling with guilt at not having rescued her sooner.

"We need to do this fast," I said to bring his head back where it belonged. This wasn't the time for regrets or anger. It was time to focus. We needed to get Mom, get back to Chase, and get home.

Dad nodded and reached inside his robe.

The problem at hand was a small, fist-size glowing symbol on the cabinet's door. Genies couldn't get through locks, hence all the magic carpets and curtains. But this cabinet was an exception. Kate had done some research and concluded that the doors were some kind of illusion, kept shut by a magic seal shaped like Chase's brand: the djinn word for *slave*. Kate had concocted a spell to neutralize the lock and had given it to Dad.

"Wait a minute," I said as an idea came to me. It made more sense to be sure Mom was inside one of the bottles before we wasted time breaking in.

Slipping off the egg pendant, I dangled it in front of the cabinet. "Have I lost my mother?" I murmured.

I waited, focusing on those words and channeling my energy toward the egg. I breathed in through my nose and let it out slowly. After a long moment, the egg swung back and forth, toward and away from the cabinet.

"Is she here?" I asked. The egg circled, then began to swing slowing, side to side. I moved the necklace horizontally along the cabinet until it started circling again. I lowered it and it stopped moving. I raised it toward the top shelf and it began to swing again. "Here?" I said, holding it in front of a deep sapphire bottle with a gold rim. The chain vibrated in my hand. Mother. She was in that bottle.

Joy soared through me. I wanted to grab Dad and give him a huge hug. But I forced my excitement down, slipped the necklace back on, and stepped aside so Dad could work the spell Kate had given him.

He pushed back his sleeve and a small metal tool appeared in his hand.

Not a spell. A glass cutter.

Even without seeing his face I knew he was grinning. I also suspected this was no common cutter. I mean, cutting the glass was the perfect way to bypass the glowing lock, but these doors for sure weren't normal either.

As if by magic, a handful of iridescent sand appeared in Dad's other hand. "Crystal, quartz, diamond, gossamer. Unyoke, divide, sever, cleave . . ." he chanted under his breath—

A swish of movement sounded behind us, and a deep voice growled, "Break that spell and Malphic will be here in a second."

I swung around and found myself nose-to-nose with a tall, broad-shouldered eunuch. The hood of his brown robe hid his face, but the leather gloves and short whip hanging from his belt revealed what I couldn't see: a black man who had once been as handsome as Chase, his face now warped by a vicious scar that ran down from his left eye to his upper lip, giving a cruel twist to his mouth.

"Nice to see you again, Annie," he said. He rested his hand

meaningfully on a second whip, a long, coiled one partly hidden by the folds of his robe. He hadn't been carrying that one the last time we met.

My mouth went dry. I glanced at Dad, my voice quavering. "Ah—Dad—this is Chase's half brother, Jaquith."

Dad dipped his head politely, but his hand eased toward a fold in his robe as if going for a salt shank.

Jaquith rested back on his heels. "I heard you two were looking for me?"

I steadied my voice. "Yeah. The guards told you?" What else could I say to him when I didn't know if he was on Malphic's side or our saving grace?

Dad cleared his throat. "So do you have a better suggestion about how we could get into the cabinet?"

"I do." His gaze swept my body, a quick assessment. "You might be small enough to do it. Follow me." He turned away.

"Wait a minute," I said sharply. I cringed, instinctively fearing I'd spoken too loud. But the room had swallowed my voice, so I went on. "Where is everyone? Malphic. The guards. The other eunuchs . . . Everyone."

"It's the zenith—the middle of the night. Most have eaten and are bathing or resting." He paused for a moment as if puzzled I would ask. Then his voice lightened. "When you were here before, it was a festival night. There is no resting then."

My gaze darted to his, cautious hope fluttering in my chest. "So Chase is resting, too?" Had the guards and eunuch lied or been mistaken about the next fight?

Jaquith shook his head. "None of us can stop what's happening to him. But we may be able to help your mother—if we hurry."

Dad shook his head. "Annie's not going anywhere until you explain."

"We're going to borrow Malphic's key." He swiveled and started across the hall.

Dad held his ground, not moving a step.

Understanding suddenly dawned on me. The zenith. Bathing. The key. The last time I was here I'd seen the communal baths. They weren't far away. Malphic would have his clothes off and the key would be in them.

"Come on." I snagged Dad's arm and set off after Jaquith. We had to trust him. There wasn't enough time not to.

My brain took another leap of logic and I quickened my steps even more. The glowing seal on the cabinet looked like Chase's brand. That mark had been made by the retractable branding iron built into the moonstone decorated handle of Malphic's knife. Chase had taken that knife from Malphic five years ago and still had it. But I'd seen Malphic with a duplicate moonstone knife since then. It was always with him. What if—

Letting go of Dad, I caught up with Jaquith. "You're talking about stealing Malphic's knife. It's not just a branding iron, is it?"

"Borrow. Not steal," he said, very low.

My mouth dried as Jaquith headed toward a narrow, curtained doorway instead of leading us toward the communal baths. Next to the doorway a wooden screen was set into the wall. It was pierce-carved with dragon and peacock decorations. Tendrils of heavily scented musky-orange smoke drifted out through it.

Jaquith looked at Dad, then nodded at a bench that sat below the screen. "You wait there," he said.

Dad stiffened. "She's not going anywhere without me."

"You might want to think twice about that unless you truly are a eunuch." Jaquith's voice was firm. He jutted his head at the doorway we'd taken into the harem and to another large archway on the farther end of the room. "The main entries are safe for any male. But if an intact male enters this one, it would feel like a camel had bitten his testicles. Then the organ would drop off."

I cringed. But it did partly answer something I'd been wondering about. I'd always believed men weren't allowed in harems, and yet I'd seen warriors walk through this room before. "So this isn't the harem?"

"This is the harem gallery," Jaquith clarified. "Malphic grants gifts here and"—he hesitated, as if searching for the right phrase—"no disrespect intended, but this is where he displays his most favored acquisitions. Beyond its walls is the harem proper."

Display. Grant gifts. His words made my head swim. It was almost unbearable to think of my mother being used like that, not to mention all the other women and possibly men as well.

Jaquith gestured forcefully at the bench under the pierce-carved screen. "We don't have time to debate this. Sit. Let the smoke fumigate your clothes and body. Your daughter will be right back."

CHAPTER 23

Abilities lurk within the nooks and crannies
of our mind and souls, lost continents of
knowledge and power awaiting our discovery.

—Persistence Freemont, "Introduction to the Arts"
In *Compendium of Psychic Sciences (Vol. 1)*
Boston, Massachusetts: Coryphacus Press, 1982

I stepped through the curtained doorway and into a closet-size room so dense with plumes of musky-orange-scented smoke that I had to cover my nose to keep from choking. Overhead, the ghostly shapes of towels and robes hung in the haze. Everywhere, earthenware jugs and bowls weighed down racks and shelves, each labeled with line drawings of plants and symbols that resembled the ones on the poison ring, the djinn's magical language. In this case I suspected the words were fairly common: orange oil, myrrh resin, cinnamon bark. Incense waiting to be sprinkled on the hot coals that glowed in a pan that spanned most of the floor.

Jaquith touched my shoulder and nodded ahead. Squinting through the smoke, I made out another pierce-carved screen, nearly wall size. On the other side of it, a small alcove and pot-ted rose topiaries shielded what lay beyond from my view. But the unmistakable trickle and slosh of water suggested it was a communal bath. As I tiptoed closer to the screen, what Jaquith had in mind became obvious.

A stone bench was shoved tight against the farther side of the screen. A gold robe and long white tunic were draped across it. Next to them lay an assortment of sashes, belts, and weapons, including Malphic's moonstone knife. There was no way to reach through the pierce-carved screen. However, the screen did not go all the way to the floor. If someone were small enough they might be able to wiggle under the screen and come out on the other side, beneath the stone bench.

I took off my dagger so it wouldn't clink on the floor and tucked it into a pocket. Whether I could fit through the slender gap was a good question. Lotli could have done it with ease, but right now she was—

Images of Lotli walking her fingers down Chase's sweat-slicked arms wormed their way into my head, her bending close to the fight cage's bars, licking her lips and whispering lies about me, about him and her.

Clenching my teeth, I willed Lotli from my head. I dropped down on my hands and knees, and started belly-crawling under the screen. It was only once I was halfway under the screen—and too late to retract—when another thought rose. Could this be a setup? A clever way to separate me and Dad and make capturing us easier?

My shoulder bumped the screen. It jiggled. I froze, not even daring to breathe. One second passed, then two. I let out my breath, flattened myself as much as possible, and wormed forward until the front half of my body was through to the other side and beneath the bench. I couldn't worry. I just needed to get the knife as fast as possible. It wasn't like I was out in the open. The rose topiaries did partially shield me from their view.

The air was hotter and more humid on this side of the screen. The sound of the water sloshing was louder, too. I caught a glimpse of palm trees, white sand, and a waterfall trickling into a scallop-shaped pool. The Sovereign Mistress Vephra lay naked in the pool's shallow end, her black hair sprawled out across the water. Malphic was breaststroking toward her like a dark-eyed barracuda, the waves from his movement lapping against her very pregnant belly. Water shone on his shaved head and trimmed black beard, the tattoos that covered his face and body glistened.

I bit my lip, an evil thought forming. What would happen if someone dumped a few sandwich bags full of salt into that water? I frowned. For that matter, why were beings that were made of smoke-less fire paddling around in a pool?

Malphic went under the water, resurfacing a second later next to her belly. A wicked gleam sparked in his eyes. He scooped her from the water, carrying her out of the pool and toward a mound of embroidered floor pillows. She struggled against him and let out a playful squeal. I closed my eyes. I really didn't want to witness whatever was about to happen. But this was perfect timing for me.

I pushed even farther forward and twisted onto my back to where I could see the clothes and weapons. One inch at a time, I reached toward the knife until I wrapped my fingers around its handle. It was thicker and heavier than I expected. I slowly brought it downward.

Vephra murmured. I heard a shushing noise. A cushion moving? A footstep?

Heart in my throat, I began to slither backward. Jaquith's hand pressed my leg, holding me still. His other hand appeared from under the screen. "Give it to me," he said, barely audible. "Don't move. I'll be right back with it."

As the weight of the knife left my grip, an uneasy feeling washed over me. I wasn't thrilled by the idea of leaving everything in Jaquith's hands. What if he had totally different plans for the knife than he claimed? Even if he didn't, what if something went wrong? I had no way of knowing if Dad was okay or not. Still, if Jaquith was trustworthy and all went well, then my waiting made perfect sense. The less movement I made, the less likely we'd get caught.

A flump-flump noise, as if someone were pounding bread dough, came from the general direction of Malphic and Vephra. I shifted ever so slightly and glanced their way.

Atop the cushions, she lay on her side. Malphic knelt over her, working his forearm against her buttocks, rolling strokes, firm and determined. He picked up a lavender bottle, poured oil onto his hands, and then moved downward, his fingers working against the tattooed cords of her legs. She stretched out and I got a full view of her swollen stomach, the tanned skin of her taut belly painted in a spiraling design like a maze. As Malphic massaged the inside of her thighs, her whole body began to shimmer brilliant blue. An image of Chase glowing when we made love flashed into my head, like brilliant blue diamonds.

Chase. I rubbed a cramp from my neck. I hoped with all my heart that his next fight was over with and that he was fine. Not that I wanted him to kill someone else, or be alone with Lotli.

An image of them alone in a cell burst into my mind, her stroking his body, caring for his wounds.

A headache pulsed in my temples. I scrunched down and nibbled on the willow bracelet that Selena had given me. Not a lot, just enough to stop the ache. I glanced back through the pierce-carved screen. Freaking hell. What was taking Jaquith so long?

Malphic moved on, his fingers anointing Vephra's calves, her ankles, her feet, each toe, his fist rolling against the arch. She rolled onto her back. His hands slid up her hips. His butt was taut, muscles flexed. The air around him shimmered vibrant blue and began to crackle and vibrate just like when Chase and I made—

I clamped my hands over my mouth, a sour tang creeping up my throat. Oh my God. I really didn't want to see this. But like the worst kind of voyeur, I couldn't stop watching. This man had kidnapped my mother. This man was Chase's father.

Something hard nudged my leg. Malphic's knife. I took it from Jaquith's hand, snaked out from under the bench, and put it back where I'd found it. I started to wriggle back under the screen, but I couldn't stop myself from taking one last look.

Vephra lay on her other side now, Malphic's hand just retreating from under her hips, as if he'd helped her roll over. Her body glistened from head to toe, shades of pale blue and lavender. Her eyes flickered closed as he began to massage her exposed hip, rolling his forearm against it, gentle and firm. A fluttery feeling tingled in my stomach, a strange mix of uneasiness, joy, and fear. I was glad and surprised to see this gentle and caring side of him. But what kind of man could do this and at the same time force his son to fight for his life and sanity?

I shook the sight from my mind and wormed backward under the screen. Jaquith pulled me to my feet. In a second, we were through the curtained doorway, sprinting across the harem gallery toward where Dad stood next to the cabinet, holding the deep sapphire bottle.

Thick gray smoke spiraled out of it, widening and narrowing as it curved downward and solidified into a tall, willowy woman in a deep crimson sari, golden skin, full lips. A ribbon held her hair up in a tousled twist. Mother.

She stared at Dad and he gaped at her. As we hurried toward them, I wasn't sure if they were going to embrace or simply stand there forever.

Suddenly an oily black puddle of darkness skimmed across the floor toward them.

"Look out!" I screeched as the puddle rose up, a shadow-genie as brawny as Malphic's most vicious spies.

Dad flung the bottle onto the divan and dove at the shadow, a salt shank in his hand. There was a wet *thwack*. Black goo flew from the shadow's arm. The shadow staggered backward, yanking the shank from his flesh. Dad pulled a knife. The shadow charged, a trail of dark ooze spewing out from his dissolving arm.

I grabbed my flashlight, pinpointing its beam on the shadow's face. He swung toward me and Jaquith, his face a whirlwind of anger and pain. I pocketed the flashlight and went for my bags of salt. He rocketed at us. I shot forward, throwing all my bags at the same time.

They hit him square in the chest, salt spraying out. His body exploded, a million black sparks. They splattered to the floor in an oily mass, then sucked back together, distorting into a gyrating version of Edvard Munch's screaming man.

Mother's face went white, her gaze flitting from the writhing shadow to me and back.

"We need to get him confined," Jaquith said.

Dad's eyes darted to the sapphire bottle. "Too bad we can't put him in that."

A bottle. An image of Selena flashed into my head, her standing in my bedroom not long before we left. She'd tapped a finger against the side of her head. "*Magic is partly about focus and accessing energy, about self-control. But it mostly involves discovering spells and remembering words. . . .*"

My ears rang, my thoughts jumbling as two other memories fought to find their way to the surface at once. I snatched the bottle from the divan, my breath coming in short pants. Somewhere in the background Dad said something, so did Mother and Jaquith. But their voices hummed like bees in the soundproof room and beneath the roar of the memories that vied for me to recall them and understand.

I circled my finger around the bottle's gold rim, focusing with every ounce of my being. *Guide me, Hecate. Keeper of the Gateways, show me the path,* I prayed.

A strange tightness played behind my ears and they began to ring. That sound transformed into words I didn't understand. It was an incantation I'd heard spoken twice before: once when Grandfather used it to return Culus to the poison ring, and again when Malphic commanded my ethereal body into the decanter the last time I was here. I didn't know the language, but the words formed on my tongue, readying to be made audible by my lips.

I closed my eyes and raised the bottle. My mouth filled with the taste of salt and mushrooms, and the incantation flowed out, a living thing slithering into the air with an electric prickle. The scent of sandalwood, like Mother. The smell of roses, like Vephra. The rhythm of the incantation spun my thoughts into a fine thread, a single, focused line pulling the shadow-genie's writhing body toward the bottle's mouth, an irresistible tug and as strong as spider silk, a single pulsing vibration plucked on the string of a violin, a whistle in the dark, a ringing in my ears—

Every sensation vanished: the prickle, the sounds in my head . . . everything. Numb and overwhelmed, I stared at the bottle in my hand. Oily darkness circled the bottom. It spun into blue threads of flame, spiraling toward the open top.

Dad whipped the bottle from my hands and corked it with its stopper. He shook his head at me. "I don't know when you learned that trick. But I'm impressed."

Jaquith's eyes were wide with amazement. "You know the old language?"

"Ah—" *Know* wasn't exactly the right word for it.

Mother took me by the elbow. "This way. We need to hide the bottle and get out of here."

That brought me back to my senses. I wrenched my arm

from her grip, refusing to budge. "We have to get Chase and Lotli."

"After we go to my chambers," she insisted.

Heat flooded through me. Who was she to suddenly take charge? This wasn't her rescue plan. Come to think about it, why hadn't she tried to escape on her own? "No," I said tartly. "There isn't time for side trips."

She flinched back as if I'd physically assaulted her. A pained look hovered in her eyes.

"Annie," Dad said. His voice was hushed, but stern. "We'll do as she says."

I shot Dad a hard look. "Seriously, we don't have time," I mumbled. But as Mother headed across the harem gallery, I followed with everyone else. I should have been excited to see her after so many years, and I was. Sure, her stubborn abrasiveness rubbed me the wrong way and it made me wary. But the resentment I harbored toward her surprised even me, and I hated myself for it. She was my mother. We were together again, finally.

Mother reached the farthest wall and stopped in front of a curtained doorway, her stance once more confident, her composure regained. "Wait here," she said to the men. "Annie, follow me. We need to adjust our outfits."

My anger returned, blood boiling. But I kept my voice calm. "You go on. I'm fine just the way I am."

Dad pressed his hand against my spine, propelling me forward. "I'm sure your mother has her reasons."

"I suppose," I said, exasperated. Saying no would only delay us longer.

On the other side of the curtain, Mother and I entered a small vestibule. From there we went into a massive bedroom, heavily draped in crimson silk. A wide doorway shielded by a beaded curtain opened onto a terrace piled with tasseled pillows. Everywhere crystal bowls held single water lilies.

I folded my arms across my chest, standing back and watching while she opened a curtained wardrobe and stashed the bottle behind the line of clothes. As she yanked out veils and sarongs and flung them over her arm, a deep sadness began to replace the resentment and wariness inside me.

The moonstone knife embroidered on all the curtains and pillows, and carved into the headboard made it painfully clear who shared this room with her. I also now suspected she hadn't ordered Dad and Jaquith to wait outside for modesty's sake. It was more out of habit or perhaps it even was a djinn law. Only one man was allowed in this room—and maybe others he favored.

I swallowed a lump in my throat. The last fifteen years had to have been hard on her in ways I didn't even want to imagine. Ways that perhaps had made her feel unworthy of freedom, even when she'd had the chance—like when she chose to stay behind so Chase could have his freedom. Perhaps Dad's love for her was beyond the borders of sanity. But after everything that had happened to her, how would she feel toward him or any man?

I gathered my nerve. It had to be said. "Dad realizes it's not going to be easy once we get back home. He knows . . . Well, you've been separated for a long time. He feels horrible about not helping you."

Mom glanced over her shoulder at me. "None of us can afford to live under regret's shadow, Annie. No guilt. No remorse. Love—even if it's just a memory—that's where we'll have to start."

The sadness swelled inside me, extinguishing what remained of my anger and resentment. I nodded. She was right. And I was glad it was out in the open. If nothing more, it would make things easier between us. "I'm sorry I was an ass out there," I said. "I don't know what came over me."

She turned back to the wardrobe, her shoulders rising like

she was taking a deep breath or biting back tears. Then she plucked out a pair of slippers and carried everything to the bed.

"Both of us need to change our clothes," she announced, laying out two jeweled sarongs.

I eyed the fancy clothes. This was her idea of *adjusting* our outfits? "I've got a woman-warrior's tunic on under this robe. It would be faster than changing into all that."

"Are you built like a warrior? If not, you'll get us all caught." She set a silk head mask on top of each set of clothes.

My stomach lurched. She wasn't laying out just any kind of outfit. These were the *robes* worn by the human concubines, to give their ethereal bodies form when they appeared in public or serviced their masters.

I scowled. I could lie and claim that changing clothes would mess with the Methuselah oil's effectiveness.

Mother rested one hand on her hip. "Beyond the walls of the harem, women are required to have two escorts: a eunuch and a guard. One woman with three eunuchs or a woman with two eunuchs and a scrawny warrior would be instantly detained. Two robed women with two eunuchs is inappropriate—but it will most likely be overlooked, especially since our party will include me and the head eunuch."

My skin crawled as I picked up one of the head masks. It was creepy. But once I pulled it on, instead of my normal features all anyone would see was smooth silk with hollows where my eyes should be and rises in place of my nose and cheekbones. It was the perfect disguise.

"You can keep your underwear and jewelry, but remove the tunic and mitts," she said.

I shut my brain off and dressed quickly. In truth, the sarong and silk head mask fit more comfortably than the brown eunuch's robe with its rough fabric and massive hood. I could see better, too.

Mother helped me drape the veils over my head. The scent

of her sandalwood perfume drifted off of them and from the sarong, enveloping me in its embrace. I closed my eyes, breathing in her smell. Once she was done, I adjusted my necklaces to make sure the egg pendant was as hidden as the flashlight and dagger that were tucked into the folds at my waistline.

"Perfect," she said. Her voice gentled. "If I'd known you were coming, I wouldn't have asked you to wear this. I'd have acquired an herbalist's or a weaver's smock for you. That's what I wear when I slip away to tutor the boys. Chase was one of my favorites, bright and always caring for the others. A little hardheaded, though."

My face heated and I smiled at her. "I really like him, too."

Her gaze trapped mine, her expression hardening. "You do realize it might be too late for Chase?"

A sick feeling twisted inside me, but I kept my head raised and my voice inflexible. "No matter what, he's coming home with us."

She smiled, a reaction that took me by surprise. "You certainly do remind me of your aunt Kate." A glint of pride touched her eyes. "But not just her, you're very much like my grandmother. If she'd ever been attacked by a shadow, she'd have handled herself exactly like you did. You've heard the story about the blacksmith and King Solomon, right?"

I nodded, vaguely recalling something about the blacksmith being a toolmaker and sitting at King Solomon's right hand, though I couldn't understand why she'd bring that up right now.

"We descended from that blacksmith, you and I. Did your father ever tell you that?"

"No," I said. But maybe he had and I'd passed it off as one of his made-up stories. I'd only recently discovered that those wild stories were in reality true.

She looked straight into my eyes. "One of Malphic's favorite stories is about how Solomon's genies bestowed a gift upon the blacksmith in honor of his bravery and cunning, a gift that allowed him to instill *his* magic into the tools and knives he created."

I blinked at her, my head whirring from what she'd said. *Our ancestor. His magic. His knives. Malphic's favorite story.* I longed to ask her what it all meant, but this wasn't the place or time to get into it.

She touched my arm. "I wanted to make sure you knew. In case something happens."

I glared at her. "Don't even say that. We're all going to be fine."

"I hope you're right, Annie. I really do."

As she turned and began pulling on her robe, I hugged myself against a sudden chill. Maybe I'd sounded confident, but fear had gripped me until I could barely move.

Please, Hecate. Please get us all out of this alive.

CHAPTER 24

Lost in darkness, your touch I cannot feel.
Copper closes over my eyes. I cannot taste.
I cannot hear. Oblivion offers a glistening
star, relief from a prison with no bars.

—From "Lost in Darkness"
www.NorthTunes.com

Once Mother was ready, the two of us joined Dad and Jaquith in the harem gallery. Dad cleared his throat as if startled by our strange appearance, but none of us wasted time on questions or explanations. We just took off, racing out of the harem and through the reception hall.

When we reached the weaving room's curtained doorway, Mother slipped inside. We swept after her into the room's dim red light, zigzagging between looms, around baskets and stacks of carpets. She ducked behind a machine covered in spikes and into a slender doorway, all but invisible unless someone knew it was there.

At that point, Jaquith took over as the lead, down steep staircases, out into a palm-sheltered courtyard, and down again to the lower levels of the palace and into a narrow hallway. This might have been the route Mother used when she snuck off to teach the slaves, but clearly Jaquith often took it as well.

Mostly I was grateful that his feelings for Chase had made him an ally instead of our enemy.

Servants appeared. First one and then more of them, rushing back and forth with slop buckets and baskets of laundry in their arms. Zenith, or whatever they called their siesta time, had to be over, at least for them.

Ahead the hallway opened into a wide chamber. Banners and shields decorated its walls. At its center, a ceiling-high cage held a massive black eagle. Near the cage, an elderly guard slouched in a chair. He snapped to his feet as we entered, his gaze darkening as he studied Mother and me.

Sweat drizzled down my temples, sticking the silk head mask against my face. This wasn't good. Not at all.

Mother flicked her veils back, left me behind, and strode straight at the guard. "We've been waiting since before the zenith for our escorts. What's going on down here? Stuffing your bellies instead of following orders? Malphic's going to be furious."

"I—I just came on duty, Mistress," he stuttered, scuffing backward.

Jaquith swaggered forward, his hand resting on his whip. "Aren't there supposed to be two guards at this post? Where is your partner?"

"He's in the latrine. He ate some bad meat, sir."

Dad scoffed. "More likely he drank too much wine."

I slipped up next to Mother. It was time to top off this bit of playacting and move on. I tugged her arm. "We need to get going. I'm dreadfully late and *he* doesn't like to be kept waiting."

"Yes, come along," Mother said, ushering me past the guard. It was easy to guess what he might assume: two concubines in robes sent to meet a man, most likely a favored guard or officer since we had to be near the barracks by now.

Mother and I swished down another hallway, veils flying

out, silk slippers shushing against the floor. Dad and Jaquith trailed behind with heads bowed like humble eunuchs. We kept on going, moving quickly. It wasn't until we came to the top of a rather bleak circular stairwell that Mother slowed and stepped into the darkness at the edge of the hallway.

She leaned close to Jaquith. "This is the staircase, right?"

He nodded and drew us into a huddle. His gaze went from Dad to me. "Below are the berserker quarters. Its cells lie within the outer wall and run its entire length, interspersed with stairwells. Chase will be in one of these cells. Once his change is complete the cell will become his home, unless by some miracle he comes out of it sane. If he becomes uncontrollable, it will be his tomb."

His home. His tomb. I shuddered at the thought. The staircase already reminded me of the bone-laden catacombs I'd seen in Paris, forbidding and unnervingly ominous. No matter what, I wouldn't leave Chase in a place like that.

Dad rubbed his hands together. "All righty, then. How are we going to get in these berserker quarters? I'm sure there are guards. But what else is down there?"

"Getting in isn't the issue," Jaquith said. "It's getting out that's the problem."

Human howls reverberated up the stairwell, followed by manic laughter.

My heart leapt into my throat. We all looked at one another. *Chase.* Oh my God. That couldn't be him.

I toughened my voice. "But there is a way to escape, right? You wouldn't have brought us if there wasn't."

"I wouldn't have let Chase get trapped in the first place, if I could have prevented it." He lowered his voice. "There are wards on the stairwells. Anyone can walk down them, but going up them is similar to crossing the veil between realms. As long as we have your flutist, she'll be able to get us out—" He stopped abruptly, smoothing his hands down his sides.

Dad pushed his hood back. "But they wouldn't just leave a eunuch in a cell with a warrior on the verge of going berserk— that's the problem, right? We're going to need to figure out where Lotli is as well."

Jaquith shook his head. "No, they would do exactly that— whether the eunuch was willing to care for the warrior or not. One live berserker is worth hundreds of our lives. And, if Chase makes it through the change with his mind intact, then no cost would be too high in Malphic's eyes. Chase would be a Death Warrior, a rare half-ifrit survivor, a victor as well as his son."

"So what's the problem, then?" Dad asked impatiently.

"It's not exactly a problem. There is another way to escape. The berserker cells have exits into the desert, so they can patrol the perimeter of the fortress. It would get us stranded outside the walls—and it's harsh out there, beyond Malphic's protective spells and wards. But it is another route."

"Shush." Mother raised her hand to silence him.

The far-off clip of boots sounded, coming toward us down the hallway. More than one pair. Maybe more than a dozen.

We bolted for the forbidding stairwell, fleeing downward as quietly as we could. Shimmering silver symbols coated the dark walls. Under my feet, the stone treads vibrated. A creepy-crawling sensation prickled up my legs, but disappeared when I reached the bottom.

The clip of boots passed in the hallway over our heads, re-verberating down the stairwell before fading as they moved on.

"That was close," Mother whispered.

I glanced around, getting my bearings. In both directions, a gloomy, catacomb-like tunnel lined with black carpeted door-ways stretched off into darkness. Jaquith had said the berserker quarters spanned the entire length of the fortress's outer wall. That left us with miles of tunnel and potentially hundreds of cells to search.

"We'll need to break into two teams," Mother said. "It's the fastest way to find him."

I smiled. "Not necessarily." I pulled the egg pendant out from the neckline of my sarong and let it dangle. I focused my energy and a tingling sensation sparked in my chest, sweeping toward my arm. "What direction do I go to find Chase? Right? Left?"

The egg hung motionless. But the same crawling sensation I'd just felt in the stairwell prickled the soles of my feet. An intense hum filled my ears.

"Something wrong?" Dad asked.

I shook my head and the hum as well as the sensation vanished. "I think the ward on the stairwell is interfering."

Jaquith nodded. "Quite likely. It's powerful. But its effects should weaken once you get farther away."

"How far?" Mother said.

"It's impossible to say. Maybe never down here." He turned to Dad, his voice becoming somber. "We should break into teams, like Susan suggested. You and her should go check in one direction, while Annie and I do the other. A concubine and eunuch. Someone who has lived in the fortress with someone who hasn't."

"I don't like it," Dad said.

I gathered the necklace up in my hand, curling my fingers around the egg and pressing it against my chest. I didn't like the idea either, but—"It makes sense and it'll be a lot faster. If you two find him first, one of you can come and get us. If we find him, we'll let you know."

Mother glanced to the right, down the tunnel. "But how are we going to know which cell they're in? We can't just blindly walk through every carpet and hope for the best."

I nibbled my bottom lip, a touch of moisture clinging to my head mask. There had to be a solution. Chase was counting on us. He was hurting, mentally and physically.

An image of Chase, looking at me through the fight cage bars, flooded my mind: His face darkened by beard stubble. One of his eyes bruised and swollen shut, blood crusting along the lid. His nose flat. His lips split open. Bruises. Blood. So much blood—

That was it! "Blood," I said. "Chase was hurt. There'll be fresh blood on the floor you can track him with. We can do the same or use the pendulum if it starts working."

Jaquith nodded. "This is the section closest to the fight cage. If we're going to see a blood trail, it'll be somewhere in this general area."

Dad and Mother took off down the right-hand tunnel. Jaquith and I went left.

Luckily, there were only doorways on one side of the tunnel. So I crept along close to that side of the wall, letting the egg dangle and trying to ignore the sensation and hum as I murmured, "Where is Chase? Help me find what is lost."

The egg moved, but it was a natural sway, keeping time with my footsteps, almost brushing each carpeted doorway as I passed.

"*Aiyeeeeeeee!*" A bloodcurdling scream ripped out from behind the carpet closest to me, sending my pulse into hyperdrive. Almost tripping on the hem of my sarong, I bolted away, egg clutched in my hand, my heart hammering against my ribs.

The carpet began to thump in and out, in and out, harder and harder, as if fists were pounding against it. It stopped moving and a voice mewled, "I can smell you. Your meat. Your blood. Tasty. Tasty."

Jaquith grabbed my arm, towing me to the next doorway. "Don't worry about that one." He gestured back at three white X's chalked at the top of the carpet. "He's been in there a while. He's not going to make it."

I shuddered and I wished with all my heart that I didn't

know what Jaquith meant. The guy was berserk, uncontrollably so. Soon Malphic's magi would drain his energy until he died.

"This is taking too long," Jaquith grumbled. "Before we know it, Malphic will be down here to check on Chase."

He said it offhandedly, almost to himself. But it made getting back into the zone nearly impossible. Still, the crawly sensation was barely noticeable now, the hum fading, and a slight tug from the pendulum insisted we were going the right way. We'd find Chase at any moment. I was sure of it. *And Lotli,* I reminded myself.

I took a deep breath, trying even harder to channel my energy toward the egg.

The next carpet was decorated with copper coins and embroidered with ravens. I held the egg in front of it. It swung back and forth, back and forth, showing no sign of wanting to circle, like it should have done if Chase were behind it.

Still, I felt drawn to study the carpet again. It was dirt free, every thread perfect. It had to have been made and hung recently. When we'd first arrived I'd found Chase easily through a carpet in the inner sanctum. But this carpet didn't look like that one or any I'd noticed before. What if it was messing with my abilities, like the stairwell ward?

"Jaquith?" I said sharply. "Maybe we should check behind this one."

"No," he said without a trace of emotion. "That one's a tomb."

My chest squeezed. Okay. So it wasn't Chase's cell. Still, it seemed whoever they were, they deserved at least a drop of sympathy. I bowed my head, a moment of respect—

My gaze caught on a dark fleck next to my feet, then a larger spot and another, a whole trail of black-red droplets.

I swooped down and ran my fingers across the drops. Their tips came away sticky and as red as they'd been that night on the clifftop. But this time there was no rain to wash the blood away. No chance it wasn't real.

"He's here," I called to Jaquith. No need for my egg now. My heart screamed that he was super close. I scoured the floor and found more drops. A piece of blood-smeared yarn with a tiny silver starfish threaded into it—a charm off Lotli's flute—lay directly beneath a carpeted doorway.

Almost unable to breathe, I pushed my hand against the carpet's darkness. The static shock of its magic prickled my skin. I stepped through it and into a tomb-like chamber lit by a single flickering candle. A chair sat beside a table. On it were a bowl and large stoneware jug. Scattered across the dirt floor as if thrown or torn off in a hurry were a white sash, arm gauntlets, and men's boots.

A flicker of light came from a keyhole-shaped doorway to my left, its brightness casting shadows in my direction. Clearly this wasn't a single-room cell like I'd envisioned. But it was just as tomb-like as I'd feared.

"Chase?" I called, my voice weaker than I'd have preferred. *You promised to forsake him,* I reminded myself. She'll hurt him if you're not careful.

Jaquith stepped out from the carpet and moved up next to me, his voice stronger than mine. "Lotli. Chase. Are you in there?"

Nothing.

A soft, erotic moan whispered out from the other room.

"Lie still." It was Lotli's voice.

CHAPTER 25

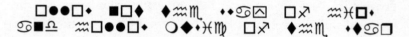

Follow not the sway of hips and hollow music
of the stars. Fear them as you fear oblivion.

—Attributed to Megast-el Zea, Djinn historian
and High Magus

Jaquith seized my arm, but a million berserkers couldn't have held me back. I twisted free, flew to the keyhole doorway—and came to a dead stop on its threshold.

Just ahead of me, in a candlelit bedchamber, Chase lay naked on a thin mattress. He was on his back, his head lolled to one side. His unfocused eyes stared out from a mass of swollen bruises. His arms hung limp. Blood and dirt splattered every inch of him. His pants, scimitar, and knives lay in a pile on the floor between where I stood and the mattress, mingled with Lotli's robe and tunic.

She knelt beside him, nude except for her tiny talisman bag. Her deep-golden skin glistened, pristine and perfect. She pressed her fingertips just below his sternum, pushing upward toward his rib cage. "Relax. Give in to it. Let go," she chanted.

Paralyzed, I could only stare, one hand gripping the doorframe, my heartbeat thrashing in my ears. I knew what I was seeing, but my mind reeled, desperate to block it out.

She slipped up onto him, straddling his abdomen, sliding slowly backward, fingertips pressing even harder. Chase still didn't move, though one part of his body clearly wasn't immune to the wriggle of her hips.

"Chase!" Jaquith barked, drill sergeant tough.

Chase's head and shoulders lifted from the mattress. Lotli drove him back down with her fingertips. She swiveled our way and smiled sweetly at Jaquith. "Give us a moment. We are almost ready to come."

Deep, cold hatred sank into my core. I stepped stiffly toward the mattress, every muscle taut. My fingers tightened around the handle of my dagger. Somewhere behind me, Jaquith shouted for me to stop. But his voice was distant and surreal, an unimportant whisper in a nightmare where I could see nothing except for Lotli.

She smirked at me. "Nice outfit," she said. Then she sliced a glance toward the floor, where her flute lay atop the discarded clothes in a none-too-subtle threat of what she'd do if I tried anything.

Heat raged through me, melting the heavy cold.

"Fuck you!" I screamed, diving for the flute.

But she was faster. Before I could reach it, she was off Chase and on her feet, facing me with the flute in her hands. She ground her fingernails into the threads of hair and corded yarn.

Spasms seized my guts, the lightning strikes of pain knifing every part of my body. My knees buckled. Unable to stand against the pain, I crumpled to the floor, hunching and groaning as I rode the waves of agony.

Lotli brought the flute to her lips and began to play a shrieking melody. She sashayed past me and straight at Jaquith. He clamped his hands over his ears and stumbled backward through the keyhole doorway and into the other room. She prowled after him, hips swaying, each step punctuated by a piping screech.

"Stop it. Stop," Jaquith wailed, sinking to his knees.

A fresh wave of anger surged into my blood. I clenched my teeth against the spasms of pain, sprung to my feet, and charged through the doorway after her. I slammed into her back like an enraged bull. The force sent her flying away from Jaquith and into the table. It toppled, and the bowl and jug thumped to the dirt floor. She went down hard on top of them, the flute soaring from her hands.

I hurtled past Jaquith, snatched the flute, and retreated to the keyhole doorway. Jaquith was shaking his head, no doubt trying to regain his wits. A yard away from him, Lotli was crawling back onto her feet, eyes on me, dark and deadly.

I glanced over my shoulder at Chase. He hadn't moved. He just lay there as if every ounce of life had been drained out of him.

Drained? I did a double take. Despite the dirt and blood, I could make out six dime-size black marks right below Chase's sternum—right where Lotli had pressed her fingertips.

In an instant, I remembered. I'd seen marks like that before. The one time I'd met Zea. I'd thought they were shrunken tattoos.

I gasped. Not just six dots. They formed the shape of an irregular hexagon. The constellation Ophiuchus!

Lotli grabbed the stoneware jug by its handle and staggered toward me, her dark eyes glistening. "You should not have done that."

I clutched her flute against my chest and stood my ground in the doorway. "What the hell are you?" I demanded.

"Hexad! She's a hexad," Jaquith shouted, struggling to his feet.

"A what?" I said to him, totally confused.

Before he could answer, Lotli slammed the jug full force into his face. With a loud *crack,* the jug splintered into pieces. Jaquith's hands went to his face, blood weeping through his fingers as he dropped to the ground, groaning in anguish.

Now empty-handed, Lotli slunk toward me. "We have business to finish with the warrior. And you promised not to interfere."

My mind spun, struggling to put everything together. The egg pendant she'd given me was designed to collect and store energy. The truth was, I'd felt physically better after I'd smashed it. Maybe I'd watched too many science fiction movies, but all I could think of was an energy vampire—or an outer-space succubus of some kind. Jeffrey White hosted a show on history and ancient aliens. Was that why he'd had Newt and Myles kidnap her? Had he suspected something about her origin that we'd missed? My mind sifted through the ancient alien TV shows I'd seen. Stars. Symbols. Interconnections across the globe. Pyramids . . . Oh my God. The Aztec calendar stone in Moonhill's secret tunnel. Now I knew why the face at its center had drawn my attention. The cheekbones. The nose. They resembled Lotli's.

She held her hand out. "Give us our flute."

I stepped back, out from under the doorway and into the bedchamber. My free hand fumbled for my dagger while my other held tight to the flute. "Take one more step and I'll smash it. Seriously, I'll do it."

Rolling her shoulders, she inched closer. "You are too late. He is already ours. Now give us the flute."

"I don't believe you." I pulled the dagger's blade along the flute's length, peeling off a long wedge of waxy yarn and hair, praying it might break her spell, praying it wouldn't do something horrible to me or Chase.

"That will do you no good." Her voice remained steady, her face calm.

Droplets of sweat slid down my rib cage. I peeled off another section and another, slivers of wax sprinkling the silk of my sarong and veils.

Her expression didn't change. But she craned her neck, making a show of looking past me toward Chase. She licked her lips and stroked her talisman bag.

The bag. I'd never had a chance to study it up close and if she hadn't inadvertently drawn my eye to it, I might not have looked at it then. But I had and what I saw made me swallow a gasp. It was decorated with a hexagram.

I stole another look to make sure I'd seen right.

Lotli launched herself at me, snatching the flute. Using it like a bat, she wacked the dagger from my other hand. I whirled on her, grabbed the talisman bag, and yanked, breaking the thong it hung from. She smacked my wrist with the flute. Pain flashed up my arm and the bag went flying.

"I won't let you have Chase," I growled.

She sneered. "He is not yours to save."

Panting, I backed to the center of the bedchamber. Through the doorway I could see Jaquith. His face was smeared with blood. But he was on his hands and knees, and gripping a jagged pottery shard. I had to buy him time to get to his feet. He was stronger. He knew how to fight.

I took another slow step back, toward the mattress and Chase. My soul, my heart, everything screamed for me to jump at her and strangle her with my bare hands. But we needed her to open the veil; without her, none of us would be able to get back up the stairwell and escape this place.

Lotli raised her flute to her lips, a soft whistle sounding as she sidestepped me and headed for Chase.

I had to focus. There had to be a way to turn this from a battle of magic to something I was a master at. Bluffing. Dickering. Dealing. Those were the things I knew the best—

And I did have something to offer her.

As if I were manning a booth at an upper-end antique show, I took a deep breath and straightened my spine. This wouldn't be an easy sell.

"Wait a minute," I said, facing her squarely.

She turned to me. "We have nothing else to say to you."

"What if I could give you a more powerful genie?"

She glanced at where Jaquith was crawling toward the doorway and snorted. "We do not think so. He is not even fully male."

"I'm talking about a different son of Malphic. A full-blooded genie. A true prince. Powerful. Handsome—and fully endowed." I took the poison ring out from my bra. Looking at her steadily, I slid the man-size ring over my middle finger, slipping it back and forth suggestively, while I gave my lips an erotic lick. "He's prepackaged and ready to go."

Her eyes widened. Her lips parted. I had her attention now. *Yeah, come and get him. His name is Culus. He's Malphic's loser son, but you have no way to know that.*

Lotli's head swiveled toward Chase, a lingering gaze. He shifted upright, half-sitting. A feral growl emanated from deep within his chest. His eyes were no longer unfocused, now they looked more fierce and wolfish. Oh God. Was she right? Had I already lost him to her—or the change?

Steadying my voice, I sweetened my tone even more. "Do you really want a berserker when you could have a full-blooded ifrit, as powerful and sane as Malphic? If you want, I'll let you touch the ring. Feel its power before you decide. Once we get back to Moonhill, he's all yours—if you forsake Chase now."

Spittle glittered at the corner of her mouth. She plucked her robe up off the floor and flung it on. One slow step at a time—like an egret stalking its prey—she moved toward me.

Out of the corner of my eyes, I saw Jaquith using the door-frame to pull himself up.

I extended my hand to Lotli, fingers fisted to keep the ring secure.

She slipped up closer than necessary, way too close. I could see the sheen of sweat on her forehead and the pulse of the blue veins beneath her skin. I could even smell the scent of Chase on her. But I stood still as she touched the ring with her fingertip. Her breathing quickened. She tucked her flute under her arm and then curled both her hands around my fingers. Her eyelids closed, lashes fluttering as if in ecstasy.

"Forsake Chase and he is yours," I whispered. "All yours, once we return to Moonhill. I promise."

"This one, he is delicious. Powerful." She moaned. "Yes, I forsake the others. Oh, yes."

Her fingers tightened around mine, a firm handshake to seal the deal. Relief swept through me, so strong it left me light-headed. We could get out of here now. Find Dad and Mother.

"Did you hear that?" Jaquith said.

I glanced to where he stood in the doorway, the pottery shard held at his side. At first I heard nothing. Then my ear caught the sound of distant shouts coming from beyond the cell's carpet-doorway, getting louder by the second.

"Guards. Malphic." I gasped. The room tilted as my light-headedness increased, darkness and stars whirling around me. I felt sick to my stomach, on the verge of passing out. I could barely stand. I felt . . . Holy crap! Drained.

Lotli released my limp hands. She yanked the poison ring off my finger and slid it onto hers. Instantly the wooziness began to subside. But it was too late. She had the flute between her lips. High whistles and shrieks reverberating as she swept toward Jaquith. He dropped to his knees and clamped his hands over his ears, agony written on his face. She skated past him and into the other room. She was leaving. But she couldn't!

I stumbled across the room and past Jaquith. "You vowed to Zea. You swore a blood oath to me," I shouted at Lotli.

She slanted a triumphant look my way, took the flute away from her lips, and smirked. "I have never and will never vow to anyone." She laughed, high and haughty. "Humans are such ridiculous creatures, easily misled with their peculiar devotion to honor and curious moralities." She jutted her chin toward the bedchamber and Chase. "Try to save the boy if you can— and keep the other as well. I have no use for either."

She raised the flute once more, screeching louder than ever as she disappeared through the carpet, crackles of electricity following in her wake.

"Get her!" the men's shouts now echoed right outside the carpet.

Flute music screamed.

"Bitch," a man bellowed.

"That way!" another one yelled, his voice and footfalls dissipating into the distance.

I rushed to Jaquith, taking his arm to help him stand. "Are you all right?"

Two dark figures rushed in through the carpet. I snagged the pottery shard off the floor and flung myself between them and Jaquith, attack ready.

My pulse froze.

Not guards. Not Malphic. It was a brown-robed eunuch and a concubine.

"Annie, it's us," Dad said.

My mind staggered, searching for a place to begin explaining. "Lotli. She—Chase . . ."

"Not now." Dad glanced at Jaquith. "You said the cells have exits that lead into the desert?"

He nodded. "In the bedchamber there's a carpet."

"Let's go," I said, turning toward the other room.

Chase was gone.

CHAPTER 26

On the eve of castration I watched the moon,
dreaming of scrolls and tablets, of magic at
my fingertips instead of a sword in my hand.
I feared not the sacrifice. I feared not
reaching for impossible dreams.

—Jaquith, Son of Malphic and High Eunuch

Not only was Chase gone, but so were his pants and weapons. And there was only one place he could have gone—out through the only carpet that hung in the bedchamber.

We all rushed for that same carpet, Dad helping Jaquith stumble along, Mother and me bringing up the rear. But before I stepped into it, I swooped down and grabbed my dagger and Lotli's talisman bag off the floor. Considering how her music had incapacitated Jaquith, I had the suspicion she'd manage to escape from the guards. That said, no way was I leaving the bag where she could return and reclaim it.

I stepped into the carpet. A waterfall of static shocks prickled my skin. Air pressure built in my ears, popping when I came out the other side and walked into a wave of whirling sand.

The wind pushed me back against the fortress's outer wall. I shielded my eyes with my hands, blinking against the half-light and haze, hoping to catch a glimpse of Chase. If the world inside the fortress was eerie, nighttime beyond the protection of Malphic's walls and wards was a hundred times freakier. Sand snaked along the ground and rose up in twisting waves, shifting from pitch-black to red where the aurora illuminated it. It curled around the outline of battered palms and all but wiped out the glow of the waning moon. Behind me, the *snap-crack* of the fortress's wind-blown banners echoed down from the parapet high above. But there was no trace of Chase. Nothing I could hear or see.

I glanced around and found everyone else about a yard away. Dad had an arm around Jaquith's waist, both of their faces hidden in the depths of their hoods. Mother was winding her veils around her silk-masked face. I followed her lead, looping any loose fabric around my mouth and nose; then I scrunched in closer to them.

"Where do you think Chase went?" I said, my voice barely carrying above the wind. "He can't have gotten far." I left it at that. What I really wanted to know was *why* he'd left the cell without waiting for us. Because he'd been afraid of being cornered by the guards? Or had he fled to protect us from what he was changing into?

"We can't stay here," Dad shouted.

Mother raised her voice. "The storms usually calm at sunrise."

My stomach tensed. *Sunrise.* I'd almost forgotten about that. How long did we have until the oil wore off? Maybe three or four hours tops. Once we turned ethereal, would Malphic need to find us, or could his magic command our bodies even from a distance? And what about Mother? Had she already turned ethereal? Her ability to stay solid was limited, and it was impossible to tell what state she was in through her robe.

Jaquith pointed away from the wall. "There's a shelter. Not far. Chase might be there."

Leaning on Dad's shoulder for support, Jaquith forged

away from the wall and into the blowing sand. Mother and I stayed as close as we could to them. Even with my face protected by the head mask and veils, the sand and salty air battered my eyelids and clogged my nostrils. But it was only a few minutes before Jaquith and Dad disappeared into what looked like a dark cranny in a drift of sand and brush. Mother and I hunched and wormed our way into the gap.

The place was dark, except for where the aurora's light sifted in through holes in the broken boards that formed the roof and walls. Jaquith's head brushed the ceiling. It was more like a windbreak or a child's fort than anything else. But those things weren't unbearable, especially compared to the one thing that was painfully lacking. Chase.

Dad pushed his hood back and I swallowed hard, once again startled by how foreign he looked with his shaven head and tribal paint. He rubbed his neck. "Any suggestions about how we can make this place berserker-proof? They're out there, right?"

Shit. I'd been so focused on Chase, I'd forgotten about them. I folded my arms across my chest, a shudder running through me.

Jaquith slumped down onto the ground. "If Malphic suspects Chase is out here, he'll call the berserkers inside to hunt for Lotli. He'll want Chase left alone until . . . until it's over."

Mother nodded. "I agree. We're safe for now. But we need to make plans right away."

As the rest of us settled down on the floor, a cold sense of wariness seeped into my bones. I glanced at Mother and Jaquith from under lowered lids. I wanted to feel hopeful about Chase, that he hadn't changed and that we'd get to him in time. But I had the sinking feeling they were going to suggest we leave him here.

Jaquith removed his hood. In the low light, sweat glistened against his dark skin, gathering along the crease of his scarred cheek and mouth. He pressed his fingers first against an enormous goose egg bruise on his forehead, then to a gash up close to his hairline. The bleeding had subsided, but I suspected he had at least a mild concussion, considering how he'd needed help walking and sat down as soon as he could. He probably had a wicked headache, too.

"Are you feeling okay?" I asked.

He straightened his shoulders. "I'm fine. It was just a glancing blow."

I wriggled my willow bracelet off and held it out to him. "Bite off a piece and chew. It'll help with the pain. Seriously."

He squinted at me skeptically, then took it and nipped off a piece of bark. The first time Selena had forced me into using the willow, I'd been just as hesitant.

"Keep it. You might want more later," I said. "Just don't chew a lot at once. It can cause hallucinations."

His scar bent his lips into a sneer instead of a smile, but his voice sounded stronger. "Thanks. I think it's helping already."

"All righty, then." Dad sanded his hands together. "As I see it, there's one way out of this mess. We're going to have to lie low until sunrise. Once the oil wears off and Annie and I are ethereal, we can get through any weak point." His voice hesitated. "Unfortunately, without Lotli and her flute, we'll need a weak point that isn't warded. Our best bet is Malphic's inner sanctum. We broke that ward when we entered. He may not realize that yet."

Jaquith nodded. "That's possible. I was with his magi earlier and they didn't mention it. But now that the guards are aware of the hexad—" His voice dropped off. It went without saying that the chance of the broken ward being discovered and fixed was rising with each passing second, especially if someone noticed the missing inner sanctum guard.

I glanced at Jaquith. "What exactly is a hexad?"

He hesitated, scrubbing his hands down his legs as if deciding where to start. Finally he said with full sincerity, "They're nomadic parasites stranded on the earth by their kind, long before King Solomon's time." His voice deepened. "There are lots of djinn myths about them. They're capable of draining energy from anything around them, stones, plants, animals . . . However, they prefer to live in symbiosis with a magic-rich entity like a genie or half genie, a sort of mate. When that happens, they mark their mate with six marks in the shape of the constellation that they once called home."

Dad chuckled. "Tell a story in the right tone of voice and no one would believe you. Right, Annie?"

I scowled at him. This wasn't funny. All my life, Dad's tone of voice was what fooled me into thinking the wild stories about his family were made up, when in fact they were true. Still, Jaquith's mention of the six marks in the shape of a constellation—Ophiuchus no doubt—had reminded me of something very important. Some of Dad's craziest home-brewed stories were about Samuel Freemont, an ancestor who was an explorer. Dad had mentioned a specific story about him in a phone conversation when we'd first discovered Lotli and were discussing her magic.

Excitement fluttered in my stomach. I took out Lotli's tiny talisman bag from a pocket in the folds of my sarong. "Remember what you told me about Samuel and the cursed fur coat?" I said, showing him the bag.

His eyes widened. "You're talking about the Native American he met who kept a living nature spirit inside his medicine pouch."

"Exactly. What if that Native American was in reality a hexad? Then what do you suppose it kept imprisoned in the bag? Its mate?"

"Sounds plausible," Jaquith said.

"Sounds horrible," Mother corrected. She shuddered and snugged her veils close around her shoulders.

My mind flashed back to the last time I was in the realm, to when I'd turned ethereal at sunrise and Malphic had trapped me in the decanter. Tears had slid down my cheeks as I'd stared through the decanter's glass at Chase fighting two bloodthirsty warriors. I'd heard Mother's glacial-cold voice choose my freedom over Chase's. So many emotions had overwhelmed me: sadness, anger, guilt, but above all else I'd felt utterly helpless.

I looked at the talisman bag. Luckily, right now, I was anything but helpless. I took a deep breath and let my eyes go back to Dad's. "Before Lotli escaped, she told me that I could try and save Chase and keep *the other* as well. I had no idea what she meant by *the other*. In fact, I didn't even really think about it until now. But if your story about Samuel is right, then this bag might not be full of crystals and dried leaves." I took out my knife, cut away the string that held the bag shut, and let it fall open. "No matter who or what was in it, they deserve their freedom."

Thin blue threads of flame spiraled out from the bag. They rose upward to the ceiling, before coiling downward into the misty blue shape of a small person. Their faded blue glow looked like the shadow-genie I'd forced into the bottle.

In a second, the misty shape solidified into a shriveled old man in a loincloth with six black marks just below his sternum.

"Zea?" I said, shocked. I don't know what I expected, but he wasn't it.

His thin legs wobbled. I leapt to my feet, catching his arm before he fell. He didn't look good. In fact, I expected him to just drop dead, like a firefly released too late from a child's net.

Jaquith lumbered to his feet. He lifted Zea's chin, studying his features. He touched Zea's ear. Part of the lobe was missing. "This is Megast-el Zea. He's been missing—since before I came here. He's one of the most brilliant genie magi. We can't let him die." He held Zea by both shoulders, staring into his eyes. "Is it you?"

Zea dipped his head, put his thumb and forefinger in his mouth, and whistled. It was a series of faint sounds that followed the pattern of human speech. When I'd met Zea at the campsite, Lotli had claimed he only communicated with whistles. Apparently that was one of the few things she hadn't lied about.

"Looks to me like there was a good reason Lotli went after Chase," Dad said. "She was almost done with this one."

Jaquith wrung his hands. He paced toward the slit we'd entered through, then turned back. He looked steadily into Zea's eyes and whistled an aria of warbling notes.

Zea whistled back, a soft argument.

In return, Jaquith's warbles grew staccato, insistent.

Mother raised her voice. "Do you mind translating? Some of us would appreciate knowing what's going on."

Jaquith stopped whistling. He waved at his crotch, indicating his absent manhood. "I never wanted to be a warrior. But I wanted to be more than this. I've dreamed of studying magic. But even if I was allowed access to the magi library every day for the rest of my life, I'd never learn a fragment of what Megast-el Zea knows. He is an enlightened master. I've offered to be his vessel."

The air went out of my lungs. He couldn't be suggesting . . . "You mean—you're going to let him possess you? You can't do that. It's a horrible idea." I turned to Dad. When Culus had possessed him, Dad's personality had remained intact at first, but over time it had disappeared as Culus took over control. I looked back at Jaquith, determined to change his mind. "You won't simply gain knowledge. Everything about you will be gone, except your body."

Dad raised his hand as if solemnly swearing. "She's right. Trust me, I've been there. It isn't good."

Zea whistled softly. I'd been so focused on Jaquith I'd almost forgotten he was listening, and he did understand English. He went on, his notes liquid and gentle, a beautiful trill that reminded me of a wood thrush's evening chorus.

"He isn't like Culus," Jaquith insisted. "Megast-el Zea will allow my voice and spirit to remain intact. I am not the first to be his vessel. I've read about the others. This is a blessing." Without giving anyone time to argue, Jaquith's voice rose loud and confident. "I offer myself to you, a humble vessel for your spirit. Welcome, Megast-el Zea. Take my body. Make my home yours."

Zea reached up, resting his shaky hands on Jaquith's broad shoulders. Blue light emanated from his fingertips. The air vibrated as if a million invisible moths whirled around us. And the pungent scent of sulfur hit my nose as Zea's body shimmered and transformed into fiery blue plume.

"Welcome. May my breath be your breath. May your thoughts be mine." Jaquith closed his eyes. And the fiery plume became a red veil. It settled over Jaquith, sinking and vanishing into his body.

Jaquith dropped to his knees, holding his hands over his face. He groaned and trembled. Then he drew a deep breath and smiled.

"Are you all right?" Mother asked.

Dad peered at his eyes. "Maybe you should have another bite of that willow Annie gave you."

"No, I'll be fine," he said. "Just give me a moment."

Dad chuckled. "Zea doesn't happen to know how to get through a warded weak point, does he?" He let out a loud breath. "Just kidding. I know being possessed doesn't mean you instantly gained access to his thoughts and abilities. It was weeks before Culus started to communicate with me at that sort of level. You—or should I say both of you—still want to leave the realm with us, right?"

"Very much," Jaquith said. His voice quieted. "I'm sorry. I should have asked him about the weak point before I took on his spirit. I was just so afraid he was going to die."

As he closed his eyes, we all fell silent, retreating into our thoughts. Chase and how much time had already passed went through my mind first. I was glad for Zea and in a strange way happy for Jaquith. I was relieved. But we needed to get back out into the desert and find Chase. After that, we could make a mad dash for Malphic's inner sanctum. Hopefully, we'd get there right at sunrise and be able to cross. But if the weak point's ward had been restored, then we'd be screwed.

I scrubbed my hand over my silk-covered face. It seemed like there had to be another answer to our situation, a way to ensure that we'd be able to get through the veil no matter what. In fact, it felt like I already knew one.

"*Magic is . . . remembering . . .*" Selena's voice whispered in my head.

I concentrated harder, sifting through my memories. My pulse quickened, a ringing sound hummed in my ears, just like it had in the harem. I closed my eyes. *Hecate, show me the way. Let me find the answer I already know.*

A memory burst into my head. I was five years old in Moonhill's gallery.

My mother. Her hands over her eyes. "Ninety-eight, ninety-nine, one hundred."

Her hands part. "Ready or not, here I come."

The room is hot now. My mother's tanned face is white, pale as the wide scarf wrapped around the man's waist. Pale as the moonstone in his dagger.

He walks toward her. Broad-shouldered. Shaved head. Bare chest. I've seen him before. Kissing Mama in my moonlit bedroom. They thought I was asleep. Dad wasn't home.

My heart is racing now. Racing and I cannot breathe. This isn't the game we were playing.

He holds out his hand. "No," she says, backing away. There are broad-shouldered men all around her. Dark men, like black paper cutouts. Black like shadows. "Stay away!" she screams.

"Mama!" I shout, running toward them. The glint of moonstone and a knife's blade flashes in my face as he wraps himself around her. A heartbeat later, he vanishes, turning into smoke, a whirling tornado of shadows. I can't see Mama anymore. Just darkness, as thick and real as congealing blood. So real it burns my nose and eyes. "Mama!" I scream.

My eyes flashed open.

"Malphic's knife," I blurted out.

Everyone stared at me expectantly.

"What are you talking about?" Dad asked.

"He uses it to slice the veil open. It's at least as powerful as Lotli's flute. We could use it to open any weak point we want."

Mother nodded. "I hadn't thought of that before, but you're right." Her shoulders slumped. "But there's one huge problem with that idea. Aside from when he's undressed, Malphic keeps the knife on his person all the time."

I grinned. "But Malphic isn't the only one with a knife like that. Chase has its twin." My voice lifted, strong and confident. "I'm positive he has it with him. I saw it beside the mattress in the cell with his other weapons. He took everything."

"Annie," Mother said, her tone gentle. "I know how you feel about Chase. But it would be even harder to get something away from him than Malphic. He's not the same man he was. He'll lash out at anyone who goes near him."

My face went hot. Chase loved her like a mother and it took so little for her to abandon him. . . .

I bit my tongue. As much as I wanted to let my resentments toward her resurface and lash out, it was wrong. I knew she didn't want to abandon him. She was upset about Chase. But she wanted to protect me more. And I appreciated that, but I couldn't go along with it.

I swiveled to Dad. "I'm not going to leave him out there to die in the desert. The knife just gives me another reason to find him."

Dad's eyes lingered on my face for a second. "I know. I'll go with you."

"You can't," I said. "I know you want to. But he'll feel less threatened if it's just me. I can find him easily."

Jaquith gave a heavy sigh. "You do realize he could be dead. He had some severe wounds and he's not immortal."

I rubbed my chest, the weight of what he and Mother were saying aching inside me. I pulled the egg pendulum out from under my neckline. "If that's the case, then he won't be a danger to me. Seriously, with my pendulum it'll only take a minute to locate him. I'll get a general direction in here, then go outside and do it again." I faked a smile. "Promise, I won't even approach him. I'll just find him, then come back and get help."

CHAPTER 27

Strip away the skin of regret and the sinew of
revenge. Bury me in the desert. A cage of bones,
I await the rain, a seeded oasis biding my time.

—Excerpt of poem by Josette Savoy Abrams
Beach Rose House, Bar Harbor, Maine

I lied. I told them the egg showed me where Chase was. Not
far, just over the dune outside the shelter. If he was beyond
reason, I'd return and get help. Then I wrapped my veils around
my head and forged my way out of the shelter and back into the
storm.

In truth, the tug I'd felt on the egg was faint and erratic at
best. I'd faked its larger movements with slight twists of my
fingers and wrist. This time it hadn't been a matter of magic
interfering with my energy, like when I was near the staircase.
My gut told me it was probably stress. But another voice whispered that perhaps Lotli had done more damage than just temporarily weakening me when she held my hand.

I turned on my flashlight. Its beam reflected against the
blowing sand, brightening only the first few feet ahead of me.
Still, it gave me a measure of comfort from the fear of what I
was doing.

The wind snapped my veils. As I climbed the dune, the sand
shifted and tumbled beneath me. When I was certain the flash-

light's brightness couldn't be seen from the shelter, I knelt with my back to the wind, braced the light between my knees, and pulled the egg pendant out.

My mouth dried. I had to be careful. If the chain broke and slipped through my fingers, the sand would swallow any trace of it in a second.

I let the egg dangle and hunched over to shield it from the storm as best as I could. Still the wind pushed it away from my body, then to one side and back, never giving the egg's weight a chance to get centered.

Frustration knotted inside me. I closed my eyes, sand and tears sticking my lashes to the head mask's gritty silk. "Please," I moaned against the wind. "Please, Hecate, show me what I've lost."

I shoved aside the sensation of my lashing veils. I tuned out the sting of sand against my shoulders. I focused and breathed deep, the vapor of my breath hot and humid against the mask. "Hecate. Show me what I've lost. Where is Chase?"

The wind spun the egg away from my body. But beneath that, there was the slight draw of something else, an independent movement, gathering strength.

The chain arched against the wind, the egg undulating back toward me. A hard pull, intensifying as adrenaline rushed into my veins. *Chase. Where is he?*

I held my breath and refused to let my focus waver from the egg, but some distant part of my body took the flashlight from between my knees. With the flashlight in one hand and the chain in the other, I rose to my feet.

Unwavering and fierce, the egg's pull led me farther from the shelter. The wind screeched in my ears. My legs strained against the sucking sand. And as I pressed on, a memory seeped into my thoughts: Once, when I was maybe eight or nine years old, I'd gotten caught in a snow squall in the woods behind our house in Vermont. Sleet and hard snow drove against me, blinding me as I struggled to find my way home. That day, I hadn't been scared. I'd known I'd make it as long as I didn't give up. I wasn't going to give up this time either. I was a Freemont, named after Stephanie Freemont, a woman who had braved the high seas, an explorer, a woman who had excavated a cursed tomb and unearthed jars filled with Solomon's genies. A woman who had faced Death herself off the shores of Madagascar.

The wind whirled faster around me, a cyclone of stinging red and black. The egg stopped pulling me forward and began spinning in the same direction as the wind, a tight spiral spinning closer and closer to a center point. "No!" I shouted. "Don't stop. Show me what I've lost!"

The egg went motionless.

The wind died without warning. The silence that followed was deafening after the roar of the storm. Waning moonlight and the aurora's smolder now illuminated the world around me.

I stood at the top of a dune. Behind me, the muted outline of the shelter sat about fifty yards down the slope, half-covered in sand. Beyond it, Malphic's fortress loomed. Ahead of me were only peaks and valleys of rippled crimson sand, shadowed in black.

"Please," I murmured, straining to see just a little farther.

On the summit of the next dune there was a glimmer of blue: the lone shape of someone kneeling.

The moonlight brightened for a heartbeat and I caught the glint of a knife in his hands. The point of a blade held against his chest, readying to thrust.

"Chase!" I screamed, running toward him.

He didn't glance my way. He lifted the knife outward, two hands firmly gripping it.

Time slowed down. The flashlight fell from my hands. I pumped my arms. I pushed my legs, running as hard as I could. The distance between us stretched out, miles of red and black, the dune as tall as a mountain. The aurora illuminated his face, darkened by shadows. Eyes vacant. Blue fire undulating along the marks on his skin. I'd never get to him in time. Never.

He looked skyward, howled, and thrust the knife inward.

I dove, shoving him to the sand.

He was on top of me, his eyes wild with fury, his knife now aimed at me. The knife slammed downward. I rolled out of the way, the blade slicing the air beside my head. A fist flew toward my face. I flung my hands up, shielding the blow. A crack and pain erupted across my knuckles, sharp in my wrists. I crabbed backward. I couldn't win this. I couldn't fight him.

He prowled toward me on all fours, his head, chest, and shoulders all bare. His ocean-blue eyes, black with rage. His mouth, a vicious slash. An aura of blue flames crackled all around him. The loose fabric of his white pants twisted in a sudden surge of wind.

I reached for my dagger. There had to be an answer here. There had to be.

My dagger was gone.

But his moonstone knife glinted in the sand a yard away from me.

I sprung toward it. My fingers closed around its handle. His hand clamped my ankle, yanking me toward him. Readying to kick, I rolled onto my back.

My brain engaged. Chase had been raised as a slave. He'd been trained to follow orders. I pulled myself upright and looked him straight in the eyes. I hardened my voice and snapped, "Warrior. Halt!"

He blinked and went rigid, his fingers an immobile band around my leg.

"I am on your side," I said, more gently.

His brow lowered, casting deeper shadows across his eyes.

I pushed the moonstone knife under my body, hiding it in

the sand. "I am Annie. I am here for you. I would never desert you. . . ." I spoke slow and firm, enunciating each word with sharp authority.

He stared at me, his grip still tight. I didn't dare pull off my veils or remove the silk mask. I barely dared move at all.

"It's okay. I'm here to help you."

His aura's flames settled into a hot glow. More than anything, he looked confused and terrified. I eased my hand forward, toward where his hand clamped my leg.

"Relax. Breathe deep. Calm, peaceful, focused, and in control." I was grasping at straws, but at least he wasn't trying to kill me now.

He blew out a shallow breath, his chest rising as he sucked in a deeper one.

I scrunched forward and wedged my fingertips between my ankle and his stiff fingers, loosening his hold. He withdrew his hand and looked at it, his brow furrowing as if he wasn't a hundred percent sure the hand belonged to him. His gaze shifted to me.

"I'm Annie," I said, super hushed. "I love you."

He cocked his head and something fluttered through his eyes. Recognition?

His eyes went blank. He seized his head between his hands and leapt to his feet, yowling as if his skull were exploding from the inside out. He dropped to the ground in a quivering ball, yowls transforming into moans.

I grabbed the moonstone knife, shoved it into the folds of my sarong. Then I knelt down and wrapped my arms around him, hugging him as tight as I could, trying the only way I could think of to give him comfort. Desperation ached in my chest. "Shush. It's okay. Relax. . . ."

The wind surged again, the sand rising with it in biting waves, crashing all around, burying us in its blood-red weight.

Beneath my arms, Chase shook with spasms and blazing heat. He curled up and whimpered, like he did when he had nightmares about being kidnapped as a child.

"Annie, I can't hold on." He groaned.

Tears washed down my face. He'd said my name. He knew I was here. "You have to hold on. I can't lose you."

Sweat slicked his head, his back, and arms. His aura flared, a wildfire crackling against my skin. The brand on his collarbone glowed white-hot. Chase. My Chase. I didn't want him to die and become nothing more than a body laid to rest behind a carpet garlanded with coins and ravens. I didn't want him to lose his mind and go berserk.

Inevitable, a voice whispered inside me.

I held him tighter. No, it couldn't be.

When I'd first met Jaquith he'd told me that all genies went through the change, but that it was worse for half ifrits. Chase had said he could slow the change down, delay it. But he couldn't stop it from happening. It was as inevitable as him growing from a boy to a man, from a child to a father.

My stomach sank. Then my pulse quickened.

I let go of him and sat up, the wind chilling my heated body. Perhaps the change was inevitable. But its outcome wasn't. There was another choice. The one Malphic was hoping for. Chase could beat the odds and survive. He could become a Death Warrior.

Hope sparked in my chest. Chase had told me Death Warriors were gladiators who fought to entertain the genies, but I now had the feeling that was an understatement. A Death Warrior was something more highly honored, rarer and harder to achieve than just a warrior simply beating the crap out of other combatants to reach the top of the food chain. It had little to do with reaching a specific age or being allowed to wear a special uniform. A Death Warrior was the victor in a battle against his own nature, a warrior of genie blood who'd survived the change and not gone berserk.

Chase moaned, his fingers and bare feet digging into the sand. I spooned in behind him, sheltering him from the storm. If Malphic thought Chase could make it through this, then I should, too. Another thought came to me and a sour taste crawled up my throat. Malphic hadn't been the only one pushing Chase toward the change. Lotli had as well.

"I'm here. I'm not going to desert you," I whispered. "Let go. Let it take you." I pressed my cheek against his back. Even through the wall of his muscles and skin, I could hear the heated rhythm of his heart. What I needed was a way to make the change easier for him, something other than just words.

Beneath my cheek his skin twitched. Feverish quivers. He stiffened and vomited, clamping his arms around his middle. He began to convulse, spittle foaming from his mouth. His groans and screams echoed in my ears, as piercing as the wind.

With one last gasp, he rolled over onto his back and went dead-still. His eyes were wide open.

Horrified, I could only stare. And beyond him, through the settling sand, I glimpsed a trace of brightness on the eastern horizon. Oh my God. Sunrise couldn't be more than an hour away.

A hollow sense of inevitability took root in my chest. But this feeling wasn't about Chase or the change this time. This was what I'd felt weeks ago in Moonhill's cemetery, the first time I'd seen my ancestors' graves. A sense that I was exactly where I belonged, that everything I'd gone through had been building toward this. I just needed to find the next step.

My gaze swept to the six dark marks, right below Chase's sternum.

Without giving myself time for second thoughts, I straddled him. He didn't move or cry out when I pressed my fingers inward exactly as Lotli had done. I wasn't hexad, but there had to be a reason she'd given me the hummingbird egg. That, combined with the way my pendulum had moved against the storm, had made me wonder if it had been my energy and not the realm's that she'd wanted to acquire. And there was another thing. I wasn't just a Freemont. I was my mother's daughter as well.

I wet my lips and whispered, "Relax. Focus. I'm here. We're going to do this together."

I slowed my breathing, bringing to mind what it felt like when Chase and I made love. I thought about the time on the clifftop when he came to me and kissed my palm: nothing else in the universe except him and me.

His aura began to shimmer like blue sapphires. I pressed my fingers harder against him. Focusing, channeling my energy into him, nothing else in my mind, nothing else except us.

Despite the Methuselah oil, my fingers turned ethereal, melding into his skin. My arms, my shoulders, my forehead followed, gray wisps of light penetrating the cells of his body, filling his veins, his heart, his mind, loaning him my strength. My love. Making him more than whole. My head swam from the power of it. I was warm. I was ecstatic. I was ethereal.

"Let it take you," I murmured. "Give in. Accept. I'm with you." My voice was breath in his lungs, my words warmth in his ears. His lips were on mine, the kiss slow and long and deeper than seemed possible. The red and black of the sand rose up around us, cascading down in pinpoints like rain, like the fountains in Rome, like sharp ashes drifting from a jar.

His aura flickered and went out. His body rigid. His voice filled with hurt. "She said you didn't—"

I pressed a finger to his lips. "She lied. I'm here. I need you."

I kissed his throat. I kissed his chest. I rolled him onto his stomach, working my forearm against his buttock, rolling stokes, firm and determined. His corded muscles flinched, then loos-

ened under my fingertips. I worked them against his thighs, his
calves. I rolled my fist against the arch of his foot. His aura burned
like a comet, sparks and heat. And he surrendered, letting my energy inside again. And it occurred to me that perhaps we both
had died. This didn't seem like it could be a part of life.

Our sparks joined. There was no him or me, only light and
warmth, both of us ethereal—

White light flashed.

And I was lying on the sand, my body entirely solid once
more, gasping for breath.

I clawed at the veils, ripping them off. I dug my fingernails
under one edge of the face mask, peeling myself free from the
grit-coated prison.

Fresh air hit my lungs. I gulped a breath, and another and
another until my head stopped spinning. *Chase.*

He sprawled on the dune beside me, bloody, bruised, and
motionless. And alive?

His body jerked and shuddered—and he began to cough,
wheezing like a drowned man returning to life.

Relief flooded through me. I was about to drop down beside him and throw my arms around his neck, when panic hit
me. The aurora still fluxed overhead. But how long had we
been out of it? An hour? A day?

I whirled toward the eastern horizon.

A faint thread of light spread along it. As impossible as it
seemed, no more than a heartbeat of time could have passed.

I pulled Chase up. "We have to go."

He blinked at me, his eyes coming into focus. "What happened?"

"I'll tell you on the way. Mother, my dad, and Jaquith are
waiting in a shelter. We've got an hour at the most to get to a
weak point."

Filled with renewed energy, I found one of my castoff veils
and used it to quickly bind a gash in his arm. I wiped off the

worst of the blood from around his nose and eyes. It wasn't much, but hopefully it would let him see and breathe easier. Then I gathered up his scimitar and scabbard, and helped him strap them on. I retrieved two of his knives from the sand and gave those to him as well. But my stomach tightened as I reached for the moonstone knife hidden within the folds at my waistline. He had changed. I was certain of that. My gut told me he was a Death Warrior now. But I'd only guessed what that meant.

Ignoring a whisper of guilt, I let my hand drop away from the moonstone knife and fall loosely at my side. I loved Chase. My blood sang from what had happened between us. I couldn't believe he wasn't okay. He looked sane. Still, I couldn't afford to take chances with this knife, not now.

Jogging close together, we hurried down from the low dune we were on and started up the next one. As we neared the peak, the loose sand pulled against our feet. But the wind had died down, only faint gusts remaining. When we reached the summit, I stopped to catch my breath and gestured toward the outline of the shelter below, a crisscross of gray and black in the predawn light. "They're right over—"

My voice died in my throat.

A troop of a dozen or more dark-robed figures were moving away from the darkness along the fortress's outer wall and toward the shelter, their unsheathed swords glinting in the last of the moonlight.

CHAPTER 28

Respect strength, but honor the victor.

—Djinn saying

"Run to the shelter. Warn them," Chase shouted, unsheathing his scimitar.

Fear burned inside me. Even if he was a Death Warrior, a dozen men were too many for him to fight. I grabbed his wrist, fingers digging in. "No, you'll get killed."

His eyes trapped mine. "Don't worry. I was trained for this."

The confidence in his voice said he was determined. But one hand swept his branded collarbone, a motion that told me he didn't fully believe it himself. Sure he'd been raised to be a Death Warrior, told what he'd be capable of if he survived the change. But knowing and wielding skills were two different things. Still, did we have a choice?

"Okay," I said. "But be careful, use your head."

He nodded and then charged down the dune toward them. With each step, he sliced the air with his scimitar. In response, the sand sprayed up all around him, like music rising to the strokes of a conductor's baton. He pivoted his scimitar and the sand coiled into a dust devil, gathering size and strength, circling around him like a blood-red shield.

I raced for the shelter, the whine of Chase's dust devil echoing in my ears. I could barely see anything through the flying sand, but I found the shelter just as Dad and everyone were coming out from it.

"We have to help Chase," I shouted. My pulse drummed in my head. Adrenaline screamed for me to fight. Maybe I'd die. But I wouldn't let Chase go down alone.

"What's going on?" Dad said.

A cloaked figure dashed out from the swirling sand, and then another, running toward us fast.

I pulled the moonstone knife, ready for their attack. But Jaquith leapt at me, pinning my arms behind my back. The figures darted by us and I realized my mistake. Not guards. Not berserkers or even men.

"They're teenagers!" Mother screeched. "Boy-slaves."

"Oh my God." I gasped. My throat was raw from the battering sand, the taste of blood tainting my mouth. Chase had attacked them, intent on slaughter. But they weren't warriors. They were boys in training. What if he realized too late—what if he killed . . . ?

A lanky boy flew past. He was twelve years old, maybe thirteen at the most.

"Stay strong! Stay proud! Stay free!" Jaquith yelled after him, as the boy careened up the dune Chase and I had come down from.

The boy's voice echoed back. "Stay strong! Stay proud! Stay free!"

The whirling sand thickened, wailing and darkening the air around us. My gut told me Chase was causing this and that the real storms had passed. But my head reeled with confusion and fear as the outline of a younger boy hurtled by, heading up the dune and deeper into the desert.

The cycloning whine silenced.

The sand around us settled.

But when I glanced toward where the boys had gone, all I could see was a dark wall of sand, like a thundercloud moving up over the dune, shielding the boys from sight and rushing deeper into the desert.

"What the hell was that?" Dad said.

"They're escaping." Jaquith gestured at the vanishing sand cloud. "If they can get to the mountains, they'll be outside Malphic's territory. Some have made it."

My heart lightened for a second. Then a sick feeling chilled me to the core. *Chase.* He'd attacked teenagers, boy-slaves like he'd once been. When we'd first spotted them, I'd seen at least a dozen. But I'd only spotted a few getting away.

I turned, searching for Chase.

He stood on a dark-red hummock halfway between us and the outer wall. His scimitar hung limply in his hand. His shoulders were slouched, his expression grim.

Shoving the moonstone knife back into the fold of my sarong, I sprinted toward him, not knowing what to say, not daring to look anywhere other than his face out of fear of what I might see.

"I almost killed them," he mumbled when I got up to him.

Almost killed? I glanced around, peering intently into the half-light. There weren't any bodies. Not even a cast-aside sword or any sign of a battle.

Pride swelled in my chest. I stroked my fingers down his face. "But you didn't. Instead you created that sand cloud to hide them—like a smoke screen. You didn't hurt them. You helped them escape."

His fingers cupped my chin, lifting it until our eyes met. His voice quaked. "I almost killed them."

"But you didn't," I repeated firmly. "You didn't even come close."

CHAPTER 29

*The fact of the matter is that guilt, love, revenge . . . and
all their ilk affect the nature of the human body, both the
mental and the biochemical aspects. In turn, this can
dramatically alter a spell or experiment, for better or worse.*

—General notes on alchemy
Hector Freemont

Dad, Jaquith, and Mother hurried over to us.
Mother pressed her palm against Chase's face. "Are you
okay?"

"Sure he is." Jaquith cuffed Chase's bicep. "Tough as iron,
this one."

"Yeah, I'm fine," Chase said. But his voice was choked
with emotion and, even in the dim light and through the scruff
of his beard and the dirt on his skin, it was impossible to not
see how battered he was. He nodded at the goose egg on
Jaquith's forehead. "You don't look so good yourself, brother."

Jaquith touched the lump. "I owe this to that hexad, Lotli.
I'll tell you about it and a lot more, once we get out of this
place."

Chase frowned. "Hexad? What the hell is that?"

"You really don't know?" Jaquith said. He waved off the
question. "I guess I might not know either, if I were still living

in the warrior barracks instead of hanging around the magi's library. Trust me. Hexads are dangerous."

Dad cleared his throat. "I hate to interrupt this reunion. But does anyone have a suggestion about how we're going to get back into the fortress? We need to get to a weak point, and fast." He cocked his head at the outer wall a few yards away from us. It was solid stone, sheer, and four or more stories high.

I glanced right and left as far as I could see. There was no entryway or carpet, nothing to indicate where we'd come out from the cell. But we had to be in the right area. Last night, it hadn't taken us long to walk to the shelter.

I reached for my egg pendulum. "I can probably locate—"

Dad's hand landed on my shoulder, silencing me.

Chase was walking stiffly toward the wall, one hand out in front of him like a TV version of a sleepwalker. Of course, it was his cell and designed to give him access to and from the desert.

He reached the wall and pressed his hand against the stone. His fingers, then his entire arm vanished through the wall. He withdrew his arm and smiled at us. "I'll go first and make sure the cell's empty."

"Wait a minute," Jaquith said. "I'm betting the rest of us aren't going to be able to enter that easily, like the way we can't get back up the berserker quarters' stairwell without the hexad and her flute." He pushed his hand against the wall right where Chase had and the stones remained impenetrable.

Dad tried with the same result and so did Mother.

I raked my hair back from my face. There had to be a way. I nibbled my bottom lip, thinking. Earlier, when Lotli had escaped from Chase's cell, she'd used her flute to get through the carpet and into the tunnel. For all practical purposes, there had been no difference between what she did then and when she opened the veil between realms. So logic told me, if Malphic's knife could open a weak point in the veil like her flute, then it might do other similar things. Such as getting us through this warded entryway.

I stepped up to the wall and drew the moonstone knife from my waistline.

Chase eyed me. "I was wondering why you were hiding that from me."

Not wanting to tell him the real reason, I faked a smile. "You have to watch out for us Freemonts," I said teasingly. I glanced toward Mother. "Plus, it seems I might just have inherited a few talents from the other side of my family."

Closing my eyes, I took a deep breath. I had Malphic's knife, but I needed the incantation that went with it. I couldn't believe there wasn't one. I just needed to remember the words.

I visualized Moonhill's gallery and from there forced my mind back to the day of Mother's kidnapping. Malphic must have said something when he opened the weak point.

"No," Mother says, backing away. There are broad-shouldered men all around her. Dark men, like black paper cutouts. Black like shadows. "Stay away!" she screams.

"Mama!" I shout, running toward them. The glint of moonstone and a knife's blade flashes in my face as Malphic wraps himself around her. A heartbeat later, he vanishes, turning into smoke, a whirling tornado of shadows. I can't see Mama anymore. Just darkness, as thick and real as congealing blood.

Malphic. Mother. The knife. But no incantation.

Frustration balled my fingers into fists. I ran the memory through my head again to be sure. Not a single word, though logic screamed that Malphic must have whispered something. A short incantation. Something easy to remember.

Frantic, I swung toward Jaquith. "Ask Zea what words go

with the knife. I know you're not that connected yet. But if he senses your desperation, maybe his personality can come forward or something. He's a magi. He must know how to open doorways and veils."

Jaquith's gaze met mine. He shook his head. "It's way too soon. Even if I could let him come through, you wouldn't understand his whistles. Things could get a lot worse."

I gritted my teeth to keep from screaming at him to at least try.

"I'll figure something out," Dad said.

But I barely heard his voice. Another one whispered inside me. *You know it*, the voice insisted. *You know the words. Look for them.*

It didn't make sense. I hadn't heard what Malphic said. I couldn't find it inside me any more than Jaquith could get through to Zea. I hadn't heard—

Or maybe I had.

My mother's kidnapping wasn't the only time I'd witnessed Malphic open the veil.

"Don't worry," Chase said, glancing up toward the top of the wall as if he were contemplating climbing. "I'm not going to let you get stuck out here, like a bunch of trapped animals."

Trapped. The word sang in my mind. Back in the harem gallery it had been the memory of being trapped in the decanter that had given me the words I needed to command the shadow-genie. Maybe. Just maybe if I followed that memory one step further, to just before Malphic ripped open the veil and hurled me out of the realm. That had to be it. There wasn't any other time.

Through the decanter's dark glass, I see Chase, a blue fluorescing outline as much liquid fire as man, fighting the two genies glowing just like him. Tears wet my cheeks.

*Malphic reaches to his sash and draws his knife. There is a flash of
moonstone as he raises it upward into the air.*

Not letting the memory slip from my mind, I lifted the
moonstone knife and pointed it inward until its tip rested
against the fortress wall. In my head, the memory of Malphic's
voice bellowed. And I repeated his words one at a time, each
inflection, each rise and fall of my voice mimicking his: "*What
tears also opens. What burns also builds.*"

I sliced the knife downward.

Blue light flashed and the wall unzipped like a tent flap.
Electricity snapped around the opening, white sparks crackling.

Chase rushed in first, his scimitar at the ready. The rest of
us followed close behind. No sooner were we all through and
into the empty cell than the opening sealed shut and vanished.

We sprinted into the other room. Chase grabbed his discarded boots off the floor and tugged them on. Then I used
the knife again to get us out of the cell and into the tunnel.
My voice was stronger now, my confidence branching inside
me, energizing every portion of my being.

Chase led us to the left, deeper into the tunnel's labyrinth.
According to him, it would take us to the chamber with the
fight cage in the middle of it. I shuddered at the thought of
seeing the room again, at the memory of having to leave him
with Lotli and at what he had endured in there, fighting
against the change and killing to stay alive. But Chase insisted
that the fight cage chamber was the fast route to Malphic's
inner sanctum and we needed to go there. It was the closest
weak point. A place I knew I could use the knife to get us back
home.

The tunnel grew dark as we hurried, only a few torches

still burning. Berserkers hammered on their carpeted door-ways as we passed. Their screeches and howls boomed down the narrow passageway, drowning out the clip of our footsteps and the huff of our breaths. Even if every guard was busy hunting for Lotli, there was no way they could miss the riot of noise rising from this place.

Dad slid his arm around Mother's waist, helping her keep up. Jaquith took his longer whip from his belt. We came to a short set of warded steps and once again I sliced an opening for us. Five yards more, and the mouth of the tunnel bright-ened. The fight cage chamber, no doubt.

Chase glanced back and put a finger to his lips, hushing us. We slowed to a tiptoe, creeping forward along the wall.

A deep voice echoed out from the chamber ahead, a guard most likely. "I wish those maggot-brained berserkers would shut up. All that noise, you'd think it was the full moon."

"You don't think that bitch with the flute circled back around?" another one said.

Chase motioned to Jaquith. He slipped by me and up to Chase. The two of them whispered, then slunk forward on their own, no more than shadowy outlines, rippling down the last yards of the dark tunnel toward the brighter chamber.

A jittery sense of terror and anticipation jumped inside me. I blocked out the noise of the berserkers behind us and fo-cused on the sounds coming from ahead. There was the scrape of chair legs. Footsteps moved across the fight cage chamber toward the tunnel. Something swished, like a sword leaving a scabbard.

"Did you smell something?" one of the guards said.

I felt myself pale. Oh my God. *Dad.* Jaquith had thought he smelled bad, so had the Hulk when he stopped us on the way to the main palace. I sniffed my arm and caught a faint whiff of cabbage, lanolin, and cloves. The Methuselah oil. Whatever Kate and Olya had done to make it scent-free wasn't working anymore. With their superior sense of smell, it would only be a second before the guards knew someone unfamiliar was here.

The guards' outlines appeared in the mouth of the tunnel, muscles tensed, ready for a fight.

Chase sprang from the shadows. *Crack.* In one motion, he broke the first guard's neck. He slammed the second guard in the kidney. Jaquith snapped his whip, jerking the second guard to his knees. Light flashed off Chase's scimitar and the guard slumped to the floor dead, blood gurgling from his throat.

I scuffed back, my stomach lurching at the swift brutality of what they'd done. But my shock vanished in an instant. This wasn't a random act of violence or uncontrolled. They were both warriors. They'd spent years in the training yard. I'd attacked Culus and his shadows minion to save my dad when he'd been possessed. I'd attacked the guy at the yacht club. The truth was, I'd have helped Chase and Jaquith now, if they'd needed it.

Whomp! Whomp! Whomp! The throb of the berserkers beating on their doors amplified, followed by more screams and howling.

"Hurry." Chase waved us forward.

We raced past the guards' bodies and into the chamber. A woman in warrior leathers crouched inside the fight cage, her face and hair clotted with blood. She snarled and hissed as we ran for the stairs. Halfway up, we met another guard, a lealaps with the face of a wolf. He leapt at Chase, claws like daggers. Chase ducked. I reached for my bags of salt. They were gone. I'd thrown them all at the shadow-genie. "Salt," I yelled to Dad.

His hand dove into his robe, too slow. The lealaps spun away from Chase, his eyes narrowing on Mother.

Fuck this.

I yanked the moonstone knife from my waistline and threw myself at the lealaps, stabbing him in the side. Once. Twice. Jaquith was on top of him now, his dagger buried in the lealaps's stomach, one jerk upward and the lealaps collapsed and tumbled down the stairs.

Chase raised an eyebrow at me. "Remind me never to get you pissed."

I laughed and shoved the blade back into its hiding spot, but inside my relief had already vanished.

We sprinted up the rest of the stairs to the stifling-hot dining hall. Sweat drizzled down my face. The remains of my sarong clung to my skin, dirty and smeared with lealaps blood. I took a deep breath, gathering my strength.

The dining room itself was empty and quiet. But below us the sounds of the berserkers still reverberated like a heartbeat and other shouts echoed in the training yard, loud enough to come from a small army.

In the distance a bell began to toll, fast and tinny.

"The alarm," Mother said. "Malphic knows there's more of us here than just the hexad."

Dad shoved back his hood. "Any suggestions?"

Chase nodded. "I'll go into the yard first. Once I've got their attention, all of you can run like hell for the inner sanctum."

I grabbed his wrist. "Don't even think about sacrificing yourself." I let go and pinpointed my gaze on Jaquith. "That goes for you, too. You still plan on coming with us, right?"

His eyes brightened. "If you're willing to have me—and Zea."

"Of course we are," Dad said. "Now let's get this show on the road. . . ."

As Dad quickly mapped out a more elaborate version of Chase's plan, I became aware of a subtle cramping low in my body.

I swallowed hard and tucked my hands into the fold of my

sarong so no one would notice their shaking. The last time I was here and sunrise had come and the oil had worn off, my transition from solid to ethereal had happened hard and fast— very much like the sharp, painful anguish of Lotli digging her nails into the coils on her flute. This was just a twinge, but there was no mistaking what it meant.

I tugged on Dad's sleeve. "We need to go *now*."

CHAPTER 30

When I held him there was a yielding inside me. Malphic saw
it, as did eunuchs who wiped the blood from my legs and laid
him in my arms. My fourth son. My fifth. That mattered not.
There was a diminishment inside me, of which we never spoke.

—Sovereign Mistress Vephra

As Chase stepped into the doorway, I stood off to one side
just out of sight of the training yard. One of Mother's
veils was wrapped tight around my lower face to protect my
mouth and nose, but my eyes weren't covered and I longed to
watch Chase and make sure he was okay.

Instead I concentrated on the feel of the chain in my hand
and channeled all my energy toward the egg pendulum, while
in the background I heard the shouts coming from the yard,
and the swish of Chase's scimitar and the whine of the dust
devil rising to his command.

"Show me where east is," I murmured. "Show me the rising sun."

Jaquith's hand warmed my back. "Go," he said, nudging
me forward.

Together we stepped out of the dining hall into the training yard, Dad and Mother tucked in close behind. All around
us darkness and sand whirled. Firelight flashed. A riot of war-

riors flayed and shouted, fighting against Chase's storm, trying to regroup.

I directed all my energy toward the egg and whispered, "Show me the inner sanctum weak point."

It tugged straight ahead and I followed. Mother held tight to the back of my sarong. Jaquith gripped my waist, his head bowed against the wind and sand.

The cry of Chase's dust devil rose, an earsplitting screaming off to my left. Out of the corner of my eye, I glimpsed warriors struggling with their face scarves, flashes of gold blades, black blades. A turban flew past. A palm branch struck Jaquith and careened off in the opposite direction. Eerie green darkness descended, the fires smothered out by sand and debris.

I pushed between eunuchs, their brown robes snapping in the wind. A warrior blindly lunged out from the darkness. Jaquith hurled him aside. The egg pulled against my grip, unrelenting and strong.

Finally, the battering of sand against my face subsided and the chaos of noise came from behind rather than surrounding us. I dropped my attention and looked up.

Through the gray haze I could make out the wide stairs to the inner sacrum a few yards to our left and even the landing at its top. There were no warriors or guards. Not even a single eunuch there. Our path to freedom was totally clear.

The hairs on the back of my neck prickled. Something was wrong.

Behind me, the whine of the dust devil stopped. Chase materialized out of the haze and took me by the elbow, urging me toward the inner sanctum's stairs. My knees locked, legs refusing to budge.

"What is it?" Dad said.

The dust was settling, the haze clearing. Men and boys

stumbled through the training yard wreckage, coughing and spitting.

"I'm not sure, but it's too easy." I pulled free from Chase's grip and took off, fast-walking straight ahead, following my gut with them trailing behind.

I jogged through the colonnade. The arena stretched before me, wide and empty as a grave built for a legion of soldiers. It wasn't lit by the aurora and moon like it had been earlier. But the sky was brightening, the east sides of the pillars and grandstand seats transformed to slate gray by the encroaching light, dark shadows stretching westward.

Adrenaline pumped into my veins. Determination clenched my jaw. I sprinted for the raised platform. It was vacant now, but the night Malphic had trapped me in the decanter it had held the banquet table, where he and his cronies had feasted and watched while performers strained and fighters died.

Another memory from that night flooded my mind: glass spears, their shafts sharp with thorns, hounding me across this very spot, separating me from Chase. I shoved that memory aside and hurried faster.

Mother ran beside me now, skirts in her hand as we went up a set of stairs and onto the platform. She and Jaquith had to know what I was thinking. They'd both been on the platform when Malphic trapped me. Chase would know as well.

Not even pausing to catch my breath, I went to where a line of columns ran along the rear of the platform. Beyond them the ocean stretched, punctuated by an outcrop of rocks. Faint fingers of light splayed upward from the horizon.

I raised the moonstone knife. No way could I ever forget this spot, the weak point where I'd watched helpless from the decanter while Chase battled for his life. And I could feel him now beside me, warm and very much alive, changed, but still the man I loved. And Mother was with me, too. And Dad and Jaquith.

"Nice try," Malphic's voice said, a little ways behind me.

I resisted the urge to turn toward his voice, brought the knife down, and bellowed, "What tears also opens. What burns also builds."

A blast of cold hit my face as the air crackled open, a wide gap with electricity snapping and popping all around it. Jaquith was the first one through, then Mother.

Malphic tsked. "You think you're a clever little thing, don't you?"

I wheeled toward him, straightened my shoulders, and shoved the knife into the folds at my waistline as if I weren't afraid of him at all.

His white and austere gold robes billowed as he strolled away from a narrow carpet that hung suspended in midair, no doubt where he'd come out from. A scarf was looped around his neck. His moonstone knife gleamed at his waistline. He stopped a few yards away from me. A frown creased his brow. "First you avoid returning to my inner sanctum. Now I see you've stolen my spell."

My hands went to my hips and I scoffed. "You're the one who gave it to me—don't you remember the last time we were here?"

"Yes, I suppose I did."

A half dozen of his shadow-spies seeped out from the columns' gloom. Dad and Chase moved in close to me, battle-ready as the shadows crept forward, broad-shouldered and twice as tall as even Chase or Malphic.

Vephra materialized, dressed in indigo veils and black leather. She drew a silver rapier from its sheath and strode to Malphic's side.

I could hear the opening in the veil crackling behind me. I could feel the weight going out of my body, cramps growing stronger as sunrise sent brighter shafts of light across the floor. We needed to make a run for it, but I didn't dare take my eyes off Vephra and Malphic. I didn't dare move until I was sure Dad and Chase would do the same.

Malphic took another slow step toward me. "It wasn't very nice of you to bring that hexad here. But we've managed to drive the pestilence back to your realm."

"You should have killed her," I said, holding my ground.

He cocked his head. "That would have been preferable. Unfortunately, the creature slipped through our fingers. I believe she came out in a lovely little garden." He pressed a finger to his lips as if thinking, then pointed it at Chase. "If I remember correctly, it used to be your mother's favorite place. Lilac trees and peonies."

Chase remained motionless, his jaw tensed, his scimitar ready in his hands. But I knew what Malphic was referring to, and his smugness made me want to rip his eyes out. The garden was where Chase's mother had been hiding the first time Malphic insinuated himself into her life. The garden at Chase's childhood home in Bar Harbor, where his abusive stepfather still lived.

One of the shadow-spies swaggered forward, the stench of bleach emanating from him, his voice harsh. "I claim the girl. Skin for skin. It's the law," he roared.

In horror I realized half his face was burned off, his body puckered and oozing. *Fuck.* It was the shadow I'd attacked in Moonhill's gallery. His burnt skin was my doing.

Dad jumped in front of me, a heartbeat after Chase had done the same. Dad's hand went into his robe, palming something. A salt shank. I caught another movement, a slight twist of his hips and shoulders. The burned-faced spy wasn't his target. He knew Chase would protect me. Dad was readying his revenge.

I moved fast, grappling Dad by the neck of his robe before he could lunge at Malphic.

"No," I screeched, yanking him back. "He'll kill you."

Dad glanced over his shoulder at me, eyes pinpoints of anger.

I gritted my teeth. "You can't. Our family will never have peace."

Behind Dad, Malphic drew his moonstone knife. He pointed it skyward and intoned, "Weave and bind, mend what's mine. Weave and—"

The crackle of the veil weakened. *Shit.* He was sealing it.

"Stop!" I shouted, tough and hard, a command, not a girl's plea.

Malphic lowered his knife. His gaze slowly swept over me, then went to Dad and Chase. An amused smile twitched at the corners of his mouth. "She is a feisty one."

Chase planted his feet. "Let her go. She's nothing to you. Let her father go as—"

I didn't let him finish. I couldn't let him say something foolish. I narrowed my eyes on Malphic. "I have an offer," I said.

Malphic chuckled. "This should be interesting. Go on, child."

The shadows broke into a chorus of snickers and chortles as if Malphic patronizing me was the funniest thing in the world. That was, all of them except the burned-faced spy. He folded his arms across his chest, clearly not amused. Vephra also crossed her arms.

I turned to her. "Actually I believe this offer is something that may interest you." I lowered my gaze to her belly. "Congratulations, by the way. What is it? A daughter or another son?"

She glared.

Chase touched my arm, a warning not to toy with her. And I knew he was right. Malphic was powerful, yes. But there was one being more powerful. A being who was as rare as a half ifrit surviving the change, the most treasured thing in the djinn realm—a healthy and alive, full-blooded female genie. Vephra. There was a reason why everyone called Malphic the First Husband of the Sovereign Mistress and no one referred to her as his wife. She was the ultimate power here.

I let my gaze return to her belly. "My guess would be a son. But can he replace any of your others?"

"Of course not," Malphic snapped. His lips pressed into a white slash. He was getting annoyed, seriously pissed in fact.

I smoothed my hand down my arm. The veil sputtered behind me, its crackle weakening by the second. Still, I didn't let my composure slip. "If that's true—if all your children are so valuable, then tell me one thing. Where is your son Culus?"

Vephra's face went expressionless. I had her now. Culus wasn't unloved, a disowned and detested son as Grandfather believed. At least not by her.

"If you swear to let all of us go—my father, Chase, and me—then I'll tell you where Culus is." I rested back on my heels, arms folded.

"Don't listen to her," the burned-face spy snarled.

Vephra tilted her head. "How do you know where he is?"

A ray of sunshine illuminated her rapier. My guts cramped, a fiery stab followed by white-hot spasms. Out of the corner of my eye, I saw Dad hunch and waver from solid to ethereal. But I kept my head up. Another second, that's all I needed.

I steadied my voice. "Let my father go. Then I'll answer your question."

Dad swiveled toward me. "I'm not leaving without you."

"No, I want you to go. Please," I said.

Chase took ahold of my arm. "None of us are leaving without you."

"So noble." Malphic sighed. His expression darkened. "Now, answer the question."

"Do we have a deal?" I said. My voice sounded firm, but a wave of vertigo sent dark flashes rushing across my field of vision. I couldn't keep this up much longer.

I glanced at Vephra.

Her deep copper skin had paled to saffron. Her rapier trembled in her hand. She gasped and the words rushed out as if she could no longer hold them back. "Tell me! Where is my son?"

I lifted my chin. "He's in a poison ring with a black onyx stone. Catch the hexad, Lotli, and you'll have your son."

With that, I wheeled. The slit in the veil was no more than a lightning strike wide. But I leapt through, gripping Dad's arm and holding Chase's hand.

The air crackled with electricity. Pressure sang in my ears. Behind me, Malphic's voice thundered through the air. "We who were cast out return, live in blood and bone of those who are great."

CHAPTER 31

The darkest places are where the most light is found.

—From the Scroll of Zitherod
Translation by Dr. Rupert Bancroft Walpole

Dad and I only got scrapes and bruises from our fall into the Pirate's Coffin. Mother twisted an ankle. We were all lucky, except for Jaquith. He broke a wrist.

Of course, there was Chase. If he'd gotten hurt in the fall no one would have been able to tell. He was acting like everyone else was worse off, but he was a mass of crusted blood, bruises, and gashes.

We made our way from the Coffin to the beach and up the stairs to the clifftop. As we started across the lawn to the house, Kate and Grandfather came flying out to meet us.

Grandfather gave Mother a huge hug. He clapped Dad on the back. "Bravo," he said. "Well done. Beyond well done! Simply outstanding." He glanced at Jaquith. "Looks like an introduction is in order."

Kate rushed over to Chase and me. "Take him straight up to the Orchid Room," she snapped. "Get him undressed and into bed. Use pillows to elevate his head and shoulders." She scanned my body, pausing on my tattered sarong and various abrasions before returning to my face. "You do feel well enough to do that, right?"

I nodded. Maybe I should have been offended by her brusque commands or concerned about my aches and pains, or even felt like popping a bottle of champagne and celebrating our success. But the truth was, all I wanted to do was make sure Chase was going to be okay and to be with him.

Without taking a breath, Kate went on. "Laura will give you a washbasin. Sponge him off, but be careful. I'll get Selena and be right up. We'll need to get his nose realigned. That gash in his arm is pretty nasty, too."

Chase rested one hand on my shoulder to steady himself as we went into the house and up the servants' stairs. Considering how many bedrooms there were in Moonhill, I was surprised Kate picked the Orchid Room. Its pristine white rugs and pink satin bedding were hardly the best choice for a makeshift emergency room. It was, however, next to my room and I was grateful to her for that.

Chase helped me get his boots off and his various belts and weapons. But after that he slumped down on the bed, his energy gone.

My stomach went queasy when I peeled off his blood-splattered pants and saw deep whip marks across one of his thighs. I got him situated in bed and pulled a light sheet up over his lower half. Using the washbasin and a sponge, I dabbed dirt and blood off his face, then moved on to his arms. He winced when I got near the larger wounds, but mostly he lay quiet. In fact, it wasn't until I was sponging his chest that he spoke at all.

"Annie," he whispered. His voice was deep and hoarse. "You're not going to leave?"

I kissed his shoulder. "I imagine Kate and Selena will want me out of the way when they work on your nose. But I'll stay if you want."

His hand captured mine, pressing it and the sponge I was

holding tight against his chest. "That's not what I mean. I don't want to wake up and find out that you and your parents have gone home."

"Ah—you're talking about home to our house in Vermont?" My head whirred under the weight of my exhaustion and the enormity of the question. "I don't think we will. Certainly not until the Sons of Ophiuchus threat is over." I met his gaze. "You don't even know about that yet. But, *no,* not right away. I don't know, I haven't really thought about it. I'm taking a class in London this fall. I've wanted to do that for a long time." I took a deep breath, surprised by how the question had upended me.

He closed his eyes and mumbled, "London's a long ways away."

I looked down at his hand, still lying on top of mine. He was right about London. It felt like a zillion miles away. But it also was the only thing in my future that I was sure of, the only guidepost for me to move toward. "Once I finish taking classes and become a licensed fine art appraiser, I'll be able to live and work pretty much anywhere," I said. But it was as much for me as for him. He'd already drifted off.

Not long after that, Kate and Selena arrived. As I'd thought, they ordered me out of the room. Selena whispered they were going to give Chase something and that he'd be knocked out until probably late afternoon. I was grateful for that. His genie blood would quicken his healing, but he needed to rest, without dreams or nightmares.

"Go on." Selena shoved me toward the door. "Take a break and get cleaned up. Have something to eat. Laura's setting up a breakfast buffet on the terrace. I'll let you know when we're done."

It was a little before ten when I went downstairs to get something to eat. I'd showered and put on my favorite jeans and a comfy shirt. Even if I'd wanted to, I couldn't have lain down to rest. I was far too wired for that. Apparently I wasn't the only one. Mother wasn't there, but Dad and Jaquith had also changed and gathered on the porch along with Grandfather and the Professor. They sat on various chairs and chaises, breakfast plates and coffees balanced on their laps or resting on side tables.

I grabbed a coffee and blueberry muffin from the buffet, and settled into an empty chair, listening while I took a long sip.

"I still say, I should have gone with Tibbs's idea and brought the black powder gun and a pocketful of cherry pits," Dad said. "Then I could have taken care of Malphic for good. If the gun didn't misfire, that is."

Jaquith set his fork on the arm of his chair. Someone had bandaged his wrist and given him brand-new cargo shorts and an L.L. Bean polo shirt to wear. The clothes looked small and awkward on such a rough-and-ready man, especially since I was only used to seeing him in a eunuch's robe. He wiped a dab of scrambled egg off his lips with the back of his hand, then spoke up. "Even if it worked, a gun wouldn't have done you any good. It's true, a pit can kill a full-blooded genie, but it requires a specific variety cherry—one that happens to be extinct."

Dad sighed. "So much for that idea."

"I'm sure it's for the best," Grandfather added.

The Professor leaned forward, hands on his knees. "I once found some ancient cherry pits at a dig site in North Africa. They were a horribly early variety, absolutely amazing. If I recall right they were in some sort of ceremonial bowl along with the remains of a slingshot."

Jaquith sat back. "That's not exactly good news, given my present condition."

"So sorry," the Professor said. "I forgot about your situation. But surely being possessed wouldn't make you susceptible to that sort of weapon?"

Grandfather peered over his coffee cup at Jaquith. "You're a hundred percent certain that Zea's intentions aren't malevolent?"

Jaquith nodded. "I've read a great deal about the High Magus. He is an enlightened djinn—devoted to magic and peace. To be honest, I feel better than I have in years."

"Interesting," Grandfather said. The jangle of a ringtone came from his pocket. He pulled out his phone. "Hello?"

Everyone quieted, so he could talk.

"Yes, I'm aware of who you are. Jeffrey White as in the Sons of Ophiuchus, correct?" Grandfather said.

I cocked my head, intent on catching every word.

Grandfather raised his eyebrows, telegraphing his surprise. "Dinner, you say. Might I suggest Bar Harbor? Yes. A private room. Yes, we are aware she is a hexad. Perhaps you could expand upon that subject. In exchange, I could provide you with adequate information to solve the unfortunate situation with that boy and his brother. My granddaughter feels horrible." Grandfather glanced at all of us and winked. "What do you say we leave the rest of this conversation until this evening? I'll make the reservations for five. We can have a few brandies beforehand. Great. I look forward to chatting with you."

As Grandfather tucked his phone away, I glanced at Dad. "I've been thinking about Lotli and the energy-sucking thing. When we were at the yacht club and Selena was helping Lotli across the boardroom, do you remember how exhausted Selena looked?"

Dad set his coffee cup down. "I thought she was worn-out from scrying. But I think you're on to something."

"Sounds very plausible to me," Grandfather said. He gave me a smile. "Fortunately, between that phone call and your clever move with sending Vephra after the poison ring, I don't believe we'll be seeing Lotli again. Unfortunately, Malphic is another story. I'm quite certain there's something else rattling around in his head."

I nodded and the last words Malphic had said echoed in my mind: "*We who were cast out return, live in blood and bone of those who are great.*" What the heck had he meant by that?

The Professor got up from his chair and smiled at Jaquith. "I very much suspect the world has changed a great deal since you were last here. Perhaps you'd enjoy finishing your coffee in the library? I could introduce you to our audiovisual selections—and show you a few catalogues of mens' clothing, if you'd like."

Jaquith's eyes met the Professor's. His scarred cheek dimpled and his upper lip lifted into a lopsided smile. "I'd like that very much."

I bit my lip to keep from smiling. It truly was surreal how normal everything felt, though in truth it all was very odd.

CHAPTER 32

*At sunrise, I let the egg fall from the shell into water
gathered from the spring. The white, he did not float.
The yoke, she did not sink. All turned into smoke
and was gone, like a shadow into darkness.*

—Annie Freemont's future,
divined by Olya Freemont

Over the next two days, Chase mostly slept and I sat with
him. Dad and Mother spent most of their time talking
quietly and taking drives along the coast. Grandfather learned
a great deal about hexads from Jeffrey White. Apparently the
Sons of Ophiuchus had hoped to use her flute-magic to access
the veil between life and death. However, as much as they wanted
that, it wasn't going to happen now. Lotli had vanished—or at
least Tibbs's surveillance drone showed her campsite as empty,
the bread truck and everything else gone. He also discovered that
Newt and his entire family had disappeared, not a trace of them
left in Bar Harbor.

Chase's genie blood must have kicked in on the third day
because he rapidly started to feel better and insisted on moving
back to the cottage and doing his chores.

"It isn't fair to make Tibbs tend the sheep and take all the
patrol shifts," he insisted. "Besides, I feel fine. Zachary needs

someone to help him with his knife throwing. Your uncle complained about the lawns getting shaggy. . . ."

I rolled my eyes and didn't argue with him. But just before sunset I drove Dad's Mercedes up to the cottage to bring him a plate of Laura's maple-glazed donuts and make sure he wasn't doing too much. All right, that's a lie. Every inch of me longed to be with Chase and I needed to talk to someone.

Watching Dad and Mother together had been wonderful. But it had left me oddly unsettled. That feeling had intensified even more that afternoon, when Dad had told me they planned on returning to our house in Vermont in a few days. Dad wanted to get back to traveling and dealing antiques. Mother wanted time to quietly adjust to everything. They made it clear I was welcome. They wanted me with them. But I wanted them to have their own time, to get their lives together. And, as strange as it sounded, I wanted to stay at Moonhill more than I wanted to go back to my old life.

I parked the Mercedes in front of Chase's cottage, snagged the plate of donuts, and started for the front door. Chase opened it before I could even knock—and he wasn't the only one waiting on the stoop to greet me. Houdini wound around Chase's legs as if they were best buddies. Strange cat. He'd never hung out on this side of the estate before, at least that I was aware of. For that matter, he'd never appeared to like Chase. I'd assumed that was why I hadn't seen him very much since we returned from the realm.

Chase took the plate from me. The bruises under his eyes had faded to a purplish green. His nose and left arm were still bandaged, but most of his other wounds had healed up. He really was looking good.

I swept my fingers down his jawline and gave him a quick kiss.

"No fair doing that when my hands are full," he said, kicking the door shut with the side of his bare foot.

"Well, there's an easy remedy for that." I smiled suggestively, took the plate of donuts from him, and set it on the coffee table next to his yarn and knitting needles.

He pulled me into his arms, his lips meeting mine in a warm, firm kiss, lingering but not that hot. A delicious promise of things to come.

Everything about the moment felt perfect, like I was in a dream. Maybe it was a dream, one that I'd had over and over again since I was a child, but forgotten upon waking. Everything did truly feel familiar: The warmth of his arms, the last of the sunlight slanting through his windows, dust motes rising from his old couch, even the hint of lilac wafting from a candle that he'd no doubt lit after I'd texted to say I was on my way. It felt like I'd been moving toward this moment all my life.

I dropped down on one end of the couch. "Did Grandfather tell you the news about your mother?"

He glanced at the yarn and knitting needles and smiled. "I can't believe he arranged everything so fast."

"That's the old boys' network for you. It's just too bad she has to stay at Beach Rose House a second longer."

"It's not that bad," he said. "The lawyer said my stepfather should be gone before the end of the week. After that, Olya and Kate are going to install wards to help protect her from Malphic. She'll be able to move back home, once that's done." Chase's eyes came to mine. "Thank you. She deserves it."

My body felt warm and buoyant, as if I might float up into the air from sheer happiness. He made us coffees and we sat on his couch, my head on his shoulder as we sipped them and nibbled donuts, talking about nothing particular, mostly snuggling.

After a while, he put his mug on the table, his face suddenly serious. "Annie," he said. "I can't promise that I'm okay.

It might be a long time before I know the full extent of what the change did to me."

Silence hung in the air between us. Houdini padded across the room and off into the kitchen. I wasn't sure what to say. I was surprised he hadn't brought this up earlier, like while I was sitting with him in the Orchid Room. Then again, I probably should have asked him about it. I should have been worried. But I hadn't been—and I still wasn't.

My heart said, everything was going to be fine.

He touched my wrist. "When I was in the desert changing, I felt so lost. It was like a nightmare where I was running and running and couldn't find a familiar place. Everything was strange. But your voice. Your lips. The smell of your skin. Your touch. Your essence." His thumb grazed the back of my hand, sending tingles across my skin. "Those things were familiar. And they led me out of the nightmare. I thought about you lying in my bed, here in the cottage. I remembered the light of the bonfire on your hair. The taste of strawberry jelly on your skin. I remembered you in the driver's seat of the Mercedes, the first night you came to Moonhill. I remembered every second of us."

I raised my eyes to his, barely able to breathe. "Chase, I—"

His finger pressed my lips, silencing me. "All those years in the realm, I hated being a slave. I hated myself and hated what I was becoming even worse. But sometimes—here at Moonhill—I longed to be back there. Strange, isn't it? But sometimes I felt so alone here."

"It sounds normal to me," I said lightly. "I felt alone when I came here, too." But inside I was quivering. So overwhelmed with emotion that tears prickled in the corners of my eyes.

"Annie." His voice was hushed now, his eyes on mine. "I'm not lonely anymore. I don't want to ever go back to the realm. Everything I want is here."

I didn't dare move. I didn't dare breathe. "I want what's between us to last," I whispered. "But I can't guarantee it—any more than you can predict what the change did to you."

"I know that. But we can try." He hesitated, his blue eyes as fathomless as the ocean. "Annie Freemont, will you stay here with me?"

Surprised, I sucked in a breath. "You mean—"

"Will you live with me? Here in the cottage. I know it's not much."

"I—ah—" An explosion of emotions crashed over me. Relief. Joy. Amazement. Tears flooded from my eyes. I wrapped my arms around his neck and nuzzled my face against his chest. "Of course, I will. I love you, Chase Abrams."

He pulled away from me, holding me at arm's length. "I don't mean right now. I want you to go to London first. Take that class. Take all the classes you want. I don't want to hold you back. I don't want you to rush into it or stop dealing antiques."

I smiled so hard my cheeks hurt, and cuffed him in the chest. "That all sounds very noble—but no way am I going to wait to move in with you. I'm thinking I've already spent the last night in my own bed. From now on it's you and me."

He laughed. "And Houdini makes three?"

"I don't think he's going to give us much choice about that."

The cool air chilled my toes as Chase ran after me up the narrow staircase to the attic bedroom. He lay me down on his mattress—our mattress, brightened by clean, crisp sheets. He pulled off my shirt. I undid his jeans, kissing each fresh scar and bruise, each plateau and ripple of his body. To say we made love would be like comparing a single star to the Milky Way or the whole swirling universe to a drop of rain. It was beyond lovemaking. It was a bonfire. It was coals and heat and love.

Sometime later, I woke up curled against him. He slept quiet and peaceful. I pulled a loose blanket around my shoulders and sat up on the edge of the bed, staring out the open window at the yard below—our yard. Everything was calm, the chime of crickets the only sound.

But in my head a low voice whispered, repeating once more the words that had woken me from my sleep. Malphic's words: "*We who were cast out return, live in blood and bone of those who are great.*"

The mattress squeaked as Chase joined me on the edge of the bed, his arm wrapping around my shoulder and snuggling me close. "Something wrong?" he asked.

I shrugged. "I've been thinking. Well, more like my subconscious was doing it while I was trying to sleep."

"You're not thinking of changing your mind about living together?" he said. Hesitantly, he added, "I'd understand if you—"

"No, it's not that. Never." I rested my hand on his naked thigh and glanced back out the window. Along the edge of the yard, outlines of trees reached into the darkness. I swallowed dryly. "I've been thinking about Malphic's last words—about blood and bones, and those who were cast out returning. I'm certain it wasn't a spell. But what do you think he meant?"

"I'm sure he was talking about genies being cast out of the Garden of Eden and their dream of one day repopulating this world. Culus's whole reason for trying to steal the Lamp of Methuselah was so he could take over this realm. Malphic has the same dream." His voice quieted and he turned to look at me, worry shadowing his eyes. "What are you thinking?"

"My dad's told me lots of stories about my Freemont ancestors. We've matched wits with genies for eons. It's like they enjoy the challenge, or maybe even admire us because we aren't pushovers."

"That's possible," Chase said. "But what does that have to do with Malphic's words?"

"In the realm, my mother told me that the blacksmith who sat beside Solomon is her ancestor. He was known for his ability as a toolmaker. But I think Mother was hinting about him being the source of her special abilities, too—just like my Freemont ancestors and their magic."

Chase's arm went around me again, a warm comfort against the chill prickling the nape of my neck.

I leaned into him. "Your mother told me that her family descended from the union between a Malmuk warrior and a daughter of Genghis Khan. She thinks Malphic was behind that happening and that he chose to have a child with her because of those ancestors, some of the finest warriors this world has seen. But what if Malphic has been manipulating my family, too, playing matchmaker with both our bloodlines?"

He let go of me, sitting back, his eyes on mine. "It's possible. If Malphic's anything, he is patient. Eons would mean little to him."

My mind spun, thoughts and pieces of ideas flying together, like leaves and twigs rejoining to form a tree. "When you escaped from the realm the first time, you beat Malphic in a fight and stole the moonstone knife. You hadn't gone through the change at that point. You were a teenager. He could have easily killed you."

Chase shook his head. "There's a code of honor. A mature warrior has to limit his magic and skills when he fights a younger opponent. That's why I won. Malphic was obeying his own law, just like he'd expect his warriors to do."

"Maybe. But I think he was testing you." I rubbed my neck, pausing to let my thoughts catch up. "What if having my mother as his mistress wasn't his ultimate goal. What if it was a small piece of a larger scheme? I'm starting to think everything—him kidnapping her, you escaping, then us going to rescue her. What if everything was designed to bring us together, to test our abilities and worthiness? To see if we had our ancestors' skills."

He tilted his head and gave a skeptical nod. "I suppose Malphic might do something like that. But worthiness? For what?"

My pulse slowed. I licked my lips. "The day your mother talked about your lineage, she told me something else." I took a deep breath, bracing myself. "She told me about when you were conceived. She claimed she knew the instant it happened. I thought that was nuts. How could any woman know that so soon? But she was telling the truth. And so was Malphic. The genies will return in the blood and bone of those who are great."

I took his hand and pressed it against my stomach. Sometimes a woman knows.

Look for me at midnight. When the darkness and Devil's hour make you fear, open your eyes to the flooding moonlight and the sting of the stars. For it is then, I reach for you, come to you. Visit you in your bed.

—Malphic, Warlord of Blackspire

DON'T MISS

A Hold on Me

Annie Freemont grew up on the road, immersed in the romance of rare things, cultivating an eye for artifacts and a spirit for bargaining. It's a freewheeling life she loves and plans to continue—until her dad's illness forces her to return to Moonhill, their ancestral home on the coast of Maine. There she meets Chase, the dangerously seductive young groundskeeper. With his dark good looks and powerful presence, Chase has an air of mystery that Annie is irresistibly drawn to. But she also senses that behind his penetrating eyes are secrets she can't even begin to imagine. Secrets that hold the key to the past, to Annie's own longings—and to all of their futures . . .

Beyond Your Touch

Annie Freemont knows this isn't the right time to get involved with a man like Chase. After years of distrust, she's finally drawing close to her estranged family, and he's an employee on their estate in Maine. But there's something about the enigmatic Chase that she can't resist. And she's not the only woman. Annie fears a seductive stranger who is key to safely freeing her mother is also obsessed with him. As plans transform into action and time for a treacherous journey into a strange world draws near, every move Annie makes will test the one bond she's trusted with her secrets, her desires—and her heart.

Available where books are sold.

Enjoy the following excerpt from

A Hold on Me

CHAPTER 1

There are things darker than night, darker than the souls
of wicked men or a woman of unchained passions.
Believe me, for I have known them well.

—Josette Savoy Abrams
Beach Rose House, Bar Harbor, Maine

Most people went to church to save their souls, but not
Dad and I. We went there to see the priest about treasure.

It was a cold day in February and the church was an abandoned stone chapel on a back road near our home in Vermont. With its gloomy stained-glass windows and carvings of gargoyles under its sagging eaves, the chapel was exactly the kind of place where antique pickers like Dad and me could find the weird treasures and the gothic furniture our customers loved to buy. And, as luck would have it, the bishop had given the local priest permission to sell the entire contents as he saw fit.

The priest glanced once more at the grungy pews and the statue of St. Anthony with its chipped fingers and peeling paint. "Now that you've seen everything, are you still interested?"

Dad gave my shoulder a squeeze. "What do you think, Annie?"

"Ah—" I let my voice crack as if my jitteriness were

nerves instead of excitement, then I met the priest's eyes. "One price for everything, right?"

"For all the contents. That doesn't include anything that's part of the structure. No windows, attached light fixtures, doors, none of those sorts of things." His tone left no room for debate.

Dad looked down, scratching his elbow while I took a scrap of paper and a pen from the turned-up sleeve of my bulky sweater. I jotted down the offer he and I had covertly agreed on when the priest had turned away for a moment, then handed it to the priest.

The priest's brow furrowed as he studied the paper. He ran a finger under his collar, cleared his throat, and finally glanced at Dad. "Perhaps you should look at this before we agree?"

Dad waved off his suggestion. "This was her idea. The offer is hers to make."

"All right, then," the priest said. "We have a deal."

I counted out a thin stack of hundreds and gave them to him. In turn, he passed Dad the church keys, all neatly labeled. The truth was, he wasn't the sort of person who would have ever believed a twenty-year-old girl with ripped jeans and a stud in her nose could know the first thing about valuing antiques—as Dad and I had hoped.

"Sorry I can't stay and help," he said, "but I have to get back to St. Mary's in time for Mass. When you're finished taking what you want, leave the keys in the box outside the door. I hope you find enough to make this worth your effort."

"I hope so too," Dad said, without cracking a smile. But, as soon as the priest went out the front door, he did a little victory dance and gave me a kiss on the cheek. "Perfectly played. If I'd given him an offer that low, he'd have thought I was up to something for sure."

Every inch of me tingled with anticipation. "So, where do you want to begin?" I asked.

Dad jangled the keys. "It appears the priest neglected to give us one very specific key. The one to the only room he didn't take us into or even mention. I don't know about you, but that makes me curious."

"The sacristy?" I said.

"That would be the one. Did you notice how he fidgeted with his collar, too?"

"I figured he thought everything was junk—that he was nervous I'd offered too much and that you'd back out."

"That's possible. But don't ever underestimate your opponent. There could be something else behind his uneasiness. Perhaps he hid something in the sacristy, something of value he hoped the diocese would forget. Priests are men, after all. They come in all shades of honesty, like the rest of us." He stroked his chin, a sure sign that he was about to launch into one of his home-brewed tales. "You remember the story about my wicked great-uncle Harmon and the Canary Island sirens? He always claimed to be a spiritual man, forthright and faithful to his wife. . . ."

I loved listening to Dad's crazy stories. But, as he began an abridged version of a tale that easily could have gone on for an hour, the word *faithful* sent my mind veering in a different direction—to me and Taj and a matinee of *Romeo and Juliet,* to his practiced fingers slipping under my skirt, up my inner thighs. The rush of desire. His words hot and moist against my neck: "*Oh, baby, c'mon. I want you so bad.*"

Men come in all shades of honesty for sure.

Shoving Taj from my mind, I smiled at Dad and cut him off. "I'm going to run out to the car and get the tool bag."

"Don't forget the thermos and flask," he called after me. Dad most always kept a thermos filled with coffee in our '68 Mercedes. He loved his cup of joe and it had become our tradition to toast successful deals by lacing a cup with a bit of brandy from his flask.

When I returned from the car, I found Dad crouched in front of the sacristy door, studying the keyhole. I set the flask and thermos on a pew, got the screwdriver and stiff wire he used for picking locks out of the tool bag, and gave them to him.

As I watched him work, sunlight crept in through the stained-glass window behind us, smearing the back of his old leather flight jacket with purple and blue. He glanced over his shoulder at me, the colored light now bruising his face. His eyes glistened with excitement. "What do you think we'll find inside—hidden treasure or a glorified broom closet?"

I hugged myself against a sudden chill. Either way the sacristy was bound to be windowless and dark, as black as a cellar or the space under a bed, black like death. I forced a smile. "Treasure," I said, because I really did hope we'd find something valuable.

"Well, we'll soon know for sure." Dad turned back to his work.

He pivoted the screwdriver and the lock clicked. Throwing me a triumphant grin, he reached for the latch, readying to open the door—

Suddenly, a thin, man-shaped shadow appeared on the wall next to the door, slithered toward Dad, and vanished.

I whirled around.

"What the heck?" I said, scouring the pews and aisles to make sure the priest hadn't returned. But there was no one in the church besides us. No one who could have caused the shadow. I turned back toward Dad. "I could have sworn—"

My voice died in my throat.

Dad was staring at me in a way I'd never seen him do before, his eyes dark and vacant.

I took a step back. "Dad?"

His tongue grazed his lips as if he was lost in thought.

"Are you all right?" I asked.

He didn't say a word. He just kept staring at me.

Trembling, I lowered my gaze to avoid his deadpan eyes.

Dad's expression was exactly how he described the faces of the sleepwalkers in the creepiest of all the stories he'd ever made up. But this wasn't one of his tales. This was real. And I didn't have the faintest idea what I should do.

My stomach twitched from nerves as I made myself glance up. I couldn't just pretend nothing was wrong. I had to do something.

To my surprise, he appeared normal. The familiar sparkle had returned to his eyes, and he was grinning.

He chuckled. "What's wrong with you? You look like you've seen the Devil."

Totally baffled by his transformations, I could only gape.

He shrugged halfheartedly like he was done trying to figure out what was going on with me, then cocked his head at the sacristy door. "Be a good girl and lend me that flashlight of yours, so we can see what we've got in here."

"Uh—sure." My voice stuttered a little as I fished my flashlight out of my jeans hip pocket and handed it to him.

He gave me a quick wink, then opened the door and headed into the sacristy.

As I watched him disappear into the pitch-black room, I shook my head. What was I thinking? Slithering shadows. Sleepwalkers. That was ridiculous. There was nothing wrong with Dad. It was me. Me and my childish fear of the dark. Plus, I was overtired and had stupidly got myself worked up about Taj again. I hadn't eaten all day and had drunk way too many coffees; enough to keep me awake for a week. No wonder I was imagining things.

Giving myself a mental shake, I inched closer to the door.

Dad's voice echoed out. "Broken cups and napkins." He laughed. "Not even enough for a bad garage sale."

I blew out a relieved breath.

There was definitely nothing wrong with Dad.

Connect with

Visit us online at
KensingtonBooks.com
to read more from your favorite authors, see books
by series, view reading group guides, and more.

Join us on social media

for sneak peeks, chances to win books and prize packs,
and to share your thoughts with other readers.

facebook.com/kensingtonpublishing
twitter.com/kensingtonbooks

Tell us what you think!

To share your thoughts, submit a review,
or sign up for our eNewsletters, please visit:
KensingtonBooks.com/TellUs.